CHASE
THE
MOON

MINETTE LAUREN

THE GUARDIAN SERIES

CHASE THE MOON

Published Internationally by Minette Lauren
Magnolia, TX USA
Minettelauren.com

Copyright © 2020 Minette Lauren

Exclusive cover © 2020 Fiona Jayde Media
Inside artwork © 2020 Tamara Cribley, The Deliberate Page

PRINT ISBN: 978-1-952387-00-5
EBOOK ISBN: 978-1-952387-01-2

This is a work of fiction. Names, characters, places and incidents are either the product of the author's imagination or are used fictitiously, and any resemblance to
any person or persons, living or dead, events or locales is entirely coincidental.

ACKNOWLEDGEMENTS

Thank you to my editors, Joanna D'Angelo and Amy Sharp. Your hard work, encouragement and grammar lessons are always appreciated.

My heart goes out to my wonderful hubby, who is always there for me.

To my best Louisiana sidekicks, Tiff and Sal. I'll always think of you when I write about the bayou area. Sometimes the best family is the family we choose.

Cheers to Cristina for all that you do.

And to my Greek Mama Mu for your continual love and inspiration. Our meeting wasn't too late. It was right when destiny said it should be…

*To all the big sisters with tag-along sisters, you
don't know how lucky you are...*

PROLOGUE

A flash in Delila's peripheral vision distracted her. It could have been anybody, but his energy lit a string of synapses that were like starbursts in her energy waves. Inexplicably drawn toward the entryway of the establishment across Canal Street, Delila looked toward him for only a moment, yet it felt as if time stood still. He didn't look as he had in the last life she'd known him. His hair was now sandy blond with streaks of warm honey illuminated by lamplight and the neon sign above. His green t-shirt clung to broad shoulders, but his frame was lean. His face was an artwork of planes and angles that made him attractive even though he hadn't shaved. The beautiful young man had been her son in her last mortal life and she had been his father. Her love for him was immense. Delila had lost him when she parted much too soon from the living. He was her eldest son, John, during that existence. The soul connection they shared was stronger than with her other children from that life.

Dying in a pool of her own blood on foreign soil, her last thoughts were not of her sweet wife, but of John and how the young boy would fare without a father to guide and protect him. His soul name was forever Venery, just as hers was Delila. He was someone she would reincarnate with throughout eternity. Venery was a soul complement, not her soulmate, but someone her heart would always yearn for. They had shared lives as husband and wife, mother and daughter, father and son. In an embodied state, the thought of their roles might seem incestuous, but in the spirit world, all souls were cut from the same cloth, destined to be woven together over and over again throughout time. Delila wasn't sure how many lives she'd known him, but their energy connection was impenetrable, and his presence was never lost to her. She was now keenly aware of Venery. The energy pulse between them was almost overwhelming. She'd only looked at him a moment, hadn't she?

Water dripped in the darkness, and Regan shivered at the eerie sense of cold without actually feeling the sensation.

"Hello! Anyone there?" Her knees were weak. She picked her way toward a pinhole of light. It was as if she was being called through a wall of water. The muffled voices somehow seemed familiar. *Am I dead? What happened?* She shook her head, trying to think. Creeping along the black, wet rocks, she held her hand out to feel her way but didn't touch anything. As if locked in a dream, the more she reached out, the farther everything slipped away.

Desperation grew with the chill inside her. "Mark? Rain? Where are you?" Fear coursed through her like electricity, making her vibrate with trepidation. Her entire life flashed before her. Her birth, baptism, first day of school, her first Mardi Gras parade when she was eight, her parents' break-up, getting her braces removed, the first time she had sex. The collage of moments seemed to exist instantaneously, like someone running a finger over a thick catalog as the pages fluttered past at lightning speed. The flicker of her life decelerated until recent events unfolded in slow motion. It wasn't a nightmare. She knew she wasn't sleeping and somehow sensed she had been here before.

It was unfortunate that only now she understood the old fortuneteller's message.

What comes next?

The voices grew louder, and the light grew brighter, beckoning her. She ignored both and retreated, retracing her steps back to the darkness. She wouldn't return to the beginning again. The pain and unfairness of living was one thing, but the endless unknown of the afterworld held its own misery, and she wasn't about to dance on puppet strings to figure out how to get back in the game. It was all a game, wasn't it? To prove yourself worthy in the afterworld, to start all over again. She refused to do it. *It's not fair.* She'd had a good life—she was going to be someone. She was supposed to be famous. In that moment, the word felt empty, incomplete. Fame held no value for the dead. All her worldly relationships exploded into shards in her mind.

She groaned with remorse and dread. *What did I do?*

She'd had everything. How did it all slip through her fingers like fine golden sand? The answer flashed through her core.

My life was stolen.

CHAPTER 1

Two weeks earlier

"Regan Hope Landry, you get back in this house and finish cleaning your room!"

Regan ignored her mother and revved the engine of the tangerine-colored Mustang. She didn't mean to peel out of the driveway, but she'd just gotten her license last week, and she was going stir-crazy stuck in the house. It was April, and school was almost out. She would graduate in a few weeks, and the bliss of freedom would prevail. The car had been a gift from her dead-beat dad who showed up once every five years to worm his way back into her broke mom's heart. He didn't have money, but somehow always came up with something to offer. Regan had accepted the car and pretended everything was forgiven. That was two weeks ago, and he was already gone.

"Where are we goin'?"

Regan swerved, nearly careening off the narrow, curvy highway headed out of Bonne Fete, Louisiana. "Rain! What are you doing back there?" She swore with a hiss and brought the car to a skidding halt. "You almost gave me a heart attack. Get out!" Her little sister had this new habit of hiding in the back seat to tag along. Regan was in high school and she didn't need her little sister following her everywhere. Making her walk home might teach her a lesson.

"You can't put me out here, Regan. Mom will kill you if something happens to me. Didn't you see that thing on the news? A girl was kidnapped last week in New Orleans, and they found her body out at Butte La Rose." Her eyes teared up. "I don't want to be gator bait, Regan. Don't put me out here." Rain's strawberry blonde hair showed their mother's Irish heritage, a stark contrast to Regan's own long, dark tresses. Regan looked like her father's side. Coon-asses, all of them. They both had inherited their mother's fair skin, but Regan and Rain shared their father's intense green eyes.

Regan blew out a breath, stirring a lock of hair that had fallen over one eye. She started driving again and turned on the radio.

"Where are we goin'?"

An older woman stared over the crystal ball at Regan. The combination of ebony skin, purple nail polish, and rumpled green clothes that were a size too big and two decades past the current fashion made the seer look like a Mardi Gras float.

"You're a new soul, ain't cha, chile?" The dark woman nodded as if she knew the answer, but Regan was sure she was full of shit. She'd left her sister sitting on the concrete bench in front of St. Louis Cathedral waiting for her so this old woman could tell her fortune. Judging by the purple turban on the woman's head and the long toenails that stretched over her neon yellow flipflops, Regan had just wasted a week's worth of allowance.

The woman was still nodding, but now her eyes were closed, and she hummed as she rocked her shoulders back and forth like she was listening to some soulful music playing in her crazy head. The only thing Regan could hear was the bubbling of water from an old fountain in the courtyard. Her hackles went up. This was a bad idea. She was alone and pretty far from the square. Why had she told Rain to wait there? No one would even know where to look for her if she went missing. Regan remembered the story of Hansel and Gretel, lured into the ovens by the old witch…. She gasped as the fortune teller's head reared back, the whites of her eyes bright against the black of her skin.

"I see a dark sky with a bright shining moon. You've been here before. This isn't your first life, but this time and place is new to you. You're not an old soul, but you did exist long ago. I see lights, lots of candlelight, and hear music. A lot of people gathered." The woman smiled as she nodded, gripping Regan's hand. She rubbed her thumb back and forth over the lined palm, though she didn't look at the lines. There was a pause and the older woman looked like she was holding her breath. "Water, so much water. The news. It's everywhere. I see your name and picture in the paper...." The woman's head flung forward, and her shoulders sagged. Her breath came in ragged gasps. Regan worried that the lady's insanity might cause her to have a heart attack, though she wanted to believe what the old crone said was true. The band she played in was surely destined for fame, and she was the lead singer and songwriter for the group. It was 1985 and Regan knew she would come on the heels of Joan Jett and Pat Benatar before the decade was over. She just needed the right break. It was one week from her eighteenth birthday and after that, no one could stop her from hopping a bus or moving to the city to get real gigs. The fortune teller had just described her fame. It would happen. Regan knew she would make it somehow. Despite her earlier doubts of the seer's gift, Regan was now convinced of the old woman's skill. How would the seer know of the band's new song, "Walk on Water"? Why would she mention the paper, people speaking her name, candlelight? The woman must have had a vision of Regan singing on stage, the crowd holding lighters and shouting her name.

Regan fished out a twenty-dollar bill from her jeans pocket and placed it on the table next to the crystal ball. The woman's head slowly rose to peer at her with bloodshot eyes. The twenty would probably buy her another bottle of wine, beer, or whatever the source of that fermented odor was.

"Thanks, lady." Regan turned to leave.

As she reached the door to the courtyard, the woman called out, "Live each day as if it were your last, sweetheart. The dream you seek won't come the way you think it will, but you'll get there. We all get there in time."

Regan paused, studying the neon-green bellbottom pants and sage print wrap-around blouse the woman brushed at as if she were wiping away cat hair or a spider's web. Clearly, she had issues and apparently spoke in riddles so no one could accuse her of not getting their fortunes right. Without replying, Regan opened the door and retraced her path back to Rain. It was eighty-four degrees, but the humidity made it feel like summer already. For Regan, summer couldn't come soon enough. She was a senior and her four years of high school were finally coming to an end. Freedom was in reach and she was itching to start her future.

Rain lay on a bench, staring at a flock of pigeons roosting in a tree. Regan bumped her foot. "Get up. We need to get back before Momma has a coronary."

"What took you so long? I was about to walk to the police station."

Regan looked at her sister's sleep-lined face. "Yeah, you look really worried."

The silver bangles on her wrist jangled as she reached in her pocket for her key. Regan didn't look behind her as she started toward the parked Mustang. Rain would never leave her shadow. They stopped at an open bar on the way. Music and cool air conditioning poured out onto the street. A saxophone blew out a soulful solo to solicit potential patrons. Regan leaned into the cool wood frame of the old door with its doorknob as low as her knee. She was only five-four. On a guided tour through New Orleans her freshman year, a historian had explained that people used to be much smaller. She was average, but the old architecture washed over her with a feeling from the past that piqued her curiosity. The old French Quarter, combined with the sultry blues the band was playing inside, made her long for a time she hadn't lived, and she wondered how it might have been a hundred years before. If it wasn't for her tag-along sister, she could have enjoyed a Coke inside the bar and listened to the music, maybe flirted with the handsome guitar player who was checking them out.

The song came to an end and the players reached for a variety of drinks, most of them amber-colored over ice in short glasses. A bearded black man holding a saxophone called to them, "Why don't you come on in, pretty young thang."

Regan smiled but lingered at the entrance, remembering the old woman's words. "I can't. I've got my little sister with me." She motioned to Rain and shrugged her shoulders.

The man chuckled with a knowing smile. "Aw, I had one of those. My little bubba followed me everywhere until I was twenty-five. Don't worry, she'll outgrow ya and get her own life. She's a pretty little thang too, but too young for the likes of me, ya."

Regan sensed the need to move on. She might not care for Rain tagging along all the time, but she didn't need older men scoping her out, either. As she turned with her hand on Rain's shoulder to nudge her away from the unwanted attention of the sax player, she heard one of the band members whistle at them.

Looking back, she heard, "You got a sweet voice. It's a little raspy. Can you sing?"

It was the one thing he could have said that made her stop. She turned, squinting through the strong rays of the summer sun pouring over them as they stood on the cobbled street. "Yeah, I sing. I play a little too."

The band let out a mix of hoots and jests. The guitar player pulled the strap over his head and held out his instrument to her. "Come on then, don't be a tease. Show us whatcha got."

Regan pulled Rain in and looked her in the eye. "Don't move! You hear me?"

Rain protested, "I don't think this is a good idea, Regan. Mom will tan your hide if she finds out."

Her face was mere inches from Rain as she blew out a warning in a sharp hiss. "I said, stay outside the bar and don't leave!"

Regan sauntered the short distance through the mostly empty establishment. A few drunk patrons sat at the bar, but no one paid attention to the amateur show going on behind them. She took the guitar from the good-looking guy with dirty-blond hair and hitched herself up on the stool where he'd been sitting. She strummed the strings, checking if it was in tune. She knew it was since he'd been playing, but she gave a show of warming up. Regan plucked through the few chords leading into the chorus without a word, just feeling the music. The song started with remnants of classical excerpts from famous composers, diced up then smashed together with modern flare. Her voice hummed over the strings as she felt the tempo climb. As the chords led into the first chorus, she started in. Her voice was barely audible.

"Louder honey. We can't hear you." Regan's head jerked up. Her gaze locked with the woman behind the bar. She missed a note but quickly recovered as she belted out the lyrics.

"You stole my head. You stole my heart. You swore we'd never part. You walk on water, baby. You know you're driving me crazy...."

Her eyes were closed, but she could feel the intense interest of the room as everything around her came to a halt. She worked over the strings, ranging her rhythm from ballad to high-tempo rock. She wooed the band members into tentatively joining in, feeling their way into the unfamiliar chords. On the third swing through the chorus, Regan let it rip, watching Rain return her stare with an emotion that could only be defined as awe. Her little sister deified her—worshiped her talent, quick wit, and ability to shuffle through the bad things in life. Regan Landry was already famous in her small back-woods town, carrying a badass reputation around school, but her grades were okay. She held a B average, which wouldn't get her into any of the big colleges, but her family didn't have big college money anyway. Regan didn't care. She knew she wouldn't need it. Her music would make her world-famous one day.

The song came to a halt and the few patrons in the bar actually put down their drinks to clap. Some even blew out raucous whistles. Regan thought the smile she was trying to tame would break her cheeks. She had trained her emotions over the last few years to hide the need to be accepted. Indifference had gotten her where she was today, not that it was super-stardom, but she knew she had what it takes. She was on her way.

"Go on, li'l girl, you got some lungs on you, cher." The man holding the sax reached out a hand and waited for her to shake it.

Regan reached out and slapped it in a low five, giving him a sassy grin that he returned, flashing a gold tooth. "Awe now cher, I like me a feisty woman, but you be a bit too young for me, too. Tell me, where did you learn to sing like that?"

Regan shrugged her shoulders, "I sing in a band." Why give away free information? She did her usual, if they don't ask, don't tell, routine. She handed the guitar back to the handsome guitar player. His unwashed sandy-colored hair and after-five shadow made him look a little grubby, but his full bottom lip and hazel-colored eyes were something from the collage of Teen Beat posters on Rain's bedroom wall. He was heart-throb material and not too much older than herself, at least, not in her eyes. She guessed he was in his mid-twenties. A hell of a lot more mature than Mark, the boy she'd been on and off with. They would both graduate this year. Regan had been crazy about Mark at first, but he was gone most of last summer, and it was then that she saw the writing on the wall.

Staring into the warm hazel eyes of the guitar player, she played it casual, reminding herself that he couldn't see the erratic beating of her heart. In her short seventeen years, she knew one thing about the battle of the sexes—men wanted most what they couldn't have. If they thought you wanted them, they might be interested, but it was only for one thing. She'd learned that the hard way. Danny Rogers taught her that ego-crushing lesson. He was a senior and captain of the football team. She'd been a freshman and a straight-A student. Regan wasn't cool because she played in the high school marching band. She hadn't cared about popularity then, but what happened that night after homecoming had made her instantly known throughout the school. After a week of sulking in her room and trying to avoid classes, she admitted she had few choices. She could remain the un-cool marching band girl who was easy, or she could quit the school band, join a real band, and own the title of Bad Girl Landry. It didn't matter that she didn't date again until two years after the homecoming gossip. People believed what they wanted. She held a cigarette while she waited for the bus every morning and played in Mark Juban's garage on the weekends. They'd made out a few times and she'd even let him go as far as second base last week because she'd grown bored with their usual routine. She was glad he'd spent the summer in Galveston with his grandparents. It had given her the time she needed to get over her schoolgirl crush. She stayed with him because it was their last year of school. Being with Mark for two years had mended her tattered reputation. Regan was even cooler now because Mark's family was wealthy, and his father was into politics.

The guitar player nodded. "I'm Chase, this is Guidry, Ronnie and that's Dax." He motioned to the sax player, keyboard, and then drummer." He waited until everyone said hello and then asked, "What's the name of your band?"

"Bon Temps."

Chase chuckled, "Good times, not bad. I'm sure there are a hundred bands in Louisiana called that, but it's good enough."

Regan gave him her best bored look. "Yeah, what do you call yourselves?"

Chase laughed again, as the band members made a few jests, oohing and ahhing. He looked back at them. "Sassy, ain't she." The humor hadn't left his eyes as he returned her stare. "Cat's Quarter."

Regan actually liked the name, but she retorted, "That doesn't sound so original to me." There was another round of hoots and Guidry threw in, "Dawg, she dissed you good with dat one."

Chase chuffed. "Me? I think that was a universal diss, ya'll."

Regan turned back to see Rain waving at her to leave the bar. It was late and she knew she was grounded already for leaving the house without permission. No skin off her back, there was nothing to do on Mondays anyway. "Look, I gotta go. Thanks for letting me sing." She turned on her heel and made her way to the door without submitting to the desire to look back. It was a mystery to her why she wanted him to call her to stay or why she worried she would never see him again. He was just a guy. Someone her mother would count as too old for her and probably no good since he played in a band at a bar.

Regan felt his hand snag hers and his hot breath pour over her in a fresh wave. He was sucking on a mint. "Don't be in such a hurry. I didn't get your number." His hold was loose, but she didn't pull away.

"Mom's waiting for us, Regan. We gotta go." Rain's untimely reminder made her want to melt into the cobbled street where she stood. Chase's knowing smile made her want to slap her sister, hard. She would, as soon as they were alone. Her Achilles heel was music, and this guy knew how to play. They might have more than this one moment in common, and Regan would have liked to explore it, but her little sister ruined her chance.

She never once looked at Rain. Instead, she smirked and tossed one shoulder back, freeing her hand. Without apologizing, she repeated, "I gotta go."

"Will I see you again? We play here on Fridays. Come back and we'll let you sing. You're old enough, right?"

Holding one hand in the air as she retreated to the other side of Canal, where they had parked the car, she waved. Once she was driving, she allowed herself a glance in the rearview mirror. He was staring after them. He'd walked out into the street as if they'd known each other a lifetime and he couldn't believe she was leaving. When he was no longer in sight, she turned on Rain. "If you ever whine at me again like that in public, I will make sure that everyone in school knows you still sleep with your dolls."

Rain's mouth shot open. "I do not!"

Regan continued, "And, if you insist on following me around like a lost puppy, I'm going to leave you out in the swamp."

"I hate you, Regan! I'm telling Mom."

"How old are you anyway? You big baby. Go ahead and tell Mom. I'll be eighteen soon, and she can't do a damn thing about where I go or what I do. And, when she finds out you were with me today, you'll be grounded from ballet."

"She won't ground me from ballet. I have a scholarship, remember?" Rain crossed her arms and looked out the window. She was ignoring her now, and that was fine by Regan. Turning the radio dial, she scrolled through the stations. Janis Joplin crooned, "Me and Bobby McGee." They drove in silence the forty-something miles out of the Crescent City and through the back roads that snaked along the swamp.

When they got home, Rain jumped out, slammed the car door, then kicked it for good measure. She made a beeline for the front door, but Regan came around the hood, tackling her as she tried to clear the car's bumper. She cried out for Regan to stop while simultaneously screaming for their mother. Regan sat on top of her sister without the true urge to really hurt her. They had fought like this most of their lives. Rain was small and Regan never hit hard, but things had gotten out of hand. The Ford was a dented up 1978 model, but it was all Regan had. Other kids had new Hondas and Camaros. Her bright neon-orange Mustang somehow fit her rebel persona.

Their mother, Rona, screamed from the porch. "Regan, off!"

Regan pinched Rain hard on the arm before standing up and turning toward their mother. A swift kick in the rump sent Regan lurching forward. Like lightning, Regan turned to claw at Rain, but she was halfway to the backyard and Regan was tired of the argument. Rain was too fast, anyway.

"Regan Landry, where have you been? You know you are grounded for a month." It was a rhetorical question. Her mother didn't really want answers. She wanted Regan to shut up and do what she was told. She had behaved, until a few weeks ago. Her mother taking their father back, to be used and thrown away again, made Regan sick. She hated her father for his white trash ways, and she loathed her mother even more for falling for the conniving bastard. Rona was weak and the last thing Regan wanted was to be like her.

She made her way inside to her room, where she slammed the door and locked it. Turning on the cassette player loud, Quiet Riot filled the small room. Regan raked the activities of the day through the sieve of her brain. She retraced her footsteps along the cobbled street, through the quarter, to the old woman's room. The crystal ball, her odd seventies clothes, and the sage words she'd spoken burned across Regan's thoughts. Her mind raced to the reunion with Rain in the square, staring up at the beauty of the cathedral, then skipped to images of Chase and his strong hands wrapped around the neck of his guitar. He'd touched her hand and asked for her number. Regan flopped back against the pillows of her bed, studying the popcorn ceiling. If she'd given him her number, she would surely see him again, but now…. Closing her eyes, her hand glided up her torso and beneath the white cotton t-shirt she wore. She remembered the sultry brown eyes with flakes of emerald dotting his irises, imploring her to stay. He had looked at her with more than musical interest, and she wanted him to undress her. She imagined how his hands would feel. The rough guitar callouses as they moved over her waist and up to her breasts.

Shoving off her tennis shoes, Regan let them fall to the floor with a thump. She unbuttoned her jeans and released the zipper. Her hand plunged under the tight material, edging under the silky feel of her soft underwear to the hot wetness between her legs. She was already drenched from thinking about him. She hadn't felt safe having sex with anyone since Danny had used her, but that experience had shown her there could be pleasure before pain. Since then, she'd explored the ache between her legs and made the subtle throb of her center grow until it pushed her turbulent emotions over the edge. The secret exploration brought her to a euphoria she couldn't define.

The sensation she felt as she touched herself crackled with a naughty, guilty feeling that made the rhythm of her wicked fingers only that much more appealing. She moaned into her pillow as she pushed deeper inside herself, closing her eyes to imagine. Her hand was his, and in the end, his full lips touched her core, suckling the hot liquid that spilled from her center, making her already wet panties soaked.

The knock at her door revived her from her fantasy. "Regan, dinner's ready." Rain called from the hallway.

Regan growled with annoyance. "I'm not hungry."

Trying to avoid Mark at school on Monday was next to impossible. He'd called her the night she met Chase, but she'd been grounded from the phone, so she hadn't had to explain why she wasn't interested in talking. A switch had flipped inside her when she'd met Chase. She didn't want to be stuck with a local high school boy who would never leave the bayou and was destined to grow up working for his daddy's company. Most girls would be happy to finish high school and marry Mark and all the money he was sure to inherit. The idea of living in a plantation home with a bunch of curly-headed babies crying at her feet didn't sound like a good time, even if the silver spoon was real. Money was nice, but that existence would be a prison to her— saddled with a life she didn't want. She'd find her own money and happiness, thank you very much.

"Regan, there you are. I've been searching the halls for you. I had to ask Rain if you skipped class." He put his hand above the locker and looked down at her with shining brown eyes. The dimple in his cheek winked at her as he flashed his Crest-white smile. He was handsome and popular, but he didn't get music the way she did. The jam sessions in his garage were amateur, and the drum solos he played for her were endless. A monkey with a drumstick could play just as well.

Regan grabbed her books and shut the locker. "Sorry, I've been grounded. Can't talk on the phone or watch TV." She looked behind her, gauging who was listening in.

"I know. Rain told me."

Regan rolled her eyes. "Nothing is secret with my little sister. What a pain in the ass."

Mark laughed. "The grounding or Rain?"

Regan smiled back at him. "Both." She liked Mark. She wished they could just be friends. She started down the hall, tossing back, "I'm late for second period."

Mark jogged to catch up with her, touching her waist. "Wanna go out this weekend?"

"I can't. I'm grounded, remember?"

He took her books from her arms to carry. "For how long?"

Regan sighed hard, blowing a stray curl from her eyes. "Mom said for a month, but I bet she lets me off in another week. I start to grate on her nerves really bad when she has to see me every moment of her nights and weekends. It's like she's grounded too."

Mark chuckled. "I get it. Well, let's do something next weekend."

Regan came to a halt in front of her second class. "This is me."

Mark made a face of disgust. "Calculus? Yuck."

Regan laughed, "I know, right? Not like I'm ever going to use it again. Well, whatever. It's my last year, so I just need to cruise through so I can get on with my life."

Mark grabbed her hand and held it. Leaning against the cold cinder-block wall, iced with mint-green institutional paint, he said, "And just what is your life's plan after high school?"

The look in his eyes spoke more than the question, and Regan didn't want to have that discussion right now. She patted his arm and took her books. "Uh-later. I gotta go."

CHAPTER 2

Two weeks had passed since Regan was grounded, and she was eighteen now. Her mother's resolve was wearing thin. Regan had convinced Rona to let her out of the house, but not with the use of the car. Rona wasn't budging on that particular privilege. Regan used her mother's given name when they weren't on good terms, like when her father had come home uninvited or now, when she was grounded.

The lines knitted in Rona's forehead smoothed as she pushed her blonde hair back and leaned against the kitchen sink. She crossed her arms and let out a long sigh. "You can go out if you want, but you better get a friend to drive. The tangerine machine isn't going anywhere."

Regan would have argued, but that gave her mom more power. Instead, she went to her room and called Mark. He was the only one with a car that could make it to New Orleans. Her mother probably hadn't counted on her getting a ride since Regan and Mark had been on the outs. She didn't want to include him, but with the keys to the Mustang in her mother's purse and the knockoff Calvin Klein bag in the room where Rona was watching TV, Regan didn't have much choice if she wanted to see the Cat's Quarter again, namely Chase. She was nervous about how things would pan out, but she wasn't officially dating Mark. They hadn't fooled around since a few weeks before she was grounded. He'd been hurt when she pulled away, telling him she needed space. He had given her space but then started hounding her again. She offered friendship, explaining it would be a shame if, after all this time, they couldn't hang around together. Regan assured him that she wasn't interested in anyone else and that she just needed some distance to figure things out. It was clear that he wanted sex.

She didn't have to twist Mark's arm to take her to the French Quarter where the band was playing. Biting her lip, she worried over the attraction she felt for Chase and taking advantage of Mark's willingness to drive her to the bar. Would he sense the chemistry between her and the guitar player?

"So, who's this band you want to see? What do they play?"

Regan shrugged her shoulders as they sped down the causeway. "Not sure. They were playing jazz when Rain and I stood out in front of the bar. They asked me to sing, so I did, and then they invited me back to see them play."

It was the truth.

"Is that what this is, an audition? Rae, you know your momma's not going to let you–"

Regan's hand flew up. "You don't know what I can or can't do. I'm never going to get anywhere singing in your garage or the off moments we get a gig at a party. This is a real band," she stressed, turning in her seat, imploring him with her eyes. "A real grown-up band that plays for money." Regan raked her hand through her hair and remembered her mother doing the same thing earlier. She placed her hand on her jeans and rubbed her knees as if to erase the memory of the conversation. "Look, if you don't want to take me, just drop me off and I'll find my own way back."

Mark moved his hand off the wheel and across the console to squeeze her knee. He took a deep breath and let it out in a frustrated sigh. "All right. Okay. I'll take you. I didn't know it was so important."

Regan stared at the road. She could feel his smile but didn't turn her head to smile back. His attention had become tiresome, and the more she distanced herself, the more he clung to her. She regretted asking him. Driving to New Orleans with Mark was a big mistake. When they got back to Bonne Fete, she would tell him it was truly over. She knew now that the possibility of friendship was a lost cause. Mark was clinging to a hope that didn't exist in her heart, and the tighter he held on, the more her skin crawled when he touched her.

The band was playing popular cover music and the bar was full. Regan was finally of legal age, but she was disappointed that no one asked them for an ID when they entered the bar. It was standing room only, so they made their way to a place by the pool tables and flagged down a cocktail waitress. Mark ordered a light beer and she ordered a cherry coke. She didn't like the taste of beer and had never really longed to drink alcohol. If she wanted to sing, she didn't want to take any chances of messing up her voice or the lyrics. Mark picked up a game of pool, and Regan watched the band play, moving her hips to the music. As Mark made friends, starting a second game, she wandered closer to the stage, hoping for Chase to notice her. Guidry smiled, then blew into his sax, impressing the crowd with his short but intense solo. He then nodded to Chase. When Chase's hazel eyes found hers, he tilted his head and smiled. Regan nodded to him, finding an edge of a table to lean against. The spot where she roosted bordered a small open space being used as a dance floor. The Cat's Quarter played a funk-infused version of Michael Jackson's "Pretty Young Thing." Regan smiled as Chase gave her a wink, never breaking eye contact, and confirming his interest in her. As they ended the set, members of the band collected around the bar, but Chase ranged in her direction. Regan felt her heart do a little somersault, but she turned to look over her shoulder, wary of Mark's interruption.

"You made it." Chase's smile was infectious.

Awareness crackled over her senses and she took in his handsome features. His straight nose, soft, silky hair and white, even teeth. His eye-teeth were slightly pointy, giving him a devilish grin. She wondered what his full lips would feel like against hers. Sipping the dregs of her soda, she nodded toward the stage. "You guys are great."

Chase quirked a brow. "Even if our name is ordinary?"

Regan held her hands up, "Okay, it's a good name, but what was I supposed to say after you dissed my band?"

"Touché." He smiled. "Look, next set, if you want to sing, I'm sure the boys would love for you to join us. You were on fire the other day. They haven't stopped talking about the angel with the lungs from heaven. Though your raspy style is something sinful to be sure." His eyes glittered with mischief.

Regan shook her head in denial but couldn't wipe the grin from her face. "Yeah, I've been told I walk on water." She cocked her head to the side and gave him a challenging stare. Surely he hadn't forgotten the title of her song.

Chase's head fell back with a hoot of laughter then he looked at her with wonder. "Who are you?"

She shrugged her shoulders with a casualness she didn't feel. "Regan Landry, bonified badass."

He flashed a wide grin, dazzling her with his perfect teeth. "I don't know where you came from, but stick with us and I'll tell you where you're goin'." His hand touched her arm with a light squeeze that turned into a soft caress.

Instruments tuned up to play, and he told her to give him a moment as he backed toward the stage to join the band. After a pause, the music started with a roar. Chase's cool voice came across the microphone loud and clear. "Ladies and gentlemen, welcome to the Club on Canal. We are the Cat's

Quarter, and tonight, we have a very special treat. Everyone, please put your hands together and give a warm welcome to Regan Landry!"

Mark forgotten, Regan didn't waste time jumping onto the stage. The band must have practiced her music over the past two weeks because the spiffy lead-in almost threw her for a loop with its rendered brilliance. Why hadn't she thought of it? She'd never heard her song like this. Its pounding drums rolling with the guitar and sax were over the top. A few hoots went up, but all eyes focused on her. Pulling the mic in close, she belted out the first few lyrics, sending the room into a state of awed silence. Energy surged through her, and as she dove into the chorus, Chase leaned into her with the guitar. All the hair raised on her forearms as static electricity raced over her in amorous awareness. Chase was fulfilling all of her rock star dreams. She was actually singing *her* song in front of a crowd, and they were eating it up.

The small disco ball in the middle of the bar scattered specks of light around the stage. The sparkles over her hands and arms entranced her as she pulled the microphone closer. The dazzling globe was a stark contrast against the dark wood floor and dated wall paneling. It was the only fancy element in the bar. Regan felt like a star, and she immersed herself in the moment, soaking up the approving nods of strangers gathered around the stage. Regan let go of her troubles and bled the words of her song through the intense vibration of her voice. She climbed the scales to a final wail, reaching an all-time record-breaking pitch, then crashed to an abrupt halt. She waited for a beat. Patrons clapped and called out for more, then she crooned the last few words. The surge of applause overwhelmed her, and she blinked back tears. Her whole life, young though it was, had led her to this place and time. She felt like she had waited an eternity, not just a short eighteen years.

I am meant to be here, in this moment, singing this song. This is the beginning of everything.

Regan caught a glimpse of Mark through the crowd, beating his hands together. She could tell he was genuinely enthused for her, and it warmed her mood toward him. For a moment, he was the boy she'd thought she would love. Chase leaned close and told her she was great. Grabbing her up in a surprising hug, he crushed her to him.

It was what she wanted but at the wrong time. She pushed away. "I gotta go. Thanks."

Chase looked at her in confusion. "Now? No, stay. Please. I don't even have your number or a way to get in touch with you."

Knowing it wasn't a good idea, but afraid she might not see him again, she ran to the bar and asked for a pen. Jotting her number down on a napkin, she raced back to the stage. The band was already playing, but she pushed it into the tip jar at Chase's feet. He smiled, nodding. Regan nodded back and then turned to find Mark. He was already outside. The hot summer night air stirred her hair and she studied his bent head as he stared at the sludge along the edge of the street.

"Ready to go?" She didn't want to ask what he was thinking. Regan already knew and she didn't want to hear the breaking of his heart. She didn't want to feel more guilty than she already did for using him tonight, but what was done was done and she couldn't take it back.

Mark nodded, and they walked to the car in silence. He peeled out of the parking lot onto Canal Street and sped up, running a red light. A car almost careened into them.

"Mark, slow down!"

He ignored her, his jaw muscle jumped, and his hand gripped the gearshift. The whites of his knuckles showed under the streetlights flashing through the windows. He downshifted as they hit the ramp to the interstate. The BMW sped along the causeway as they rode in silence.

Regan tried to stay calm. She knew Mark was in pain, and she was the one responsible for it. "Mark, I'm sorry. I didn't mean to hurt your feelings tonight. I just wanted to sing so bad. I shouldn't have—"

"No, you shouldn't have!" He roared with indignation, cutting off her ill strung apology. "He was all over you, Regan, and you didn't pull away. You liked it! You wanted it!" Mark downshifted again, jerking the car as it slowed, then lunged forward as he punched the gas.

"Slow down! You're scaring me. It was just a hug." Regan's arm shot out, gripping the dash. "You are making me nervous, and you're way out of control. Besides, we aren't together anymore. We're just friends, remember?"

Mark dashed away a tear, sniffing in defense. "You're the one who wanted to be friends, but I can't. I can't sit back and watch you with someone else. Either you are with me, or you aren't with anyone."

Regan's head snapped around in indignation, "What? Who the hell do you think you are? Stop the car! Let me out. We're over. I'm done with your high school boy ways and your temper tantrums. I said I was sorry. I truly was, but now you've gone too far." She reached for the door latch, expecting him to pull the car to the side of the causeway.

"You want out?" his voice was eerily calm.

Regan was beginning to feel frantic. "Yes, pull the car over."

He punched the gas, wrenching the wheel hard to the right. As the car careened over the guardrail, he yelled, "Fine!"

Doom settled over Delila as the couple sped down the causeway hurtling toward the bayou. The soul watcher knew the future held disaster. As the car careened over the guardrail, Delila's energy was ejected from the car. Surveying the empty highway, she plunged into the bubbling water where the BMW sank. She wouldn't give up on Regan. Maybe there was still hope.

Regan's surprise instantly turned to fear, but the one piece of the puzzle that truly paralyzed her was Rain's scream. As the car dove into Lake Pontchartrain, Regan braced herself for the impact. Tamping down the panic as the water quickly surged into the vehicle, she reached to unclip her seatbelt, but it wouldn't budge. She looked over at Mark, but he was sloped across the wheel, his neck at an odd angle that she knew wasn't normal. She needed to focus.

Wrestling with the belt, she called out, "Rain?"

At first, there was silence. Then, as if waking up from a slow dream, she heard, "I'm–I'm okay, I think. You? It's really wet back here, Regan. The door won't open." Rain's voice turned to panic. Regan heard her tugging the latch of the BMW.

"Rain, you have to wait until the car fills up a little more. Then the door will open. Don't panic, but I'm stuck. I can't get out, and I need you to go for help." Regan tried to keep the tears out of her voice. Rain had to think there was a chance if Regan expected her to do the unthinkable.

"I'm not leaving you, Regan! What about Mark? I can't. I'm scared."

"You have to, Rain. I can't get out. You need to swim out and find some-one to help us. It's our only chance." She tried to keep her voice calm. "Go, Rain. Leave now before it's too late." The water was to her chest and rising. Rain was tugging at the strap holding Regan's shoulders captive. "Now, Rain!"

Regan heard the rush of water as the back door opened. Rain's soft cry broke her heart. "I love you," she heard as the water rushed over her ears.

CHAPTER 3

Regan trudged through darkness away from the light, which was only a pinhole now winking at her in the distance. Fear and determination were at war with her senses. She wouldn't go there again. This life was not over yet.

A quiet voice, soft and lilting, beckoned to her through the darkness. "Luna."

Against her will, she turned to view the glimmer quickly approaching. A flash blinded her, and when her vision cleared, a beautiful woman with long golden tresses appeared. White flowing wings protruded from her shoulder blades and she wore a luminous, flowing gown. Regan studied the hem of the garment but couldn't see the angel's feet.

The apparition's voice was a balmy comfort as she approached Regan. "Luna, don't run away. Not this time. Come with me into the light."

Regan shook her head and stepped back. The name and the angel's presence both seemed eerily familiar. Regan had stood here before. This conversation was not new. She tried to shut out the flashing memories as they momentarily arrested her.

Placing her hand over her eyes as if to ward off the images, she cried out, "No!"

"Luna, be reasonable. This is for your own benefit. It's all part of your journey. Do you remember the life that brought you here?"

Regan's mind raced back across space and time, taking her to the bank of a river. Shrouded in many robes and a stifling veil that covered her face, she wept with great sorrow. Regan watched herself as she dropped a baby in the water, intending to drown it in the morning light. In her present existence, she placed her hands over her heart and sobbed. Looking at the angel, she confessed, "I killed my child." No tears fell from her transparent form, but Regan was overwhelmed with grief. She couldn't recall the complete life she'd led, but she somehow understood the angel knew and wanted her to remember it now.

"Soledad, the soul watcher who spoke to you, made a mistake that day. She was punished for meddling in your journey. It was your first life, Luna. You've been forgiven."

Regan shook her head to clear the fog, "Wait, yes, I remember. I saw a different angel that morning. I didn't drown my baby. She begged me to save it and I did." Pausing, memories raced over her entranced form. "I was unwed, and the baby was a bastard. I saved the baby, only to be stoned to death with my child in the city square. It was a cruel death for us both. I shamed my father by breaking the law of chastity. The baby and I died a horrible death."

The angel's silence made Regan press on. "We were meant to die, and the angel's interference couldn't help our fate?" Regan shook her head, trying to understand the latticework of life's meaning.

"The angel you speak of is a spirit like you. She had the knowledge not to interfere. It was her choice, Luna."

"Why do you call me Luna? I'm Regan."

"Luna is your spirit name. Regan is the name you knew in your last life. You will bear many names as you live and learn the lessons assigned to you, but you will always return as Luna in your spirit form."

"Luna…."The name rolled off her tongue with definite familiarity. There was no reason to argue what she felt in her soul was true. "But I wasn't finished being Regan Landry. I was going to sing. My family… oh God, my mom, Rain—what will they do without me?" A fresh sob rolled up inside her. She choked on the thought of how her short life had ended. Regan remembered the argument with Mark, the car crashing into the lake, the seatbelt refusing to release as the car and her lungs filled up with water. Had Rain made it out alive?

"Is that why I died? Was this to teach me a lesson for trying to drown my baby in that life? That life was a thousand years ago. Why wait so long to punish me?"

"No."The angel hesitated, looking as if she was holding back some secret that was the key to everything. "You paid for that sin when you lived with the Mohawk."

Again, flashes of another place and time surged through her memory. She had been part of a wagon train. Her new husband, with hair the shade of the sun and eyes the color of bluebonnets, had bought a wagon, joining the trek with other homestead hopefuls as they traveled across the open plains. He promised her a land of their own and a new way of life for their family. They were attacked by Indians, and her husband was scalped alive, then set on fire. She was married to the chief of the Mohawk. Eight months later, she bore a son with pale bluebonnet-colored eyes, like his father. When the baby's eyes didn't change, and his skin remained white, the chief demanded the baby be tossed into the great falls above their camp. When the baby plunged to the water, she'd broken free and followed her child to his watery grave.

"Your sacrifice forgave you for your prior sin."

"Was I forgiven for committing suicide? Isn't that a sin?" The angel didn't answer. Regan knew they had discussed these topics before in this dark place. "Why did I drown again? Why was my life so short? What could I have possibly learned?"

The angel fidgeted with discomfort and Regan wondered if she was just another spirit like herself. The blind leading the blind? Of course, Regan didn't sport the fancy white wings, yet. Maybe she never would. They were standing in the dark. Maybe the light was heaven.

And she had just told it to go fuck itself.

She turned, darting away from where the angel beckoned her. Somehow her gut told her that when she went into the light, her knowledge of the life of Regan Landry was over. She wasn't going to let that happen. She had to save Rain and help her mother. Marching on, she didn't dare look back. Regan could no longer feel the angel's presence. Loneliness slithered around her somewhere in the in-between world of darkness and dread.

It felt like an eternity had passed, but Regan didn't have any real sense of time. In the eerie darkness, she was lost, but had a sense of familiar loneliness. Tamping down her fear, she tried to stay the course. If she trudged far enough, something had to change. Why couldn't she remember what this place was, or what came after? Fear wracked Regan's existence and prevented her from moving farther. She'd churned up memories of two past lives and flashes of other lives that she couldn't fully recall. The knowledge terrified her. She didn't want to be recycled and clung to the hope that she might somehow find her way back to her mother and Rain. They needed her.

It smelled wet, and she could hear water trickling in the distance. She followed the sound and eventually found herself standing underneath an overpass. Concrete pylons held up a massive roadway and there was nothing but swamp surrounding her for miles. The lights in the distance looked like the city. Relief flooded her core. She was under the causeway, near the accident. She heard a loud sob and a small, scared cry for help. Rain was gripping a pylon. No telling how long she had been there and with nothing to cling onto except for the causeway itself. Drivers couldn't see Rain. Regan called out to her, but Rain couldn't hear. Regan's new presence was without physical substance, and no one of this earth could hear or feel her anguish.

Regan had to find help. Rain was clearly in shock and might succumb to the lake if no one came to her aid soon. Gators weren't as thick in this part of the bayou area with the usual traffic overhead, but her sister was an easy meal in her weak condition. She wouldn't last long if she tried to swim. Help had to come soon before it was too late. Regan concentrated on lifting herself above the causeway. If she could surface to the highway, maybe she could summon a trucker who needed to stop for a leak. Standing in the middle of the road, she tried to flag an eighteen-wheeler. Pouring out her lungs, she yelled and pleaded for the trucker to stop to no avail. Even if he had gotten her message, he would have braked too far away for Rain's cries to be heard. She needed to range farther out. It felt impossible to leave Rain there all alone. After all the time Regan had searched for a way back to her sister, leaving was something she must do to summon help.

She floated about a mile, calling to different vehicles to slow. Popping into a taxicab, she grabbed at the old man's arms and tried to get him to pull over. "Please, please, you have to hear me. My sister's life is at stake. I need your help." When he didn't seem to hear her cry, she sighed heavily and looked at the dash. A pretty card with a school photo was attached near his cab license on display. The grade school handwriting was made out to say, "Happy Birthday, Papaw," signed, "with love, Brandy."

"For the love of Brandy, please stop! Please, please hear me. I need you to save my sister."

The man stayed quiet but looked in his rearview mirror. She noticed the hair that rose on his forearms in the light of the dawn that crested the bayou. There were no cars behind them, but he still signaled as he pulled to the side. Regan followed him as he exited the vehicle, standing there watching the sunrise. "Over here! That's the wrong way. She's over here." Regan's excited energy couldn't be heard, but she was sure the man in the car sensed her presence. He shook his head and started back to his car. "No," Regan wailed. "Please don't give up. You wouldn't give up if it was Brandy." Pushing her energy at him, a small breeze stirred, catching his ballcap and tumbling it across the cement, closer to Rain.

The old man stumbled after it as Regan used all her might to push the cap farther down the causeway. He paused and then she heard Rain's tired, troubled voice call out for help. "Is someone up there? Please. I'm down here." It was faint, but he'd heard it. He stopped, clutching the cap, and quickly looked over the rail. He couldn't see her from where he was standing, but he could hear her faint call. Another car slowed and parked behind the old man's sedan, and the rescue relay began. The cab driver sent the vehicle to call the police. Regan wanted to weep with relief, but no tears fell upon her ghostly face. A deep throb in the place she would have called her heart, if she had a body, thumped with pain. It pierced her soul.

Three police cars, a boat called in from the nearest marina, an ambulance, and even a fire truck arrived in a short span of time. A team of men rappelled from the interstate and pulled Rain to safety. Regan knew her sister would be okay but dreaded what they would find when they dredged the lake to extract the emerald-green BMW. Forcing her spirit state below the water, she had to see. The car tires were buried in the silt of the lake, and the door to the car still hung open. The body she had inhabited while she called herself Regan Landry was hunched over, hair splayed out like an ostrich feather fan as her tresses floated around her head. Her arms and legs dangled from the front seat. Her torso was still tethered by her safety belt. Mark's form now leaned toward her dead body, as if still trying to claim what was already lost. It was a scene out of some sick movie, an unrequited love story, a modern version of Romeo and Juliet. Regan hoped her mother would never have to see her remains. A diver joined her, inspecting the sunken vehicle. Bubbles rose from his tank, flowing through her invisible energy. She thought it might tickle, but alas, she felt nothing. She wished she could feel anything besides the emptiness that she could only define as a hollow ache.

Regan wanted her body back. She wanted to sing in front of large crowds and make her dreams come true. She wanted to be crushed in Chase's arms one more time, like tonight after she'd sung. There was something more to him than just good looks. They shared chemistry in their love of music, and something in the depths of his sherry-colored eyes beseeched her to want more.

Was he my soulmate?

She'd been drawn to him instantly, and she ached now for the missed opportunity. A life where they might have connected. Now she was forever alone in whatever this in-between world was. There was so much she didn't understand.

I should have asked the angel more questions. Like how to find my way back to reality.

Maybe this was reality. Thinking back on the old seer's vision, Regan now knew the true meaning of her divine message. She'd wanted to believe her picture in the paper and water meant her song would be famous, that the light was surrounding a stage. The old woman was warning her of her ill-timed death. She had told her to live each day as if it were her last, and her voice had been somber. The woman had known.

CHAPTER 4

I
t was the second time Regan had appeared somewhere she was thinking about with no recollection of getting there or knowing how much
time passed in between. Standing outside her mother's bedroom, Regan
heard muffled sobs and curses beyond the door. Someone had told her
mother she was dead. How could Regan let her know she was okay? She
wasn't okay.

The door to her sister's room opened. Rain crept to the kitchen in
darkness. *Is it the same day? How much time has passed?* Following Rain,
Regan wandered around the island. On the table was the local newspaper. Her face and Mark's were plastered across the front page. Rain
was given credit for recounting the story of how it all happened. She
described the argument to the reporter, and the paper declared the event
as a murder-suicide, a lover's quarrel. Lovers? They weren't even dating
anymore. Regan slapped the table with fury. The pages fluttered. Rain's
head snapped back from the fridge, looking at the table and around the
room with suspicion.

"Regan?" she whispered.

Regan grabbed at her nightshirt sleeves, "Rain? Can you see me?"

Rain's eyes darted past her ghostly energy to the backdoor locks and the
window over the kitchen sink. After a pause, her sister grabbed her snack
and scurried to her bedroom.

Regan noted the date on the paper. It was three days after the accident.
She followed her sister back to her room and sat on the bed next to her. Rain
took a bite of her cheese sandwich then a large sip of the soda, followed
by a deep intake of breath, and an unladylike belch. Rain teared up, setting
the plate aside. The dark circles under her eyes were hollows where smooth

unlined skin used to be. Her pajamas were rumpled like she'd been in them for days. The phone rang and Rain lunged for the receiver.

"Hello," she whispered.

"Hey, is Regan there?" Regan heard the voice and recognized it. Chase wouldn't know about the accident unless he'd read the paper. Shock, then regret, rushed over Rain's face in tandem. Regan ached to hug her sister.

"I'm so, so sorry, Rain," Regan whispered to the empty in-between world she belonged to.

Rain's voice was barely audible, "She's not here."

There was a pause. "Uh, okay. I'll call back."

"Don't!" Rain rushed before he could hang up the phone. "Please don't call back. My mom can't handle these phone calls anymore. My sister is dead." Bursting into tears, Rain hung up the receiver, not waiting for more questions. She obviously didn't want to explain how she'd died. How many times had Rain and their mother had to do this? *Poor Rain.* Regan glanced toward her mother's room. She had really messed up this time. Regan hadn't hugged her mother or told her that she loved her for so long, and she'd give anything to do it right now. She floated out of Rain's small room and down the hall to her mother's. Passing through the closed bedroom door, Regan watched her mother sleep. Wet tresses of blonde hair stuck to her cheeks, and her breath fell in rhythmic inhales and exhales as she let go of the stress and pain she'd had to endure that day.

Regan lay next to her, wrapping her arms around her mother. "I love you." She whispered. "I never knew I wouldn't get another chance to say it. I'm so sorry for not telling you more often. I'm so sorry for all the pain I've caused. I'll stay for a while and watch over you and Rain. I won't let anything else bad happen. You can count on me for that."

Her mother sighed in her sleep and mumbled her name. "Regan, come home." Rona sobbed and rolled over, opening her eyes. She was staring right at Regan. "Why, God? Why?" Pressing her eyes shut tight, Rona rolled onto her back. She pulled the pillow over her head and began sobbing hard. Regan's heart felt like it would burst. Even though she no longer possessed the organ associated with love, she still felt emotional pain. Maybe the heart wasn't just the core of the body, but its main purpose was to pump energy that resonated from within the soul. People were known to die of a broken heart. Would her soul evaporate into nothing from her own broken existence?

Delila could do nothing except follow Regan and try to convince her to return to the light. Her moment's distraction, when she glanced at Venery, might very well warrant a penance for eternity. As a soul watcher in the in-between world, she was assigned a soul to guard and guide until their existence reached its goal. Then Delila would be granted another life—a chance to advance her spirit. Her own spirit guide had not called her to counsel yet. This wasn't good. At the end of each life phase, whether embodied or unembodied, her energy floated to a place to confer with her spirit guide.

Has Rodanian abandoned me?

She wouldn't blame him. Though so much time had passed, so many lives had been lived, and many goals had been attained, she still made blunders. Granted, it had been a long time since she'd had to repeat a soul-watching cycle for the same soul, but it obviously wasn't beyond her capacity. The problem now was that Luna still thought she was Regan, and she refused to reincarnate. For Delila to succeed, these things must happen. Without an embodied soul to guide, Delila could only stand by until Regan was ready.

She watched as her ward lay beside her mother. Tears rolled down Rona's face. It disheartened Delila that she couldn't chant soothing energy to both. It was the embodied souls who suffered most from a death. In human form, souls were filled with glorious emotions but with no cognitive memory of their past lives. They didn't conceive that their actual existence was permanent throughout time. Delila supposed it was for the best. If Rona knew she would see Regan again in her next cycle of life, then she would surely run the bathwater and plug in the toaster this very minute. Delila knew the pain of losing a child. What she wanted to know most right now was the future, since there were exponential outcomes. God's gift of free will made predictions complicated. Each soul floundered or flourished in different phases of the puzzle, making their guardians scurry about like rats on a sinking ship to save them. And if the soul watcher turned their spiritual eye for even a moment, as she had, all could be lost. This waiting in limbo was torturous. Delila might not be able to channel energy to Rona, but she could say a prayer for the mother and daughter.

CHAPTER 5

Regan remained at home for weeks, watching the daily movements of her family as routine breathed its way back into their lives. Her mother moved like a zombie but didn't have the luxury of remaining at home for the rest of her existence. Bills needed paying. Her mother's struggle and toil weren't something Regan considered much when she was alive. Rona returned to her life as a cashier at the Piggly Wiggly, and Rain went to her ballet classes every day after school. Regan wandered around the house, talking to her sister and watching late-night television with her mother. She tried to comfort them the only way she knew how — by being there. Every waking moment and sleeping moment, too, she was with them. Dread of disappearing consumed her, and she was afraid to leave the house for fear of where it might lead her, but as time passed, Regan grew curious.

She sat in an empty desk next to Rain in her homeroom class, listening to the science teacher explain Einstein's Theory of Relativity. Regan pondered the lecture and wondered if it was true. She thought about the meeting with the angel and the life she remembered from so long ago. The seer had told Regan she was a new soul. Maybe the medium meant inexperienced. Maybe there was no division of time, and everything happened all at once. If it were true, she'd just have to figure out how to get back to the past and change everything. As if feeling her dismal thoughts, Rain let out a long sigh.

The aging science teacher wore a blue plaid shirt and khaki pants. His brown hair was too long and his beard a bit scraggly. He called out, "Rain Landry, did you have something you wanted to add to the discussion?"

Rain sat up straight in her seat, tucking a lock of strawberry blonde hair behind one ear. "No, Mr. Simms. I just think it's a lot to take in."

Mr. Simms nodded. A glint of light reflected off the bald spot where his overlong hair parted in the back. He wrote an equation on the board and rattled on for the remainder of the hour. Regan could tell Rain was day-dreaming. Unless her sister snapped out of her depression soon, she wasn't going to complete the year. Regan followed Rain between classes, trying to talk some sense into her.

"You need to concentrate! Ninth grade is pretty easy, but next year will be harder, and you need this stuff as a stepping-stone to get through next year's courses. Don't screw around, Rain. You don't want to end up in summer school. Mom needs you to help out, and Lord knows she doesn't need any more worries."

Regan didn't really know what else to say. She had never been an exam-ple for other students, but in her defense, she would never have gotten into college, and if she had, they couldn't have afforded the tuition. Rain was different. She had a full ballet scholarship to the best academy in New Orleans, and she was smart enough to get into any university she wanted. Rain was a voracious reader. It was part of the reason she was such a pain in the ass. Because she knew it all, Rain didn't have friends of her own. Their mother equated her tag-along behavior as keeping an eye on Regan. Maybe it was true. But she really wished Rain hadn't followed her that night to see her die. It must have been the worst moment in her young life. Most fourteen-year-olds didn't experience heavy stuff like death unless it was an older grandparent who kicked the bucket.

Rain threw her books on the tan tile in front of her locker, grabbing at her hair in frustration. "I hate school. This sucks, and I want to die," she murmured under her breath. Two girls approached the lockers. One tapped her friend, who covered her mouth in exaggerated shock.

Their whispers echoed throughout the corridor. "Her sister died with that boy in the car crash. *She* was with them."

Rain opened her locker and swapped out the books she needed for her next period. Rolling her eyes, she turned to the girls. Regan recognized them. They were new to the cheer team and in Rain's grade, but she doubted they ran in the same circles as her younger sister. The girls were new to popular-ity and Rain never spoke to anyone.

She slammed the locker door. "I can hear you!"

The girls covered their mouths and tried to suppress the giggles that followed. Regan couldn't believe their thoughtless behavior. She was happy to see Rain stand up for herself, but worried by the sudden backbone. If

Regan had been alive, she would have yanked the girls by their French braids. But then again, if she were still alive, this wouldn't be happening. Her sister was stuck in one of the worst school years of her life, one that would define her place in high school for the next three years. She was already voted the president of the Library Club and a member of the Speech Club. Regan guessed this new morbid phase of Rain's life would shake things up a bit. It wouldn't make her popular, but it might make her edgy, and that was better than being a nerd.

Regan watched as her sister went into algebra. It was Regan's least favorite subject, so she decided to skip. She explored the hallways while things were quiet, and everyone was in class. Wandering randomly, she found herself in front of Mark's locker. It was covered in paper flowers and cards from the students. It was a shrine to his lost youth. *Asshole!*

She doubted hers would be the same. Roaming another four hallways, she made her way to her locker. Mark's shadowy figure leaned against the decorated metal door. His hair dripped water onto the tile floor. His head was bowed, but his neck was no longer at an odd angle. She stopped cold. Energy raced up her core in a prickling sensation she identified as fear.

"Mark?" she whispered, though her voice could be heard by no one, or maybe it could? Mark lifted his head and stared at her. His blue eyes glistened in the dull lights overhead. She wasn't sure if tears coursed down his cheeks or if it was the water from the lake still clinging to his dead form. He was a shadow of the past, like her. He was translucent, still wearing the same clothes from the night they'd drowned. He reached his hand toward her, but Regan didn't move. She was angry. He took her life. She wanted to kill him, but he was already dead—scratch his eyes out at the very least, but there wasn't any substance to him. He opened his mouth to reply and water gushed out. She turned away, not able to handle the ghastly vision. When she heard the bell ring, she glanced back, but he was gone. Her heart exchanged anger for loss. A fist gripped and twisted inside her. Regan knew she had to find him. Maybe if she could resolve the argument, they could both move on, but to where was the question. She wanted to go back to the past. She wanted *her* life back.

It occurred to her that the one place she might find Mark was at his home. After school let out, she followed Rain to the bus and rode with her until they reached Mark's stop. She hesitated. Regan didn't know how things worked in her new altered world. If she got off the bus here, would she ever find her way home? She could hang out and catch the bus again tomorrow if worse came to worst. It wasn't probable that she'd be lost there forever.

As Regan floated out the open bus door behind other students who made their way home, she studied her sister's profile in the dust-covered window. Regan stood still, watching the bus pull away from the curb. Rain's heated breath frosted the glass where she drew a heart. Inside she put the initials "RKL," a plus sign, then "MAJ." Rain and Mark's initials momentarily paralyzed her. Rain wasn't just mourning the loss of a sister, she was mourning the loss of her high school crush. It was then that Regan knew Rain had been in love with Mark.

CHAPTER 6

It felt odd to walk through a solid building, but there were no boundaries for Regan. She floated through the front door from habit, but she very well could have just glided into Mark's bedroom or the garage where they used to practice their music. She went into the living room, but it was empty. Regan made her way to the kitchen. Mark's mother sat slumped over a table, gripping a bottle of prescription pills in one hand and an empty beer in the other. Regan worried if Mark's dear mother had taken too many. She was out cold, but the tear-stained face and rhythmic breathing told her all was okay for now. Mark walked through the opposite wall. He stood over his mother, trying to grip the pills and pull them away from her. He railed and balled his fist, but nothing absorbed his reach or blows. His mother whimpered and moaned. Her head rolled to the side, and a string of drool pooled on the table.

Regan wasn't sure if he was aware of her presence, but she felt the ache of his sadness. His emotions vibrated in angry pulses, and she read them like a script in a silent movie.

Regan moved closer, searching the woman for other signs of life. "I think she'll be okay, Mark. She's still breathing."

Regan tried her best to reassure him, but she suddenly zinged with newly rekindled animosity. She wasn't sure if it was his or hers. This pushing and pulling of energy was confusing, and he still hadn't looked directly at her. She watched his contorted features stare down at his mother, studying the woman's incapacitated state, taking in the matted hair and tangled robe ties. Her toenails were too long and the polish chipped. The slippers she wore were the only thing that was pink, puffy, and full of life. Regan wanted to shed tears for his mother's anguish. She'd liked her when she was alive.

When Regan looked back up at Mark, he was gone. Damn, she'd lost the opportunity to speak with him. She combed the house for his presence, but without luck. He'd left the premises or was hiding. Either way, she couldn't feel him. She meandered outside and sat on the porch swing, wishing she could feel the breeze that stirred the tree leaves or smell the azaleas blooming along the hedge. Her mind sorted through possibilities and she wondered what she would be doing today if the car crash hadn't happened.

Would I be hanging out with Chase? Would I be singing in his band by now? Would he have kissed me?

He'd called her house.

Regan felt a mixture of anger, loss, and sadness for what could have been. She felt darkness creeping up from the porch's cold concrete surface. Seeping over her luminous form, it engulfed her. She was no longer at Mark's home in Bonne Fete. She heard the dripping of water once more. A steady tick, tick, ticking against a liquid surface somewhere in a blackened cave. She'd been here before, after the accident. There was just enough light to see the charcoal-colored wet stone. It was as if the rock seeped water. Her mind whirled with how she'd gotten here and where exactly *here* was. The pinpoint of light she had run from blinked at her in the distance. *No*, she wouldn't go to it. Though she had seen Rain and her mother, they weren't okay. Mark was still angry and unsettled, and she needed to make peace with him. She needed to see her family safe, and then she could ascend if she must, but she'd made a promise.

Mustering her energy, Regan pushed herself away from the light. With determination to get back to where she was before, she concentrated on floating forward and didn't look back, not even when she heard the angel call her, "Luna."

A snaking white fog floated around her like a river, and an unknown energy source ruffled through her. As if she were on a rollercoaster, during a warm summer evening, things began to drift slowly forward. Everything came to an abrupt stop and then her energy catapulted as if she were being shot from a canon. Water, cypress trees, brick buildings, wrought-iron railings—all whizzed by at an alarming speed. This wasn't something she'd experienced before. Fear of the unknown gripped her spirit. Regan found her own ethereal hands fluttering at her throat as she struggled to stop, then everything came to a shuddering halt. She found herself standing on cobblestones in front of the bar where she'd sung with The Cats

Quarter. The sun jagged between buildings, glinting off the brass door-knob of the closed door. A street cleaner and a garbage truck were the only two vehicles on the road. She could tell by the faint light in the sky that it was early morning, and the heart of the Quarter was finally asleep. Regan moved closer to the window and stared in. She didn't have the urge to enter. Chase wasn't there.

Floating along Jackson Square, Regan passed the bench Rain had lain on while waiting for her to return. Without pondering her direction, she felt pulled toward the familiar fountain in a nearby courtyard. The old woman was probably sleeping. Regan wanted to shake her awake and give her a piece of her mind. What use was the gift to tell the future if you didn't tell the entire story? The seer had left out some very important details that might have prevented Regan from ending up dead!

Regan entered the small home the same way she'd entered Mark's. The old woman sat in a dusty kitchen with green-checked, tattered linoleum that was yellowed with age. She nursed a cup of steaming black coffee that looked like sludge as she looked over the newspaper. Regan saw the picture of Mark and herself splashed across the black and white newsprint. The woman let out a heavy sigh and set the paper down, shaking her head as she made an "Um, um, um" sound deep in her throat.

"That's what I was trying to tell her. Damn chile done run off like she knowed everything."

Regan's jaw dropped. "Me! You're the one who spoke in half-truths and lies."

The woman's head snapped up, searching the corners of the room. "You be here, chile?" The woman held her coffee cup out, peering at the goose-bumps on her own arms. "Yeah, you done be watching me, trying to figure out why old Zada didn't tell you da end to your story." The old woman nodded again. "Um-hm. I'll be damned."

"As a matter of fact, I *was* wondering." She stopped and waited, but the seer didn't say anything. "I—I didn't intend to come here. It was almost like I was summoned. I was somewhere else and then…" Regan's thoughts scattered as the woman started to speak again.

"I knows what cha thinkin', but my vision isn't as clear as everyone thinks it should be. Knowing what will happen is sometimes tricky. Sometimes, the spirit world just shows me the possibilities. I could have told you that you was going to die, but then what if you didn't? You wouldn't have believed anything I ever said, and you would tell people I was a fake." She wandered to the sink, putting her cup in the stained porcelain basin and began to run the water. "Nobody wants to hear about their own death no-how."

"But if you had told me, I might not have died!" Regan railed against the old woman's cluttered rambling as she talked low to herself.

"You need to go on now with your spirit-self. You shouldn't be here. You should have gone on into the light. You is too young to be stuck in this hell hole, but I suppose you is too young a soul to have enough sense to save your sorry butt." She stared at the ceiling for a minute with her eyes closed and then made the sign of the cross three times.

"Chile, you won't find the answers you're searching for here. Only your spirit guide can help you now." Zada clicked her tongue, seeming to consider Regan's presence. "I'm too busy today to start all that channeling, but come back on Sunday, and I'll see what I can do for you. Sunday is a good day to be talking to angels. It's the Lord's day, and if he say it's okay, then I's help you."

The old woman dried the cup, put it back in the cabinet, wiped the excess water from around the sink, and went to her bedroom. She changed, then walked outside. The blazing sun almost paralyzed Regan as she tried to follow her. The woman chanted in a low hum as she departed the courtyard and turned toward Jackson Square. Regan could feel the field of energy surrounding the woman pushing her away. She must have some sort of magic power to keep the dead at bay. It made sense. If you could talk to the dead and hear their concerns, every lost spirit in the world would be hovering around waiting to speak. Regan thought it was odd that she was the only soul present. She hadn't sensed any other spirits, and she knew there must be more dead wandering the in-between world besides her.

Regan walked the cobbled and paved streets, exploring places she'd never been. The bars were opening their doors to air out the stench of stale beer and cigarette smoke from the night before. She glided through the French Market and watched the vendors uncover the wares in their stalls and talk amongst themselves about the commerce the day would bring. She saw a silver bracelet she would've loved to have bought for Rain's birthday. Her sister loved turquoise, and the silver cuff had a large oval-shaped turquoise stone in the middle of the intricate design of twisted silver loops. She summoned all her energy to see if she could lift the bracelet and transport it home, but it wouldn't budge. She would have to find another way to get it for Rain.

Delila watched Regan finger the silver bracelet, wondering if the vendor saw the turquoise wiggle on its thin, swirling band. Regan was exploring the outer realm of the in-between, and Delila had cloaked her presence for now. Her powers had grown throughout the many thousands of lives of her existence. Regan was her ward, and she would shadow the girl throughout all of her experiences until their time together was complete. Delila's luminous existence was constant most of the time, except for now. She felt herself fading and knew in an instant she was being summoned home. *It's about time.*

Rodanian was a formidable presence. He looked like a giant-sized version of the grand Buddha himself, but without the protruding belly and hanging earlobes. His kingly scowl alerted her to his displeasure.

"And what is it you think you've accomplished now?"

His great throne was a large divan draped in fine magenta and golden silk, floating in the midst of a great thunderhead. If spirit guides were allowed to have egos, she suspected his was the grandest and had sharp teeth.

"Delila?"

Her energy coiled at his tempered bellow. "I'm watching my ward, your grace."

"Save your pleasantries. If you'd been watching your ward, this wouldn't have happened, and you and I would not be having this conversation."

Delila winced. She knew it was true. "But, haven't we all been distracted at some point?"

The waves of negative energy rolled off him, and she could feel a low vibration of uncertainty. Delila wasn't where she was because of a lack of experience. She had known Rodanian her entire existence, and though his presence was not a puffy confection like cotton candy, he had lived longer than any spirit she knew. Rodanian had to have made a similar mistake at some point in his existence. She knew she had once watched over a soul that was dear to him, so many eons ago. Her success had granted her a life of her choosing. It was a grand life to be sure, but her previous success might allow her to call on his favor again now.

"I must ask that you grant me a way to correct this mistake. This soul should not suffer such great peril at her displacement because of my few seconds lapse in duty. She is vulnerable even now that I am away from her, conversing with you."

He nodded, appearing to contemplate her request. "You are right in this request. There will be a penalty in time, but if you are ready to sacrifice yourself, then I grant you this one reprieve. Don't squander it," he warned, clapping his hands twice. Thunder boomed in the distance. She was already transcending as she heard his fading voice. "And get it right this time for all of our sakes."

CHAPTER 7

Regan floated up the front porch and through the front door. Her mother was standing by the stove cooking dinner. Regan wished she could smell the aroma of the sautéed garlic, onions, and peppers mixed with the ground beef that would go into the dirty rice. The sliced French bread slathered with garlic butter graced a baking pan and would have made her mouth water if she'd been alive. It sat on the counter next to an open bottle of wine as the oven preheated. Rain walked in the kitchen, grabbed a wine glass from the cabinet, and filled her glass to the rim.

"Rain Landry, you put that glass down and get yourself a Coke from the fridge. And set the table. Dinner's almost ready." Rona didn't even glance over her shoulder to make sure her orders were carried out as she tossed the sautéed ingredients in with the rice.

Rain took a big gulp of the wine and set it down next to the stove. Rona grasped it without looking and took a large sip. Her eyes glistened in the fluorescent kitchen light. She was holding it together, but just barely. "God, help me," she whispered to no one.

Rain stared out the window of the breakfast room where they ate most of their meals. In the dining room was a massive oak table that served as a catch-all for bookbags, bills, dancewear and a car part her mother couldn't afford to have replaced.

Rain pointed out the window. "Look, Momma, it's a full moon tonight. There's a red glow around it. That's weird."

Rona brought the pan of dirty rice to the table and set it on a potholder, then returned for the bread that was starting to burn. "Blood on the moon," she said as she filled their plates. "That's a bad omen."

Rain let the curtain fall. Tears brimmed in her eyes as she sat down at the table. "What does it mean?"

Rona served them both a slice of bread and placed a dishtowel on her lap. They couldn't afford paper napkins and linen napkins were for families like Mark's. "It's some nonsense my granny used to talk about. Nothing to worry over. It's just a lunar eclipse. Some people say it's a chance to end one thing and start another, but Grandma used to say it's a warning from above. Of course, what else could happen that hasn't already." Rona's voice caught in her throat, and she paused to collect herself with a deep sigh. "Go on, honey, let's eat."

Rain didn't push the subject, and Regan was glad that some of her little sister's rebellion had quelled itself. Their mother didn't need the added stress. They ate in silence and Rona finished the bottle of wine before turning out the lights and going to bed.

Regan was glad to see Rain in her room studying. It was too close to the end of the school year to see her give up. She supposed it was a good distraction from recent events. Rain opened her notebook to copy equations, and Regan saw the swirls of doodling in the corners of her scratch work. Rain Katheryn Juban, Rain Landry Juban, Rain heart Juban. Flowers, hearts, initials and more littered the scratch sheet where Rain began her homework. Regan ran her hand over the page, and Rain shivered. The distraction was enough to dislodge Rain from algebra to beginning another heart with Mark's name in it, but instead of adding her own after the cross, she focused on making the cross larger and deeper and then began to sketch a band of daisies around it. Instead of her initials, she put RIP below. All the scribble was about Mark. It made Regan wonder if Rain was even upset by her death.

"Damn it, Rain, why didn't you tell me? You could have had him, and maybe I'd still be here," Regan blasted.

Rain's head jerked up, catching her own reflection in the full-length mirror that faced the bed. She pushed a lock of her hair over her shoulder and craned her head sideways to check out her profile. Finally, she stood and walked closer to look at herself. She undid the top button of her pajama top and lifted her small breasts to create small mounds of cleavage above her vanilla-colored flannel PJs. The roses printed on them looked like pink polka dots at a distance.

If Regan could roll her eyes, she would. "Oh, God, please don't play with yourself. I won't be able to handle it. It will totally gross me out."

Rain crossed her arms over her chest, hiding away what she barely had. "He never would have liked me anyway. Who would when they had you?"

Was she talking about her? Regan searched her features, but Rain sighed and flopped on the bed, staring at the ceiling. "I might as well give up. I'm never going to beat you. You were everything he wanted—everything every boy wants, and I'm just …weird."

Tears sprang to her eyes, and Rain turned on her side, hugging a pillow. Regan felt her sibling's heartache and wished there was something she could do to soothe the pain. She stroked her sister's hair and talked softly to her. "You don't want to be like me. Look where I am. You are so much smarter than that. You're talented and will probably be a prima ballerina one day. You could be a scientist, a teacher…the sky is the limit. You don't want to waste your time on a boy like Mark. He was a douche bag. He almost murdered you. Thank God you got out in time. I am so happy for that. Please don't waste your life feeling miserable because of my mistakes. You are going to be amazing. Rain, I know I never said this when I was alive, but *you are* amazing."

The tears subsided and Rain hiccupped softly. Her hand fluttered over the scrollwork she had done while working on algebra. She traced the heart with Mark's name in it. "Don't worry, I'm going to be there soon."

CHAPTER 8

Rain's words haunted Regan as she floated along the bayou where the car had splashed into Lake Pontchartrain. She contemplated what Rain had meant. Was she going somewhere? Maybe to the graveyard to bring flowers? To Mark's home to check on his mother? Surely, she didn't mean she would be joining him in death. Rain wasn't the suicidal type. Was she?

She's a little geeky, sure, and maybe a bookworm, but she's never been depressed—until now.

Was their death such a great burden that Rain felt she couldn't go on? Regan thought her mother might have the right to contemplate extreme measures, but surely not Rain. She was young, smart, and had everything to live for. Besides, no mother should have to outlive their children, so Rain had to live. She had so many opportunities ahead. She could have her pick at success. Surely, Rain wouldn't think about throwing it away over Mark. He didn't deserve that kind of sacrifice. Regan hadn't been the best role model, and she supposed her devil-may-care attitude is what Rain was impersonating now. *Damn Mark Juban! And damn me for not being a better sister.*

Regan watched the sunrise over the swamp as she floated above its murky surface. As she rose above the guardrail of the causeway, she watched a pair of egrets take flight. She remembered hitching a ride with the cab driver to save Rain. Maybe she could do it again now. She picked a minivan cruising along at a moderate speed, but when she stood in front of it, it whizzed through her. She tried again and popped into the cab of an eighteen-wheeler. The middle-aged man was yanking his pecker and lolling his head back against the headrest. *Gross!* Skidding back into the freeway, she lunged herself into a Jeep with the top off and music blaring. Thank God, a normal person near her age who was headed into the city. If not, it would be close enough for her to wander around and find her way. She needed to see Chase. He hadn't called the house again, and for that she was glad, but a little hurt he didn't inquire more about what happened to her.

Hell, it's in the papers. He probably knows the whole story and has forgotten me by now.

The Jeep took the Vieux Carre exit and made its way down Iberville Street, then veered off when it approached Bourbon.

Regan made her exit as the driver slowed to a rolling stop at the sign. "This is where I get off. See ya' later, alligator." She waved as the young man drove on, knowing he had no clue he'd just given a ghost a lift into the city. She pondered what he might say if he knew. Floating among the shops, she watched their keepers opening the sliding metal gates. Some swept door stoops while others dragged out display racks onto the sidewalk. She admired the shiny fruit at the grocer's and longed to push the button on the Coke machine out front. There were some things she missed about living more than others, and soda was one of them. She never smoked and hadn't lived long enough to grow interested in alcohol, but she certainly had a penchant for soda. Pepsi was her favorite, but most of Louisiana catered to a Coke crowd. Pepsi was sweeter, and she remembered how the bubbles tickled her nose as they danced off the ice cubes in her glass. As if teasing her, the machine rumbled, and a cold glass bottle of Coke rolled into the tray below. The storekeeper jerked his head around, inspecting the vending machine's bizarre behavior. Standing with his mouth agape and broom handle paused in mid-stroke, the older man squinted his eyes, then crossed himself, looking toward the sky.

"Damn," Regan cursed in wonder. "Did I do that?" She moved closer to inspect the machine and heard someone cackling from above. Turning in a circle to see where the laughter came from, Regan spotted a dark form perched high on the Spanish wrought iron railing of the apartment across the street. The shadowy figure spread its arms and twirled like a mini tornado in her direction. A dust devil swirled below them, and the old man took up a coughing fit, swiping at the air around him. Finally throwing his arms in the air with disgust, he took the broom inside. "Damn ghosts," he muttered, slamming the door behind him.

Regan lurched back as the apparition approached her. He was too close for comfort. Now that he'd stopped spinning, she could see he was luminous like her. His filmy existence sported tight, black pants, a cream-colored shirt with billowing sleeves, and a silk charcoal-colored vest with a dark hole in the left breast pocket. His black boots probably would have been shiny if he wasn't an apparition. She couldn't place what time period his clothes were from, but they were at least a century before this decade. His well-made ensemble was too expensive for him to be a pirate, she decided. He must have been aristocracy or a wealthy merchant.

He reached out to touch her and Regan slapped his luminous hand, "Back off, buddy."

Once again, she heard the same cackle as before. "Oh, pardon," he drawled out, bowing deeply. She was sure he was mocking her. He smelled like spring grass and baked cinnamon rolls. *Oh my God! I can smell him!*

"Who—what are you?"

His mouth opened in mock surprise then shut with a snap. Wait, she could hear him, and he could hear her! There *was* life in the in-between world. Chills roved over her as she wondered what other spirits were skulking about.

"I am Lord Gustave Desmarais, at your service." The swank apparition made another flourishing bow, clicking his boot heels as he righted himself.

Regan eyed him suspiciously. Not sure what he might be able to do to her spirit form, but not letting down her guard to find out. "Lord, huh? Well, Lord Desmarais, it's nice to see another soul like myself, but I must be on my way."

He didn't try to hide his chuckle, obviously amused by her words. "And what's the hurry? Decided to go into the light after all?" He paused for a moment, and Regan could feel a vibration of energy roving over her, but he was clearly in front of her and couldn't be in two places at once—or could he?

Spinning around, she inspected the street and alcoves around them. "Don't touch me!" She eyed Gustave, and her luminous hand came up between them, warding him off. He chuckled with glee. His incessant amusement at her expense grated on her nerves. She darted toward Jackson Square, leaving him to entertain himself.

"No, wait! Please, I apologize." He called after her. "Don't go! I'll behave. I promise."

Against her better judgment, she stopped. When she turned, he was already there. To her annoyance, she couldn't outrun him. She crossed her arms to defend herself from any untoward advances.

"I admit. I've been away from the physical world for a long time, and my manners are a bit rusty. I'll be on my best behavior. I promise, just stay with me awhile. It's been so long since I…" his voice trailed off. "This existence can be quite lonely, and the modern world is quite boring to an old spirit like me."

"Then why are you here?" Regan challenged.

Gustave bit his lip to prevent dissolving into laughter. Regan turned to leave. "Why are any of us here?" He called to her back. She turned and studied him. Gustave quirked a brow. "That seems to be the million-franc question."

It was Regan's turn to look inquisitive. "Franc?"

He shook his head as if to clear it. "Pardon, million-dollar. I am aware of the current currency, but alas, I do miss les bon vieux jours."

"The good old days," Regan repeated absently. How did she know that? She hadn't taken French, opting instead for Spanish, and she wasn't very good at it. Shaking her head, she began to float away from the trickster spirit. His charm and ill-timed humor grated on her nerves.

"I'm stuck," Gustave called out wearily. His humor seemed to vanish. "I walked away from the light too long ago to remember now, and it hasn't shown itself to me since. I was hoping you might tell me where to find it or at least warn you not to run from it. If the light shows itself to you again, take it, or you may be forever caught in this limbo, like me."

Regan gave him her attention once more. Something about his presence felt different, and she thought she might be crazy for stopping to listen, but his words momentarily paralyzed her. What if what he said was true? What if she got stuck here? Was this limbo? She had ignored the angel's pleas to go into the light. She had needed closure and time to watch over her mother and sister. What if she could never return to the world of the living? So far, the only souls she'd seen in the in-between were Mark, who either wasn't aware of her presence or was ignoring her, and this Frenchman, who was long past his expiration date. The in-between world seemed cold and lonely. Maybe that's why Gustave was desperate to capture her attention.

"I don't know where the light is. I left it at my crossover. I still have things I need to take care of, so if you'll excuse me."

Gustave didn't try to detain her any longer. Time stopped with a flash, then reeled forward like a cassette tape on high speed. She was propelled to the bar where she'd met Chase. It was now late afternoon. The band played, and the same three patrons held up the bar. Chase was caught up in his music, strumming the acoustic guitar. Regan's heart flip-flopped as his low and gravelly voice burrowed into her song. She moved closer, noticing the flow wasn't the same. He had added notes to the chorus, rearranged the lyrics, and played at a more soulful pace. It was a soft, crooning ballad that made her sigh with sadness and longing. At first, she was miffed that he'd changed so much, but then she was mesmerized by his performance. He sat on a wooden barstool with chipped green paint peeling from the tall, nicked legs. His body cradled the guitar as his fingers strummed the chords, and his head rocked to the rhythm of the music.

"You lift me up, spin me round, crash me to the ground… You walk on water, baby, ain't no crying this time lady. You stole my heart, you stole my mind, think about you all the time. You walk on water, baby, you walk on water—."

Sparks of energy pulsed through her. She hadn't known she could feel passion in her current state. It wasn't the lustful kind that had made her want to jump his bones in the mortal world, but a deep sizzling in the center of her being. They shared a connection. She wasn't sure she believed in soulmates, but she couldn't deny there was more than lust to her attraction, something that transcended to the in-between world. Regan ached with lost opportunity. What would her life have been like with this man? His overlong, sandy hair shielded his eyes as he played through the next song, but she didn't miss the solitary tear that slid down his cheek. Was it for her? Did he feel the same sense of loss?

The set ended and Chase went to the bar to grab a drink. Guidry followed him, clapping a hand on his shoulder. "You still caught up in that girl?"

Chase shrugged, swallowing hard. The muscle in his jaw flexed.

Guidry's voice was thoughtful as he took a pull from his own beer, "You know, she belonged to a band. You may want to get their permission before we go and record it. I don't think it's right just to play it like it's ours."

Chase's eyebrows drew together, "You're right. I've been thinking about that. The boy she was with that night was in the band, and there could be others that might have a claim, though she told me it was her song."

"Still, you should get legal permission from her family. The record label won't appreciate getting drug through a lawsuit if someone decides to dispute ownership."

"It's not even the same song anymore, really, but I see what you're saying."

Guidry clapped him on the back. "Good. Go on out and see her little shadow of a sister. Besides, it'd be nice if we could throw some money at her momma. It's the least we could do."

Chase nodded silently. It was as if he didn't trust himself to talk. Moments passed and then he said, "I know it sounds strange, Guidry, because I only saw her those two times, but I feel like I lost the only opportunity in my life to find…." His voice trailed off. "Oh, never mind. I sound like a love-sick puppy." He drained his beer, set the bottle down hard, and went back to the stage.

Guidry pressed his lips together like he did when playing an intense solo on his sax. Blowing out a long breath, Regan heard him whisper. "God help 'em." She didn't know if he was referring to Chase or her family's loss, but she appreciated his sentiments either way.

CHAPTER 9

Regan watched as Rain balanced one leg on the ballet barre, raising her arms above her head. It was clear to Regan that her sister's focus was on herself. The ten other dancers along the barre moved in unison as Rain followed a step behind. Regan watched her younger sister, thinking it odd not to see her own reflection. It made her ponder movies and books she'd read about vampires and other creatures of the night. Now she was one of them, trapped between life and death.

The instructor tapped a ruler against her palm, beating out the sequence as she called to the students, "One and two, three and four…."

Rain's detachment from the group sent her stumbling against another dancer, earning a foul look and a reprimand. "Take a break, Rain. Use the back studio to get your routine together."

Rain's silent disdain was evident in her heavy steps as she left the main studio to retreat to the back room. She hit the button on the cassette player and whisked herself into a flurry of pirouettes. She threw herself down, sliding across the slick wood floor, flipping her head forward and then back as she swung her leg around. In one fluid motion, she pushed up to a standing position en pointe. Rain was almost fifteen, but most people wouldn't have deciphered her age. Though her breasts were small, her lean muscular torso was a woman's full-grown and made for dancing. Her long strawberry blonde tresses had come loose from her bun and billowed out around her as she spun in great arcs around the room, lifting her legs in great leaps. Finally spent, she crumpled to the floor and spun around on the silky material of her leotard-covered bottom, holding her ankles high.

A single person clapped, capturing her attention. Rain jerked her head around to see who'd witnessed her abandoned behavior. From what little Regan had learned from seeing Rain practice in Mrs. Landeaux's School of

Dance, she knew the stiff instructor wouldn't approve of Rain's impromptu, non-choreographed release.

With a hand over her heart, Rain exclaimed, "Oh, it's you."

"Hi. I'm Chase. The guy who sang with your sister. I called, but—you said—I uh…" He scratched his head, shifting his weight to his other foot. "I need to talk to you. You got a minute? We could go for ice cream. I'll buy." His lame smile didn't seem to fit with his gorgeous face.

Rain shook her head in disbelief. "You offer ice cream to a dancer? How did you find me, anyway?" She stood, walking toward him. Her five-foot-two stature was shadowed by his broad shoulders and towering height. Regan was impressed by her sister's growing confidence and attitude, though not altogether sure it was best for Rain's future.

Chase sniffed and shuffled his feet again. "Yeah, right, then how about a Diet Coke or a coffee or something? The obituary in the paper listed Regan's family. It's a small town. People talk," he shrugged.

Rain rolled her eyes. "Tell me about it. I can't wait to get out of here. London Ballet or bust."

Chase looked confused. "You're going to London? Wow."

Rain snorted and went to the barre to resume practicing the routine she had failed to complete earlier. "I wish. It's a long way away, and then there's the whole money issue. I doubt I will get a scholarship to participate in the bigger schools that I would need to train in to get there. Juilliard doesn't exactly take stray mutts from the bayou, no matter how talented."

"Are you?"

"Am I what? A stray or talented?"

"Both."

Rain cocked her head as if she was contemplating the question, but maybe she was analyzing him. Regan's heart tilted just a little. Chase was meant for her, not Rain. She would have given her sister Mark, but not Chase. He was supposed to have been hers. Even in her spiritual state, Regan was still possessive. He was here about *her* song.

"I'm a coon-ass from the bayou. No one's gonna take me seriously in the world of ballet, but I'm still going to give those debutantes in New York a run for their money, even if I have to work all summer long to get there."

Chase slid over to where she was doing a plié on the barre and leaned against the mirrored wall facing her. "You need money?"

She quirked a brow at him. "Are you propositioning me? You know I'm only fourteen."

Chase pushed away from the barre and put distance between them. Holding his hands up, as if to ward her off, he said, "No way, man. I just came to ask about Regan's song. We have a record label that heard us sing and wants to sign us, but we need a family member to approve our ownership of the music first."

Rain tossed her hair and turned away from him. "No."

Chase sputtered in shock, "Are you serious? It's not even the same song. I've changed some of the chords and the lyrics. Look, I'm not even sure that we need your family's permission. I just thought I would suggest—" His words died off as if he didn't know where he'd been headed in the first place. It was obvious he'd never expected Rain to say no.

"It's Regan's song. I can't give it to anyone."

Chase gave her a cautious nod. His eyes slanted downward with understanding. "Then who can?"

Rain turned from the barre and shut off the cassette. "Only Regan can do that. It's her song and she's dead."

Chase approached her slowly. Her silent tears fell, slicing into the hollows below her eyes and down the dimple in her cheek, dripping from her heart-shaped chin. He shook his head as he blew out a sigh, inspecting the dance room's rafters. "I don't want to steal it from Regan. She shared it with me, and I love the music we made together. I'm more sorry than anyone that I didn't get a chance to get to know her. I knew the day I met your sister that there was something special about her. I know if things had been different, she would be a part of my life. I want to share that little bit of what I knew about her, her music, and her talent with the world. Will you let me do that?"

"Honestly, I think that's up to our mother. She didn't really know Regan sang."

"What about the rest of the band? Do they have any rights to the song?"

Rain bit her bottom lip, shaking her head as she looked at her well-worn ballet slippers. "Naw, she wrote the song the day before. She hadn't even shared it with them yet. She'd broken up with her boyfriend, and she'd been grounded up until the night of her accident."

"Mark, the guy who killed her?"

Anger flashed in Rain's eyes. "He didn't kill her. He was angry. People make mistakes."

"Really. And you're not angry that his temper took Regan's life?" His voice rose and he stared aghast at Rain.

A woman cleared her voice. "Rain, guests aren't allowed in the studio during practice. You know the rules."

Rain's head popped up like a military school cadet. "Yes, Mrs. Landeaux."

Chase's eyebrows came together as he studied Rain, not looking back at the instructor. "I was just going. Sorry for the interruption." When he stepped through the threshold, he turned and called to Rain, "I'll pick you up after school tomorrow so we can talk."

CHAPTER 10

Regan floated through classes, watching students take exams and teachers erase chalkboards as they droned on about their subjects. She looked out the window to the sports field, watching the senior graduation practice. A sense of longing filled her as she thought of what it would have been like to have worn a cap and gown. She hadn't planned on being at her graduation, but now that she couldn't, Regan longed to go. Just when she was at the end of so many years of school, she had to up and die.

As the final bell rang, students disembarked from their holding cells and broke free into the sunlight. Spring was here and the temperatures were abnormally hot for southern Louisiana. Most of the students rolled up their jeans and tied their sweaters or jackets around their waists. The preppy boys wore their Polo shirt collars standing up like vintage vampires, parading around the bus area in Vans shoes with checked patterns. Guys carried books loosely in one arm while girls wore colorful backpacks and totes. Drill team dancers with overlarge bows and scrunchies in their hair and cheerleaders with pure-white tennis shoes took up their respective places, shutting out all the students that they didn't deem worthy.

Rain was among the non-popular kids milling about, reading a book and ignoring the world. Regan looked at the cover. *Rebecca*, by Daphne du Maurier, a classic. Regan had read it last year. It was probably her copy from the bookshelf in her room. She wondered if Rain would read all her books now that she was gone. A morbid sort of way to connect. Regan wasn't as avid a reader as Rain. She loved music and spent too much time in Mark's garage piecing together songs she'd hoped would make her famous, but she did enjoy a good book from time to time, and several of the classics had made their way into her heart. Would Rain read *Wuthering Heights, Jane Eyre,* or her collection of smut novels as their mother liked to call them?

She doubted Kathleen Woodiwiss would agree they were smut. Either way, they were great. Regan had read most of her books before she'd had a life, while she dreamt of what life could be. She'd longed to meet Mr. Right and just when she had—.

Rain leaned against a pole under the overhang of the main building. She shielded her eyes from the glare of the sun and searched for something in the distance. Students boarded the buses and Rain stood in line, looking like she might board with them until she spotted Chase. The briefest smile lit her features before she shrouded her face again with indifference. Regan knew the look and it spelled trouble. Rain was falling for Chase. A pang of hurt coursed through Regan paired with raw jealousy. She mentally shook herself.

Why should I care? I'm dead.

But the feeling of loss still stabbed at her senses and the tingle of desire for what could have been drenched her in depression and resentment. Regan reminded herself that she loved her sister, and the age difference between Rain and Chase was at least ten years. There couldn't be anything between them right now, and Regan doubted Chase had any desire for her kid sister, but the emotion Rain felt for him pulsed like the flutter of a moth's wings beating against a glass door—slight but unmistakably there. *What about Mark? She promised to be there soon. Wherever* there *was.* Regan breathed a sigh of relief. Maybe Rain was just being dramatic? *Hormones!*

Chase leaned against a dark blue Honda, a cigarette in one hand, though it was unlit. His ripped jeans and worn seventies t-shirt weren't in fashion, but that made him more appealing to Regan. His after-five shadow wasn't trimmed, and his tattered Converse sneakers had seen better days. His lack of socks was probably from lack of clean laundry, and his hair needed to be cut and combed. The unfashionable length made him look sexy, like a rebel renegade of sorts. The sun caught the golden highlights of his beard, making him look like he could be Rain's older brother. Both of them had sculpted features with large bow mouths and beautiful eyes, though Rain's were distinctly green, and Chase's were hazel, but sometimes sherry-colored in darker settings. Their similarity was uncanny. Regan wondered if they recognized it. The difference in their height and build was dramatic. Though Chase wasn't a football player type, his broad shoulders and tapered waist garnered attention. His pectoral muscles pushed their outline through his tight t-shirt that hung loosely at the waist of his stonewashed denim.

"Hey." His greeting was casual.

Rain shaded her eyes from the sun, returning his simple greeting with a nod.

"Wanna grab something to eat? I know a place down the road. It's a bar, but they serve good food."

Rain's eyes brightened and she smiled, "Yeah, I could eat."

Chase came around to open her door and Regan chuckled to herself. *Rain probably never had that happen before.* Regan's heart somersaulted at her sister's situation in life. She wasn't an adult or a child, and her hormones probably turned her world upside down when Chase looked her way. If Regan was there, she would have given Rain a knowing smile, the kind that sisters often communicated with. She would have wanted her sister to enjoy what was supposed to be a carefree time in her life. It was also the age Regan had made one of her gravest mistakes, entrusting her own virginity to a guy she shouldn't have. Life hadn't been so simple after that. She wondered if Rain was still a virgin. She assumed so, since Rain was so young and Regan didn't know of anyone her sister had an interest in, except Mark, and he was dead.

Chase switched on the radio and let a rock station play as they made sharp turns through the pine and cypress-lined roads of the bayou. Rain looked out of the passenger window like she'd never seen the area and was fascinated by the landscape.

He studied her briefly. "Do you like rock, or would you prefer something else?"

Rain paused for a moment, "I don't really listen to music very much, not unless I am dancing, and then it's mostly classical. Music was Regan's thing." Her brow creased. "I do like Prince, and some of the pop I hear on the bus after school."

Chase rolled his eyes, "Prince, really? What is this world coming to?" He shook his head in despair but smiled playfully as Rain laughed. They were spared from any other musical disagreements as Chase pulled into the gravel parking lot of the rundown place by the lake. Coot's on the River was a popular dive where most of the senior class hung out on the weekends. Rain had probably been there only one time with Regan when they went to see about a gig. The owner wasn't interested at the time. He said they were too young, but after he tried to brush them off, Regan busted out in a rendition of "Smoke on the Water." He smiled and told them they could play one afternoon on a Sunday. That was a big deal on the lake since a lot of boaters finished off the weekends at Coot's. They'd been the opening act for the main band that played every Sunday night, but it was enough to give Regan hope.

Chase studied Rain as she sat idle in the seat beside him, not reaching for the door. "You been here before? My buddy Guidry says the po-boys are amazing."

Rain's eyes were misty, but she held the tears at bay. "Yeah, I came once with Regan, but I never heard her sing here. She wouldn't let me come, and I had dance lessons that day anyway."

Chase cleared his throat, "She sang here, at Coot's?"

"It was early on a Sunday because she was under-age."

"Well, I think they'll let us in for a bite to eat." He exited the car and came around to open the door for her again. Chase smiled at Rain, who looked dismal to be with him at best. "Regan and Rain. Where'd your mom come up with those names?"

Rain shrugged her shoulders and shuffled her feet as she followed Chase into Coot's. "Mom was a hippy. She didn't go to college, and she works at Piggly Wiggly now. My dad ran off and left her a long time ago. Our family's pretty small. It's the only reason I'm meeting you today. Do you think Regan's song might be worth some money? Mom sure could use a break, but I honestly don't know what she'll say when she sees you. She's pretty broken up about losing Regan. I'm not sure she'll want to talk to anyone. Right now, she just punches a time clock and comes home to sleep. She might not be home until late."

Chase ordered two po-boys for them with two Cherry Cokes. "I don't mind waiting for her to get home if you don't."

Rain accepted the soft drink from the waitress who was sizing them up. Regan figured the waitress probably thought Rain and Chase were a couple. Chase was way too old for her little sister, and Regan was somewhat amused when the waitress pressed her lips together in disapproval.

Rain smiled sweetly and batted her eyes at Chase for effect, "Suit yourself. I've got homework."

The waitress scowled at Chase, then moved on to other patrons.

"I never heard her sing that song until that day we met you at the bar." Rain stirred the ice around with her straw then took a small sip. "Regan was like that. She could belt out a song off the top of her head and it would be amazing, then she'd never sing it again. When I'd asked if she would sing whatever it was, she'd say, 'I forgot it. It was just something I made up.'" Rain shrugged her shoulders and blew out a long sigh. "You know, I think she would've been someone. She could've been big." Rain's words fell softly between them. The rustic wood table was scarred with carved initials, and the cushions on the bench were tattered, but the booth was cozy.

Chase stared at the small stage that was used in the evenings. He removed the straw from his soda and took a sip, crunching a cube of ice. "Well, I remember the one she sang for me, and I can't forget it." Without warning, he stood up and walked to the center of the joint. The stage was set up for the band that would play later that evening.

Regan stilled in the middle of the room as he picked up the guitar. The waitress tried to shoo him off the stage as he started playing. When he sang, it was like gravel pitching up from the pavement and catching her in the shins. It startled her to hear her song, now, here in this place she'd been before. It stopped everyone in the room, not that there were many tables around. He worked from the classical slow beginning with the soft rumbling of a salute to a lover. "You walk on water, baby—," he crooned.

Regan prickled with sparks of energy. She moved toward Rain, who sat mesmerized in the booth. Her sister's skin prickled and the hair on her arms stood up. Rain could either feel Regan's presence or Chase's amazing voice was playing havoc over her senses. They sat together, watching the muscles in his biceps and forearms ripple. He cradled the instrument, storming into the chorus with an amazing tempo that eventually stuttered to an absorbing halt. He stared at Rain. Tears pooled in her eyes, lapping around her eyeliner. The weight of a tear slid down her upturned cheek, and Rain quickly swiped it away. The light filtered through the window, and for a moment, Regan thought she saw her own reflection in her sister's eyes.

As if sensing Rain's sadness, Chase returned the guitar to its stand and made his way back to the booth as the waitress delivered their food. Looking at the young musician with a different light in her eye, she commented. "That was amazing. Where'd you come up with that song?"

Chase smiled, "It's a Regan Landry original, but I'm going to make it famous." Chase's eyes were shiny with hope, and Regan didn't know if he held his own tears back for her or if he was just feeling the passion of his own performance. That occurred when an artist got too caught up in their music. It had happened before, and she'd had to push down tears after a particularly emotional song. When she sang, she sometimes felt like her feet left the earth and she walked among the angels. For a moment, she wondered where the angel who first directed her into the light had gone. What if she never found the light again? The spirit she'd met in the quarter had warned her that he hadn't seen the portal for quite a long time. Regan wasn't ready to find the end of this existence yet, but she felt herself moving forward into a future she couldn't predict. She didn't believe that she couldn't control any of it. Regan stroked Rain's hair and looked at her beautiful features in the light pouring through the window. There had to be a way.

Chase's attention swung back to Rain. "You know, you look like her."

Rain looked at Chase as if he was on drugs. "Are you kidding? We look nothing alike." She tossed her strawberry-blonde hair over one shoulder.

Chase's eyes sparkled with something like mischief. "Besides the hair color. You both have the same fair skin, the freckles that dust your nose." His finger stretched across the table, brushing over the tip of Rain's pert nose. "You both have the same green eyes, and the attitude, oh my God." He chuckled to himself. His demeanor grew serious. "I'm really sorry for your loss. I didn't know your sister well, but I have this feeling we would have been close."

Rain nodded as if accepting the truth. "Everybody loved Regan. That was part of her downfall."

CHAPTER 11

Regan sat in the booth staring at the man she knew was her soulmate. He was gorgeous, talented, and something about his energy drew her to him. She couldn't explain the way he pulled her in and totally relieved her of her senses, but she needed to extract herself and focus on why she still existed on this plane. A movement outside the window caught her eye. With a sudden whoosh of air, the bar door slammed against the wall, and a breeze blew through the restaurant, catching at the strands of Rain's hair. Rain reached out to grasp what was left of her meal in the paper-lined basket, knocking the remainder of her soda into Chase's lap. Chase jumped to his feet, dabbing at the liquid with a paper napkin. Regan was taken back by the quick assault. Mark's milky outline loomed over the booth, and Regan railed at him. Napkins floated off the table and fluttered to the floor. As far as Regan could determine, wind was the only weapon in the in-between world. Their souls were energy pushing air in the place of all the emotions they couldn't express.

The encounter was brief. Before she could take Mark to task and pick up the topic she'd longed to dissect, namely their deaths, the backdraft of his entry recalled his presence. As if the vacuum of space and time was righting the order of reality, he was no longer hovering over the table.

Mark was following her or, at the very least, keeping tabs on Rain. Either way, it made her uncomfortable. When he was alive, Mark wasn't a bad guy, but the anger in his shadowy presence marked a menacing force that made Regan rethink forgiving him. She had thought a pardon might cure the darkness that haunted her existence, but she wasn't entirely sure now. Would he try to hurt Rain? She would have to stand watch over her vulnerable sister until his disturbing presence dissipated, descended to Hell, or whatever God intended for his dark soul.

She followed Rain and Chase back to her home and waited on the porch with them for her mother to return from work. She wondered what her mother would say in response to Chase's request. Rona never gave Regan's talent much thought and had even told her on several occasions that her desire to become famous was a pipedream. Their mother didn't believe in dreams that came true or that Regan might possess talent. In truth, she had never heard Regan sing in public. Their mother was always working a double shift, trying to pay the rent or put food on the table. Her life hadn't been easy since their father left the first time around, and it was clear to Regan why her mother had given up on dreams.

Rain jumped up at the shrill ring of the phone that could be heard through the screen door. Regan could hear both sides of the conversation. Rona wasn't coming home. She was taking someone's shift. She told Rain what to make for dinner and to clean up her room, then she apologized for not being able to drive her to ballet practice. Disappointment weighed on Rain's expression. She closed her eyes as if counting to ten, then opened them, looking longingly over her shoulder. Once more, Regan contemplated if Rain was developing a crush on Chase. He was beautiful. The sandy hair was too long, and he needed to shave, but the glint of gold in his after-five shadow made him look angelic and sinister at the same time. The contoured facial hair accentuated his full pink bottom lip, and she wondered what it would have been like to kiss it. Regan wondered what her mother would think of Chase. It didn't matter right now because she wouldn't be meeting him tonight.

Rain let the screen door slam against the frame. She held two glasses of iced tea and a look of dejection that was quickly becoming *her look*.

"That was my mom. She's working the late shift."

Chase was standing. The tails of his shirt tucked up by his hands that were thrust into his jean pockets. "Bummer." He fidgeted for a moment, staring down at his scuffed tennis shoes.

Rain handed him the extra glass, frowning. "Tell me about it. She was supposed to take me to ballet practice. I'm missing class again."

Chase took the glass, nodding his thanks. "I can take you. I mean, if you can get a ride home. I've got a gig tonight, so I can't hang out or anything."

A broad smile spread across Rain's face. "Really? That would be great. I'm sure one of the ballet moms will take pity on me." She downed her tea, then left her glass on the porch rail. She lit through the screen door, letting it slam again. "Wait, I'll be right back," she called over her shoulder.

About five minutes later, Rain returned in pink tights covered by blue denim shorts, cowboy boots and an oversized sweatshirt. A duffle bag was slung over one shoulder, and ballet slippers swayed from the woven strap. Her strawberry hair was knotted in a bun at the nape of her neck, and her lips were suddenly shiny. Rain had put on lip-gloss for him. The man was more than ten years older than she was, and their mother would have a fit. Regan didn't know how she could save her sister from further heartbreak, but unless Chase was a pervert, Rain was destined to be heartbroken—again.

Delila watched the scene unfold, acknowledging the angry spirit of the ex-boyfriend. If things had gone as they were supposed to, would he still be railing in the in-between world? His death had been imminent, but the way in which one dies is part of their destiny. His was a scarred existence. Not a part of the living and not a part of the dead. She wondered what future lay ahead for him. She tried not to ponder the question. He wasn't hers to care for or guide, but she had been a part of his demise. The threads of all souls are interwoven like spun yarn on a loom, and she had to wonder where her responsibility began and ended. If you dissected each path, unwound the threads and separated everyone's destiny, would the choices made and the details of each life be cut and dried? Delila didn't truly know the answer, but she suspected that even her mistake was part of the great quilt work of God's plan. Even now, when she knew a bit of the gift she'd been given and Regan's most disturbing future, Delila knew she had to go forth. It was her destiny as well as Rain's and Regan's. Watching the interaction of the sisters between the spirit world and the living was difficult. As Regan brushed a lock of Rain's hair, Delila reached out and stroked a dark strand of her ward's dark mane. She was a lovely, bright soul, so full of self-sacrifice. Delila knew that Regan would gladly lay down her own life and all her conquests to save her sister or her mother. It was for this reason that Rodanian granted Delila a way to correct the past.

CHAPTER 12

Regan was filled with worry about her spirit's direction and her family's safety. On the one hand, she knew the sand in her hourglass was running out. If she dallied too long, she might be stuck in the in-between world for eternity like her pirate acquaintance. On the other hand, her anxiety about Rain's safety was shaken today when Mark breezed into the restaurant. She needed to confront his spirit and find out more about his connection to her existence on this plane. She couldn't leave this reality while knowing something might influence Rain to hurt herself or fall victim to Mark's darkness. Regan also worried about Rain taking up company with Chase. When the cool guitarist dropped Rain off at ballet, she'd smiled at him with such hope, inviting him to drop by on Sunday.

"It's Mom's only day off. She likes to pretend she's religious, but we only ever attend church on Christmas Eve and Easter Sunday."

"You must be Catholic," Chase laughed, patting her shoulder. It was a small gesture and one that shouldn't mean anything, but the touch stung Regan with worry. Chase was supposed to have been hers. It was unfair their spirits were separated by different realities. He'd sat in his car watching Rain hurry into ballet class. His expression was thoughtful, and he grinned as he started the engine and drove off. Regan stayed with him until he reached the Crescent City and parked in the French Quarter. She then took her own route back to the seer and the area where she'd met the only other ghostly entity she knew besides Mark.

Gustave wasn't hard to find. He was sitting on top of the Coke machine where she'd met him.

"Ah, you're back." He gave her a small golf clap of approval.

Regan's eyes roved over his flamboyant attire. He looked like a gentleman pirate with his tight britches, tall black boots and a plumed hat. The teal feather was fluffy and matched the material of his vest.

"That doesn't look comfortable."

Gustave snorted with laughter. "My tailor made this especially for me. I assure you, it fits like a glove."

Regan rolled her eyes. "I meant your lounging on top of that Coke machine."

Gustave jumped down and swiped the hat from his head. He made a show of taking a deep bow. "I've been waiting for you. I remembered you like soda."

Regan's eyes widened. "I never said anything about soda."

Gustave waved a hand. "You didn't have to. The look of longing could be seen a mile away. The intensity with which you stared made the machine feel sorry for you. Your energy pushed the bottle from the bowels of it."

Regan's surprise was audible. "I did that?"

"Yes, you certainly did. The question is, what else do you long for with such intense need?" He swaggered toward her with slow, swaying steps, making her think of the movie, "The Three Musketeers."

She studied the Coke machine, tossing over her shoulder. "None of your business."

Gustave's hearty laugh pulled her gaze away from the machine and back to his dandy attire. Wasn't that what they called flamboyantly dressed men of his time? She had read enough bodice-ripper romances to remember a few choice terms.

"You don't want it now as you did then. The machine isn't going to spit out soda every time you look at it. You have to want it." He waved a gloved hand in the air.

"Trust me, I do want it. I'm a soda addict. I'd die for a soda if I weren't already dead." She looked at the machine again but aimed her question at Gustave. "How did you change your clothes? You're a ghost."

Gustave smiled as he brushed imaginary dust from one shoulder. "It's easy. I was longing for the time my portrait was painted. I remembered the day I stood in front of my favorite mount, and the artist put just the right flourishes on my likeness. I looked more handsome than ever. Joseph's face was a perfect arrangement of planes and angles. I loved watching him as he worked. He had this way of chewing on the end of his brush when he concentrated. I found myself wondering what it would be like to kiss him on more than one occasion." He cackled at Regan's shock. "I wasn't gay, at least not then. It was just a passing thought. We all have those, but most people won't admit it. I was married, of course, and an affair between two men was frowned upon. I knew such things existed, but I was duty-bound to be a husband and father. Don't get me wrong, I took up with the maid, a few ladies of the court, my best friend's wife, and the cook's daughter, but never a man." Gustave let out a small sigh. Regan wasn't sure if it was regret for not fulfilling his curiosity when he was living or if he was just missing his old life.

Regan snorted. "What a get-up. You actually rode a horse in that outfit?"

"This was the attire for the upper class." His hands waved over the length of his form as if he were Vanna White. "The more vibrant the color, the wealthier the owner. Besides, I didn't wear this out on a regular basis. It was made specifically for the portrait." Gustave snapped his fingers and was wearing what looked like a riding outfit complete with crop in his left hand. "This would have been my usual attire. How I do miss riding," he said with wistful longing.

He'd looked like he should be waving from the top of a Mardi Gras float before he changed. It was easier to have a conversation with him now, but she was still wary. "Gustave, why didn't you go into the light when you saw it?"

He leaned against the Coke machine, crossing his arms over his chest. His frown made his features more intense. His face wasn't model perfect any longer. More wrinkles surrounded his mouth and eyes. Deep smile lines ran the inner contours of his cheeks. He was still very handsome for an older man, but not the flawless porcelain he had presented himself as before.

His silence stretched on and Regan thought he might not answer. He pushed away from the machine, floating a little apart from her. Turning, he shrugged his shoulders as if letting go. "I did go into the light. Fair women with wings like angels greeted me. They bade me to go with them, and I went willingly. They were beautiful sirens calling me home, and I was relieved. I had sinned enough in my life that you can imagine my pleasure in knowing there was still a place for me in heaven. As we floated farther into the light, they grasped harder onto my soul. I felt their needle-like claws, and their perfect white teeth turned to fangs. They sped away with intent to capture my spirit and fly into darkness. Whatever they were about, it wasn't heaven they were rushing me toward. I managed to pull away in time to escape light and darkness. I ended up in limbo. Now I guess I'm stuck here until I can find the light again."

Regan shook her head, confused. "But Gustave, if the spirits were rushing you to hell, why would you ever look for the light? I mean, wouldn't it be better to exist here forever than to seek out what surely must've been damnation?" She stepped toward him.

"I've been here long enough to watch too many lives unfold. I do not know what's waiting for me beyond the light or the darkness, but whatever it is, I'm ready to face it now. I've contemplated my mistakes for long enough. I'm willing to try again if that's an option."

Regan's interest piqued. "You mean reincarnation?"

Gustave's energy lost all pretense. "I'm not really sure. I just know that I am tired of lingering here and watching others live their lives. Whatever waits for me, I will succumb."

"Is that why you keep showing up? Because you think I know where the light is?"

"You did see it, didn't you?" Gustave sounded hopeful.

"Yes, but like you, I walked away."

He wrinkled his brow and his jaw dropped in disbelief. "Those devils tried to pull you into the darkness?"

Regan thought about her fleeting moment after death. "It was only one angel. She seemed nice. I saw my grandparents there too. People who waited beyond the light. They didn't seem evil or ominous. I just knew I wasn't ready to go." She paused, contemplating her next words, not sure if she should say them. "It was like, I knew if I left with her, I would have to start all over again, and I didn't want to. I liked my life and I didn't want to quit being Regan. She called me—" Regan checked herself. There was power in names, and somehow, she felt she shouldn't divulge her spirit's name. By saying it, she would admit she was no longer Regan, and then she might not be able to stay on this plane. It might interfere with protecting Rain. A question rang out from her subconscious, was it really Rain she was protecting?

Gustave studied her as he took a step closer, closing the distance between them. He picked up a wisp of her hair, twirling it between his fingers. His face was polished porcelain again. He looked like the cover of a romance novel, everything most women dreamed of, but he wasn't Chase.

"How'd you do that? We are both air without substance."

Gustave smiled, bending to her, kissing her lips. She steadied herself and didn't pull away. It wasn't that she longed for his kiss. She didn't know or trust him, but she needed to know what was possible. She could almost feel him. The kiss seemed smooth and real.

Gustave chuckled. "Thanks for that, love. Your willingness to participate made it almost real. As you said, we are air, and wind moves air. If you
steady your presence and ground yourself to this point on the earth, then
the air pushes into you, and you can feel with the core of your spirit."

Regan stepped back, feeling electricity run the length of her existence.
Looking down, she saw he was holding her hand. A static shock zapped
her, and she pulled away. "What was that?"

Gustave looked longingly at her hand. "Alas, we were not meant to
be." With his sad words, he faded. Regan searched the area to see if he had
returned to the Coke machine. Convinced he was gone for now, she pushed
her energy toward the machine. The sound of glass rolling against metal
and a swish of the flap at the bottom produced the soda she very much
wished for. With all her might, she tried to lift it from the tray, but it was
beyond her capability. With a sigh, she moved away, watching a kid emerge
from the store. He stopped to open a bag of chips and saw the Coke at the
bottom of the machine. Looking over his shoulder at the store's front door,
he snagged the soda and popped the top. With longing, Regan watched him
guzzle half the bottle before moving away to finish his snack. There was one
thing waiting for her in her next life that she would look forward to. A Coke.

CHAPTER 13

Regan made her way back to Jackson Square. She meandered around the area for a while, watching artists and palm readers hock their wares to tourists. Steam rolled off a batch of boiling crawfish behind a Cajun restaurant that sold seafood and local cuisine. She could almost smell the spices. As her energy floated toward the boiling pot, its essence drifted over her. She did have the ability to move air, but she couldn't feel the steam or smell the crab-boil the crawfish steeped in. She sighed with heavy regret, and anger splintered inside her. How unfair that Mark took all of this away from her.

A big black cat lounging on the fence hissed. The old man stirring the pot looked at the cat, then in her direction. "Easy Beelzebub, she don't mean no harm. She's hungry is all."

This grabbed Regan's attention. She moved closer to the simmering concoction. The old man's eyes were covered by cataracts. He couldn't see the living, let alone the dead. Regan stood there a moment longer, assessing the man before deciding he thought her presence was another animal approaching the pot for a bit of seafood.

He clicked his tongue and shook his head. "Um-um, don't worry ol' cat. She couldn't steal your crawfish even if she wanted to. She ain't got no real stomach for it."

Regan swung back toward the old man, pushing a breeze across him that sent his Saints baseball cap sailing from his bristling gray hair. She waited, desperate to know the answer.

Regan shouted her questions. "Do you see me? You know I'm here, don't you?"

Sticking the wooden paddle that he used to stir the crawfish into its metal holder, he turned toward the kitchen. "Come on, Beelzebub, I think a storm is coming. I'll give you breakfast inside."

Regan tried to follow him, but something kept her from entering. She looked above the door at a bundle of herbs thatched together with packaging string. Did herbs keep out the dead? She'd seen such nonsense when she was alive but never took stock in it. Of course, back then, she didn't believe in ghosts either. She sent a swoosh of energy in the direction of the hanging greenery. The fern next to the door swayed, but the herbs didn't budge. It was interesting and worth taking note of, but not absolute proof that it was keeping her out. Still, in this in-between state, she had a lot to learn. She wandered down Royal Street and through the French Market, avoiding the bar where the Cat's Quarter played until it was later in the day. She watched the crowd mill around in the cooler temperatures as the sun crouched slowly behind Saint Louis Cathedral. She'd made two complete circles before resting near the bench that Rain had laid upon. The last day here with her sister would forever be ingrained in her soul, just as the bench would forever bear the memory of Rain.

"Come here often?" Regan snapped to attention, searching to see where the slow, sultry voice came from. A handsome man with dark curling hair that spiked into fashionable points and sherry brown eyes grasped a low-hanging, winding branch from an old live oak. His aura radiated warmth and his spirit was inviting, drawing her to him instantly. As real as any human she knew, he flashed a knowing smile at her, and she could have sworn a glint of light sparked in his eyes. His straight nose and symmetrical features made him too pretty to be called masculine, but he was cut from quality cloth. Any woman would stumble at his feet. In fact, Regan was sure she'd seen him on a billboard or possibly in a movie. There was something fabulously alluring in his casual attire and confident stance. She couldn't help herself. Regan floated to him, feeling a steady hum of energy race through her alert form. He was talking to her as if she were real. *He could see her.*

Regan knew the question was redundant, but she had to ask, "Can you see me?"

He chuckled with amusement. "Of course, darling. I see everyone, don't you?"

Regan looked around the Square. Just to see if they were on the same page, she voiced her thoughts. "I see the old woman with her husband eating ice cream at the parlor tables, the two men having a beer just inside the seafood place, the horsemen with their carriages waiting for their next fare, the artist with the—"

The dark-eyed gentleman snapped his fingers with flare. "All of them," he commanded with a purr. "All the souls, here and now. Do you see the pretty young mulatto woman walking, holding the knife in her breast?"

Regan's eyes widened. The living now mixed with the dead. The square was full of souls.

"Her husband worked at a shoe factory. He was jealous and thought she'd betrayed him with a work friend. He stabbed her with his shoe sole knife multiple times and then left her dead corpse lying in a pool of her own blood. Covering her with the filthy money he thought they had planned to steal from him, he went back to work. She lay dead at their home until her husband was caught at the factory with a gun. He confessed to her murder and was hanged with the two other murderers you see."

He waved a hand and Regan saw three men hanging from the same limb. The park was now crawling with souls of both worlds. She didn't confirm or deny seeing them, but the handsome man didn't need confirmation. He was smiling as he gestured to the dead.

Regan's head snapped back to the tree where the unearthly Adonis of a man had stood. She felt a tap on her left shoulder and spun around to see his flashing amber eyes. It was different than when Gustave had held her hand. It wasn't a sizzle or a warm current, but a stinging burn that made her withdraw. "Who are you?"

He chuckled again, "I'm so sorry. Did that hurt? I never remember my own strength. The truth is, I actually enjoy a little pain. Think of the pleasure we could have together. Oh, what fun." He ran a soft finger down her face, and the most beautiful fragrance she'd ever connected to the opposite sex assailed her. Hickory, fresh tobacco, cognac, clean soap and something sweet she couldn't name. His lips were full, and for a moment he was so close, she thought he might kiss her. Regan wished he would kiss her.

Naughty images seduced her vision. She was tied up naked with the devilish man touching her backside lightly with a riding crop. His long, tapered fingers traced the length of her calf, up her thigh until just before crossing any threshold that might draw real pleasure. As suddenly as it came, the image dissolved.

"Do you wish for more?" She felt his heated breath fan her own searing thoughts. She could feel his warm energy pulsing at the juncture of her thighs, the same thighs she hadn't felt since living as Regan. Her physical senses reeled with longing.

"Yes," tore from her lips before she could even think to draw back her desire. It felt forbidden. In the same way that she had pleasured herself in secret when she was an embodied soul. Regan craved release more than ever right now, so much that her rational thoughts dissolved.

"As you wish," Transported to another time and place, she lay on an elaborately carved four-poster bed with rich velvet coverings and crisp white sheets. The blankets felt like they were made up of a million hands, touching every area of her being. Many faces cascaded through the silk. They caressed, kneaded, rubbed, and suckled her with gentle languid kisses. She was suddenly seized with a tightening of inner energy that surged with a climactic release. She gasped and sputtered, amazed at the sensation. She desired more and wished the moment would never end.

The image and the sensation were snuffed out by his lust-amused laughter.

"My turn," he rasped against her ear. Another vision danced before her in slow motion with clear, concise cracks of a whip, making her mouth drop and her eyes widen. His beautiful naked form lay before her. It was like no other male specimen she'd ever seen. He moaned with pleasure under her sharp punishment. She saw the lust in her own reflection at his blissful pain, doled out by her menacing hand. Again, a tingle of energy awakened the sexual part of her that she thought dead without a body. Caught in a wave of captive desire that had her crying out for another release. His guttural moan signaled the end to his pleasure, and like a slap in the face, she was quickly dropped back into the reality of Jackson Square. Her own pleasure was frozen by his icy stare.

"Ah, so close and yet so far away, but it could be arranged, just not here." He waved to the three dead men hanging from the branch of the live oak. His eyes twinkled with sinister mischief.

Regan gained control of her composure, feeling guilty and embarrassed all at once.

"Don't be embarrassed. You think I haven't seen it before?" He cocked a brow and she was hurtled back to the bedroom she'd known during her life as Regan. Her hand thrust into her jeans, smothering her face in a pillow to silence her cry of rapture.

Mortified and angry, she shot him a look of outrage. "Who are you? Satan?"

He gave her a wide-eyed, mocking gaze of innocence, then roared with laughter. "You say it like it's a bad thing, but it's not really. Though I'm here to give you a message. If you stay on the path you are now, your soul will be banished, and you will be mine." He smiled wickedly, tiny flames igniting in each pupil.

"I don't understand. I wasn't a bad person. Everyone does—*that*." She waved a hand to dismiss the images that still heated her conscious thoughts. "Mark took my life, not the other way around," she said, coiling away from him. His glimmer of attractiveness was evaporating, and now she could see him for what he really was—dangerous.

"I don't make the rules. I just enforce them. Now be a good girl and go home to the light. I have real work to do."

Delila was paralyzed. She stood between the two souls that hanged by their necks for all eternity. She watched helplessly as the fallen angel slithered around Regan's soul. His serpent tongue tasted her, darting in and out of her spirit's core, and Delila was helpless to watch his raping of her ward's energy while Regan writhed in guilty pleasure. Delila did not know what he shared with Regan. Lucifer had powers far greater than hers or even Rodanian's. Tethered as Delila was, she remained untouched by the devil's corruption.

He obviously knew she was present. Separating her from her ward, he bound her in place with his hypnotic energy. No punishment would come from above for her inability to protect Regan. Her strength was not able to fend off the potency of his malevolence. Not even Rodanian could keep the king of the underworld at bay. Whatever his vile intentions, Delila would wait out this captivity and hopefully return to Regan when his dallying ended.

Time passed and she continued to watch helplessly as Regan was released, and her spirit returned to the place of her death. She wanted to open her existence and show Regan the light. It was what she'd pleaded for in the beginning. Seeing Rodanian had closed that door, Delila had a different assignment now. One that was becoming ever more distasteful as the moment grew near. She wondered again about the gift she'd been given and contemplated defying her own request of Rodanian, but to do so would mean a fate worse than the repetition of a soul watcher's life. It disturbed her to contemplate such an existence, and it wouldn't benefit Regan now. Some destinies had to be played out, even if it was a destiny to correct fate.

CHAPTER 14

Regan returned from the French Quarter to the house in Bonne Fete where she watched Rain sleep. She hadn't lingered to see Chase play. Before today, she thought she was one of the limited spirits stuck in the in-between world, but now she realized there were more unembodied than embodied souls. The thought of being stuck here forever was becoming scarier by the moment. The dark presence that she could only presume was the devil, or at the very least a demon, left her feeling used and shaken. After her encounter, she'd gone back to the place where she died and looked for the light. It wasn't there, and even after calling out for the angel she'd spoken to, she was left standing alone on the causeway over Lake Pontchartrain. Maybe it was too late. She wondered if Mark had spoken to the same devil spirit and if so, what had Diablo shown him? Probably endless hours of being sodomized. *She could only wish.*

She was still angry with Mark for taking her life and even more worried about Rain's vulnerability. Her sister had said she would see him soon, but Regan had yet to see Rain go to his house or to the grave. The fact that she still attended ballet meant she probably wasn't suicidal, and the look she'd given Chase in the car wasn't one of dreary innocence. What would Rain do when the musician moved on and didn't loiter around for permission to produce Regan's song? The reality was that she couldn't hang around for Rain's whole life. It wasn't like Regan could waltz right back into her old body. She was dead, and her body was decaying in the cemetery. The only way she could live again was to find the light and start over, but she wasn't ready. Not yet, and now she'd lost her portal to the next phase. Maybe she needed to fix things with Mark on this plane first, see Rain get over her schoolgirl crush, and find something to distract her mother from crying during all her waking hours. It was a place to start.

Shuffling around Rain's room, Regan tried not to stir the air with her energy. She looked over the stack of books on the floor by Rain's bed. Her notebooks with their swirling doodles lay tightly hidden beneath the weight of the school-issued textbooks. She moved to the mirrored closet with its one door hanging ajar. One of the wheels at the top had come loose from the bracket again. The interior light was left on as it had been Rain's whole life. She'd been afraid of the dark since she was a child and used the excuse of not wanting to stub her toe if she went to the bathroom during the night. Regan knew the truth, but now that she was a ghost and had encountered the devil, she didn't blame Rain for her fear. Too much of the unseen world was fearsome. Regan looked for drugs, needles, or other suicidal objects— relieved she didn't find anything.

As she passed the footrail of the bed on her way to the hall, she spotted Rain's empty book sack. It was Friday morning and Rain still had classes. The books were on the floor, and the book sack was filled with something else, but Regan couldn't unzip the backpack. Her intuition filled her with worry. She stayed by Rain until she woke. After showering, dressing and grabbing a muffin, Rain hugged their mother and waved goodbye. She walked in the direction of the bus stop but never made it to the bus.

A red sports car pulled up with a screech. Emily Fairchild was driving. Regan knew the popular girl from school but wouldn't have called her a friend. She certainly didn't understand why Emily would pick Rain up to go anywhere.

"So, you're sure this guy needs a singer?" Emily confirmed as she shifted into first and sped down the bayou road leading out to the interstate.

Chase. Rain was using Emily to go see Chase. She was skipping school to ride into New Orleans, where she had no business being. Rain was almost fifteen, and Emily was eighteen by now. Her birthday was two days after Regan's.

"He wants to produce 'Walk on Water.'" Regan applauded Rain for her noncommittal answer.

Emily shivered as she took the ramp, shifting to gain speed. "Isn't it creepy? I mean, 'Walk on Water,' and then she drowned in the lake?" She glanced at the passenger seat, but Rain just stared out the window. Emily made a small cough to clear her throat, "I'm sorry. I know you and your mom must be devastated, but I knew Regan was headed for trouble as soon as she broke up with Mark."

Rain's nostrils flared. "What do you know about Regan? You didn't even hang out with her," she shouted. It was uncharacteristic of her sister, and Regan didn't know Emily in a way that she could predict what would happen next. They had only hung out in Mark's garage a few times. Emily could sing passably, but Regan figured her real drive to sing had to do with her own crush on Mark.

Emily shifted into fifth gear and looked at Rain with wide eyes of concern. "Okay, okay. You're right. I didn't know her." Tapping her fingers on the steering wheel, Regan could almost hear Emily's thoughts before she could voice them. "I did know Mark. He was good people. He wouldn't have harmed anyone. Are you sure it was him that sent the car into the lake?" Before Rain could react, Emily rushed on. "I'm not saying you lied or anything. He was driving the car. But you said you were hiding in the back, so maybe you scared him. Is it possible Regan grabbed the wheel? Maybe she thought she was keeping him from driving off the causeway, but really, she did. I mean, the whole affair could have just been a freak accident."

Rain rolled her eyes and pressed her lips together. Emily's eyes grew moist as the silence stretched between them. "I think I was in love with him." A tear slid down her cheek, and she pushed it away with her fingers, sniffing.

Rain leaned her head against the cool glass and muttered, "Me too."

Regan watched as Chase strummed his guitar and then tightened the E string. His fingers fluttered over the chords again, and he looked at the bar's old tin-tiled ceiling. It was probably original since the day the bar was built a hundred years ago. His gaze traveled back to his guitar, and he stopped as he spotted Rain and Emily standing in front of him. Emily was tall, thin, and blonde. She was Regan's age and very pretty.

"Hey, kid. How's it goin'?"

Rain frowned. "I'm not a kid." She shrugged her shoulders. "I'm all right."

Regan smiled as Chase tried unsuccessfully to suppress a chuckle at Rain's bristling personality. She was used to her sister's sass, but she hated the permanent furrow on Rain's brow and the flat frown that rarely lifted.

"Who's your friend?"

Rain glowered, "This is Emily. She knew Regan."

Chase nodded, reaching out to clasp Emily's hand. "Nice to meet you." He sat back on his stool and strummed the chords again in some semblance of a song, then stopped. "Hey, it's great seeing you, Rain, but we open at noon and the bar can't have minors on the premises."

"What Rain means to say, is I'm here to audition." Emily wore too much lip gloss and a little Cherry-Red Shimmer had smeared onto one eyetooth, flashing iridescent red when she smiled. Her low-cut t-shirt showed more cleavage than Chase could possibly ignore. Emily pushed her arms under her breasts and leaned just the slightest bit forward to peer at something behind him. He turned his head, but she'd already moved around him to pick up the microphone. "One-two, testing, one-two."

Chase looked at Rain, knitting his brows together, then lifted his shoulders in question. Rain ran a finger in a circle around her ear, indicating Emily had lost her mind. "Just let her sing for a minute and get it over with. She's my ride," Rain hissed.

Chase nodded, waving the approaching bartender off. "She's leaving in just a minute. Before twelve. I promise."

The bartender shook his head with a loud sigh, slapping a dishtowel against his other hand, he retreated to the bar, muttering something inaudible, like, "This better be good."

Chase looked at Emily, "What'll it be?"

"Regan's song. The one you're going to produce." He nodded, strumming a few chords until she picked up "Walk on Water" and began to sing. Emily wasn't the worst Regan had ever heard, but she sure couldn't make it sound like the original version. Chase was the lead vocalist in the band, but this song required a woman's voice. Regan saw the way his eyes lit up, and she could feel the energy of his brain clicking off the possibilities. Emily had the assets to pull it off. Her voice was decent, though she couldn't reach the high notes or the low. However, she would look good on the stage, and whatever else was missing, Chase could cover it.

When the set was over, the few band members and bar staff clapped. Emily beamed, and if possible, Rain looked even more disgruntled. Regan could see by the look in his eyes that Chase wasn't blind to the budding crush. Rain was pretty, but hopefully, he wasn't stupid. She was still underage, and he didn't seem like the statutory rape sort of guy, plus he'd look terrible in orange. If Rain was jealous of Emily, Regan wondered, then why did she bring her rival to an audition?

Emily bobbed up and down in front of Chase, her full, round breasts almost popping out of her deep V-neck t-shirt. "Oh, that was so awesome! Didn't you think so? I thought it was really great. You know, when Regan came up with the lyrics, I told her how to do the chorus. That was all me," she gushed.

"Shut-up, you liar!" Rain's voice rang out over Emily's chatter. "It's Regan's song, and you had nothing to do with it. You just wanted to sleep with her boyfriend."

The loud accusation silenced the bar and the bartender called to Chase, "Get 'em outta here, Chase. I don't need trouble. Especially under-age cat-fightin' trouble. It's five 'til noon anyway." He pointed toward the side entrance, still holding his bar towel.

Chase stood, grabbing each girl by the arm before more accusations could be thrown. As soon as they reached the alley, Emily started in. "Bitch! I can't believe you tried to ruin my audition."

Chase tried to calm them, but Rain reached around him, snagging Emily's long hair.

"Ow!" she screamed, thrashing around the other side of Chase, who was firmly caught in the middle. Guidry's rumbling laughter echoed through the alley as he approached. He grabbed up Rain, holding her securely as Chase latched tighter to Emily.

"Um-um-um," Guidry shook his head. "What is it with you and women?" Regan watched as he chuckled. His belly rumbled against Rain, who tried to break free.

Chase let out a breath he must have been holding since Rain's first shot. "Thanks, Guidry. You remember Regan's kid sister, and this is Regan's friend, Emily. She came to try out for the band."

"Well now, I do remember Miss Rain. She's a pretty little thing and her sister would be mighty miffed if she could see her fightin' in this here alley. Hi there, Miss Emily. Nice to meet 'cha."

Regan watched Rain as she sat on the doorstep of a praline shop in Jackson Square for several hours. The shop closed up and she wandered around for a while before finally returning to the bar. Sulking outside, she leaned against a streetlight. Regan thought about the numerous paintings of a bum leaning against a similar pole with a Bourbon Street sign overhead. Her sister looked like a bum with her torn jeans, well-worn tennis shoes, and messy ponytail. She didn't have money or a way home. What would Rain do? Their mom was going to ground her for life, and she could kiss her ballet dream good-bye since this was her third absence.

Emily had left the alley in a huff. Regan was sure Rain hadn't intended on going anywhere with her anyway after calling her a troll. Rain obviously knew she was being used by Emily, but it didn't bother her since she'd used Emily for her car. Now that the jig was up, Rain was stuck in the French Quarter, and the sun was going down. If only Chase would look outside and notice her little sister, Rain could ask him for a ride.

As if someone heard Regan's thoughts and took pity on Rain, Chase darted out of the bar and crossed the street into the small market. Rain looked like she was holding her breath as she waited for him to return. He didn't see her and was almost to the bar entrance before she scooted into the doorway.

"Hey, Chase." Rain was acting like a stalker, and he probably thought she was a total loser for still hanging around after the fight. He didn't say anything but looked around like he was waiting for Emily to jump out of the shadows. "I hate to ask, but I'm kinda stuck here. Any chance you're headed back to Bonne Fete tonight?"

He pressed his lips together, then muttered a curse under his breath. "I can't right now. Can you call another friend? Your mom, maybe?"

Rain rolled her eyes and turned away. "Forget I asked."

Chase didn't bite. Regan watched as Rain walked slowly, waiting for him to call her back, but all that Regan heard was the music and rowdy customers calling out above the crowd. Rain spun on her heel, eyes flashing. It was apparent she was miffed that he could leave her in the street. It was getting dark. He lit a cigarette, halfway smiling as he leaned against the brick wall.

"You—you, would just let me walk off into the Quarter to try to find a way home?"

Chase took a long drag then flicked ash onto the ground. "You got yourself here, didn't you?"

Rain's voice was agitated. "Someone could rape or murder me."

"Or both," he chuckled.

"It's not funny!" She turned around. This time it looked as if she really was leaving.

Chase jogged to her and grabbed her arm to stop her. "I'll take you home, okay, but you'll have to wait two hours until the relief band shows up for the evening crowd." His expression grew serious. "I was making a point, Rain. You could get into trouble out here. You should think about that next time, before you go traipsing around the city. This ain't Bonne Fete, Louisiana." He stared at her hard, like an older brother giving her a set-down. "You may be underage, but some men around here don't care. Hell, they prefer it." His gaze dropped to her gaping t-shirt and he paused. A look crossed his features that worried Regan. He was struggling with something. "Pull your shirt up and stay here until I get off. Don't come in the bar but keep where I can see you."

Regan was in a hurry to leave the French Quarter and get home to check on their mother. This place was starting to look seedy. The bar was just off the square and the music poured raucously out into the early evening heat. She studied Rain leaning up against the same streetlight that now blinked on with the exodus of the setting sun. The look on her sister's face said it all. First it was Mark and now it was Chase.

Rain barely knew Chase. Sure, Regan had been quickly infatuated, but it probably would have fizzled out after a few weeks of bickering about music. Time in the afterlife must be dulling her senses to entertain those kinds of thoughts, because she really wanted Rain not to fall for the soul she'd previously thought was her destiny. It was hard, even now, to deny the instant chemistry and the longing she'd felt.

Earlier, her energy had quickened as Chase had darted out of the bar and jogged across the one lane of traffic. The way his muscles danced beneath his light-colored T-shirt, and his sandy hair blew in the breeze was tantalizing. He wasn't a body builder, but he was rock star worthy and beautiful. Regan was mesmerized by his presence as he stopped to talk to Rain. The way he lit a cigarette and leaned against the brick wall with smooth confidence heightened her interest. Regan knew it was popular to smoke. Everyone in school did it, even though there were huge televised campaigns against cigarettes. If she'd dated him, she'd have made him quit, but her little sister didn't seem to mind. Rain's gooey-eyed stare and then her pretend temper tantrum said it all.

In boredom Regan waited, never wandering far. She couldn't do much about anyone wanting to snag Rain or harm her, but at least she would know where her sister was. Having no sense of time, she peered into the twilight, watching the living and dead as they caroused. Apparently, the new gift from the strange spirit she'd dubbed Diablo wasn't temporary. A young male in a torn ACDC shirt and ripped denim jeans leaned on the pole next to Rain. His slippery fingers slid down and around the pole, and he tried to graze Rain's jeans.

Regan kicked up a breeze with hurricane force. He skittered back and looked at Rain accusingly.

With sudden awareness, she pulled away from the street post. "Creep, what are you doing?"

He threw his hands up. "Nothin'. What are you looking at?" He yelled to a black man who stopped playing his harmonica. The man shook his head and looked away, muttering.

Chase appeared in the doorway, staring at the guy as he backed down the street. His expression was menacing. Softly, he said to Rain, "Is he bothering you? I'm almost done."

Regan watched two large shadowy figures with blood dripping from various wounds on their ghostly forms. They flanked the asshole as he turned away, flipping the bird over his head. They moved with him as he disappeared into the crowd gathering at the end of the street. One man tap-danced nearby as another called out to tourists, "I betcha ten dollars I can tell you where you got 'dem shoes!"

"Pesky humans. That one could use a good lesson in manners. I dare say, what's happened to this new generation?"

"Gustave!" Regan was surprised and happy to see someone she knew. Sort of. He wasn't Diablo, he didn't have blood dripping from open wounds, and he was stuck in the in-between like her.

"Who are we babysitting?" he purred.

Regan wrung her hands behind her, pushing her energy from side to side. Should she tell him? Would it somehow make her vulnerable? Was Gustave in cahoots with the devil?

"Have you ever met the Prince of Darkness?"

Gustave looked aghast. "You mean the singer? No, not personally, but he played at the Superdome some time ago, and I admit I was curious, so many people and all." He inspected his ghostly fingernails.

Regan rolled her eyes. "No, not the singer, Prince. I'm talking about Diablo, Lucifer, Satan."

Now Gustave looked intrigued. "No, have you?"

Regan sucked in a breath, "Maybe."

Gustave's casual drawl turned to gossip-worthy excitement. "Oh, do tell!"

The inside of Chase's beat-up Honda was littered with fast-food wrappers and empty soda cans. Regan thought he looked a little uncomfortable as he cleared his throat.

"Sorry, I gave some of the guys a ride home last night after work, and we grabbed some grub. I was late this afternoon and—" his explanation halted suddenly as he shut his door and turned the key in the ignition. Regan supposed Chase was wondering why he was explaining himself. Rain was a kid, and he was going out of his way to accommodate her. That, too, made Regan worry.

They drove in silence for a bit and then Chase turned on the radio. Quiet Riot's "Cum on Feel the Noize" blared from the small hatchback's speakers. He quickly turned it down and fiddled with the tuner until it played something softer. Rain suppressed a smile. Regan could hear her sister's heart thudding. *Yep, she has it bad.* Chase seemed clueless enough. He wasn't leering or doing anything inappropriate, and that appeased Regan. It wasn't that she was jealous of his possible interest, she was dead. It was that she hoped he wasn't a sleazy jerk. Rain was vulnerable, and for reasons Regan could only guess, attracted to all her prior love interests. Maybe it was so she could walk in Regan's shoes. As if she felt the currents of her thoughts, Rain started humming her song, "Walk on Water."

"Yes, Rain. I walked on water, and then the water swallowed me up, and I am no more. You don't want to be me, and you shouldn't want to be with him! Haven't you figured it out yet? I didn't choose so well. Mark murdered me, for God's sake. Chase might be a good-looking guy, and he's obviously nice enough to give you a ride home, but he's way too old—statutory rape old. Surely, you get it." Regan knew she couldn't be heard by either of the car's occupants, but it felt good to rant.

Rain's forehead tilted against the glass as she continued humming the song. The car pulled into the dark driveway, its wheels crunching along the gravel drive. An opaque porchlight illuminated the front of the house.

Still venting, Regan tossed out, "Geez, Rain. Grow up! Tell him thanks for the ride, get out of the car, and quit making a fool of yourself." Searching for another angle to argue, she yelled with anguish. "Are you trying to kill our mother? She will have a cow if she finds out you're coming home this late with a grown man."

Rain didn't touch the door latch.

Chase didn't turn off the engine. "I'd walk you in, but I don't think this is a good time to meet your mother. I'd rather talk to her about the song when it's daylight." He kept both hands on the wheel, staring straight ahead. It bothered Regan that he seemed guilty of something. She picked up his heartbeat thudding in his chest. Maybe he did like Rain, and maybe he felt guilty about it.

Rain reached out and touched his bicep. "Thanks, Chase. I don't know what I would've done without you tonight. You saved me from—God knows what that guy intended to do."

Regan rolled her eyes at the dramatics. Rain sounded like a freshman swooning over a senior. Regan should know. She'd made the same goofy mistake. It was like the scene from "Vision Quest" where Matthew Modine was caught sniffing Linda Fiorentino's underwear. Regan wanted to look away, but she couldn't. It was a train wreck. Rain moved toward Chase. She put her lips to his, and for a moment, Chase sat very still.

As if a bolt of lightning shot through him, Chase jerked, pulled away, and pushed Rain back. "Hey, whoa, no-no. None of that. This was just a ride home. What are you trying to do, send me to jail?" He got out of the car, walked briskly to the passenger side door. Jerking it open, he grabbed Rain's arm and, without ceremony, pulled her out. Returning to the driver's side, he got in and sped away. No walk to the door or good night. Within seconds, he was gone.

CHAPTER 15

Regan watched Rain go to class the following day. Her sister's mood was solemn after their mother gave her a twenty-minute set-down on skipping class and getting rides from strange boys. Rain hadn't told Rona who dropped her off. The excuse of a friend sufficed.

Regan had stood against the kitchen island, smirking as their mother raged. Before now, the wrath had always been directed at Regan. Finally, it was Rain's turn. But the tears sliding silently down her face didn't help Regan's energy soar with satisfaction. Instead, a cold loneliness washed over her. Rain's bitterness over Chase's rejection saturated Regan's conscience and made her too sad to swell with the pleasure of revenge.

Regan followed her through the first two periods at school and then back to her locker. Rain's lock code was her birthdate backward. It was predictable and easy to guess. Ballet shoes hung over the inside hook, and Regan wondered if Rain would eventually go back to dancing. She guessed it might be hard for Rain to get back and forth without someone to drive her. It had been Regan's chore before her death, and now their mother was working so many hours. Mark had simultaneously killed both of their dreams.

Thinking of Mark made her angry and she wanted to send a gale of wind down the hall to slam all the classroom doors shut, but she didn't. As if someone had read her thoughts, a door flew open at the end of the hall. It hit with a thwack, startling Rain. Regan tried to ground her energy as Mark darted toward them like a battering ram. Rain tripped over her bookbag and grabbed onto a girl's purse hanging on the locker next to hers.

"Hey, watch it. You ripped my bag!"

Regan threw her ethereal arms out to stop the onslaught. Like her, Mark was in spirit form and couldn't harm anyone, but his energy was almost palpable. He came to a screeching halt in front of Regan. Something beyond anger stretched his luminous features, pulling them out of proper alignment. The flesh of his face wrenched from the bone in a zipper-like motion from forehead to chin, first revealing muscle, then his skull splintered open, and flaming energy burst out like a blazing bottle rocket on the Fourth of July.

Regan was awestruck and paralyzed by the heat he released. She stood blocking Rain from the onslaught. When the door that Mark had entered through shut, sooty ashes swirled, and his ghostly form turned to dust. Regan was stunned, and she wondered how no one else around them could miss the horror movie theatrics but was glad they had.

"You ripped my purse! You're going to pay for it." It was one of the popular girls that Regan hated. They usually stayed far away from her and her kind when she was alive. They were scared shitless of her. Regan had only been in one fight during all of her school years, but she'd made sure she won so that she never had to do it again. This wasn't her quarrel, though, and the popular prima donna wasn't afraid of Rain, especially now that Regan wasn't around to protect her. As Rain stood up, looking at the broken strap, the angry girl got in her face. "You owe me fifty dollars."

Rain blanched. "Who would pay fifty dollars for that?"

Regan could tell it was an automatic response and that Rain hadn't thought it through. Uh-oh, this might get ugly.

The girl threw the bag down and grabbed hold of Rain's t-shirt. "I don't think you should be worrying about what I buy or how much it costs. All you need to worry about is how you're going to pay for what you broke!"

A crowd was forming around the locker area when the bell sounded. A nearby teacher left her classroom, rapidly approaching.

"What's going on, ladies?"

The popular girl was now surrounded by her besties, which made up half the cheerleading team. They were older than Rain and much bigger. "She ripped my purse. It's ruined. She's going to pay for it."

The teacher frowned, looking at Rain's wrinkled t-shirt and scuffed tennis shoes, then back to the cheer team. "All right, ladies, let's move on to class before the tardy bell rings. Rain, Claudia, to the office."

Rain huffed as she shut her locker door. Regan would have sighed if she could, but releasing energy wasn't what she wanted to do just now. She placed a luminous hand on Rain's shoulder. "You got this. Don't let that bitch bully you. It was an accident, and she knows it. She just wanted to fight you to prove she can beat someone up."

Rain and Claudia were both sentenced to three days of detention, starting today. Regan didn't know how Rain would get home without the bus driving her. They lived too far to walk. Their mother would be pissed to rearrange her schedule, or maybe she would be getting off from work at that time. Damn, didn't Rain have any friends? She seemed to be sliding down the wrong path and things were getting slippery.

Regan shadowed Rain as she skipped detention, left school, and got on the bus. It wasn't a totally dumb move if she didn't have a ride, but she should have worked something out with the principal. This wasn't going to turn out well. Rain got off at the wrong stop. They weren't exactly near home. Tears fell in buckets as the bus sped away from the gas station. Rain crossed the two-lane country road and traipsed to the other side of the large culvert, forging a path through the dark, meandering pines. Regan felt waves of hurt and anger rolling off her little sister. Rain swiped at her face. The negative energy poured out of her in great gasps as she made her way to a highway, then another patch of woods that brought them nowhere close to home.

Regan pushed energy at every car that slowed down on the winding bayou road. Rain was headed in the wrong direction. This wasn't the way home. The memory of almost putting her out of the car seemed like so long ago. Wasn't it Rain who pleaded that she was afraid of getting murdered while hitch-hiking?

Luckily, they lived in the boondocks and not many cars passed this way. Rain didn't have her thumb out, so apparently, she was intent on walking to her destination. Regan didn't have a sense of time since fading into the in-between world. She noticed the light of day and night, but somehow, she couldn't tell if it had been an hour or only several minutes. She floated alongside Rain, standing between her and a car that stopped to ask if she wanted a ride. The guy wore khaki pants and a pressed button-down shirt. He looked like he worked somewhere nice, and he drove a Volvo. Nice cars were rarely seen in these parts. Regan's hackles went up as she watched Rain debating to hop in. With a whoosh of desperate energy, Regan slammed the door. The man looked startled but put the car in park and pushed the door open again.

Rain quickly shook her head, pointing to Emily Fairchild's home. "Thanks, Mister, but my house is just there." She quickly walked on, ignoring the older man's wave. Regan wasn't sure why she felt so terrified, but something about the driver's aura was off. She was relieved that Rain had said no, but where on earth was she going? The toxic energy flowing from her little sister was making it hard for Regan to push positive energy.

Instead of crossing the railroad tracks, Rain dodged the heat and walked the trestles for a while. The shade of the tree canopy and the small stream beside and below it provided an atmosphere for quiet contemplation. Rain switched the backpack to her other side for a while before finally clamping it over both shoulders. Regan wished she could smell the honeysuckle and the sandy dirt that ran along the banks of the brown water. The tracks stretched out over a long bridge as the creek grew wider and the banks sloped lower into the landscape. Rain let out a squeal as she danced out onto the bridge to avoid a long black snake with a white chin. He was too busy chasing after a mouse to notice Rain, but the moment disoriented her, causing her to sway dangerously over the edge of the tracks. She landed hard on the wooden crossties. A great horn blared in the distance, and Rain struggled to get up under the weight of her pack. Regan noticed the strap had snagged on a nail. The whistle grew louder, and Rain struggled like a turtle knocked on its back with nothing to push against to right herself. She was so close to the edge that if she turned, she would fall into the creek far below. If she didn't move fast, she was doomed.

Rain lay still with her eyes closed for a moment. Regan wished she were back in her human form so she could rail at her sister to get the hell up. *This can't be happening! I have to stop her!* Regan couldn't imagine what would happen if Rain were to take her own life—what their poor mother would do if she lost another daughter. This entire scenario was such a cliché and totally Rain. She was an extremist when it came to drama, making everyone hold their breath and boil with insanity at her infuriating actions, but this was a permanent solution to a temporary problem that time would eventually wash away.

"Rain, get up!" Regan yelled as she floated further up the tracks to see where the train was.

Rain had always been the sort to battle with one swift swipe of the blade, paralyzing all other attacks with her one tyrannical move. Regan remembered saving money for a new guitar by mowing grass all summer long. Rain had asked to borrow a new shirt from Regan's closet, and she'd said no, it was brand new. In a fit of anger, Rain grabbed the tea tin full of cash, dashed to the bathroom, and locked the door. Regan could hear her sister tearing up the money and flushing it down their one and only toilet. She had wanted to kill her. If it hadn't been for Rona's intervention, she might have strangled Rain.

Her immobile body lying listless across the railroad tracks wasn't paper money, it was her life, and Regan couldn't bring it back if Rain succeeded in flushing her young existence down the toilet. Regan couldn't even save herself. In desperation, she started to push energy at Rain, willing her to get up, but she didn't move. It was like the many times she'd played possum to irritate Regan during their years growing up together. Rain was a pro at this game. She didn't blink. The horn blared now, causing no effect on Rain, but Regan was terrified. She pushed air in circles all around Rain, causing a mini dust devil over the tracks, whipping her hair over her face. Lifting sand from the creek and blowing it with all her might, Regan pelted her sister with dirt and sand, hoping for a reaction. Mere seconds away now, the train's weight and speed vibrated the tracks with earth-shattering force. At the last minute, Rain released her arms from the pack and rolled from the tracks, splashing into the water below.

The pack was crushed beneath the weight of the train and bits of the shredded fabric blew into the air along with music cassettes. Spools of the tape blew in the wind like streamers at a Mardi Gras parade. Bits of the broken plastic splintered into the air, littering the tracks. The train was a short ten cars. It blew its whistle as it passed into the distance. Rain surfaced from the milky tan water, sputtering and making clumsy strokes toward the bank. If Regan had been alive, she wasn't sure if she would have hugged Rain fiercely or drowned her for the stupid prank.

CHAPTER 16

"If I could only go back and change that one moment!" Regan cried out to the heavens. "It's not fair!" She stretched herself toward Rain, who was holding onto a half-submerged railroad tie at the water's edge. "Don't let go, Rain!"

"Come with me." The angelic voice pierced her sorrowful wails. The gossamer-winged angel stood between Regan and Rain. Regan still hovered over the tracks. "Some things can't be changed, but much can be altered. You could go back. Time is not linear, as you might think. Many people choose to live a simple life in the past. You may have even lived in the future, but you will not fulfill that life if you don't come home."

Regan shook off the angel's request in confusion. "Are you here for Rain, or are you here for me?"

"I'm here for you, Luna, as I always will be. I'm your soul watcher." Regan looked at Rain struggling to withdraw her body from the murky waters that clung to her heavy jeans and windbreaker. The stiff material weighed her down and would've sunk her if she hadn't been such a strong swimmer. The ballet classes had paid off in spades.

Regan felt emotionally battered. "I don't need help. Rain needs you." Regan pleaded, feeling like she was the one dragging herself from the murky water. "I mean, was she trying to—?" Regan couldn't form the words.

The angel floated closer to Regan. "She's where she's supposed to be, unlike you. She's on her life's path."

"You mean a suicide mission. Look at her!" Regan looked at Rain, then back at the angel. The heavens beckoned her to look up. The sun was blinding her energy and she felt its tantalizing pull. She backed away as if trying to retract herself from its warm tentacles. "I'm not ready yet. Rain is—I don't know, she's just not well and Mom—." Regan sputtered as she floated back off the trestles and realized she was hovering over the water. Her unembodied state didn't give her the physical presence she missed, but old habits die hard. She thought about herself as walking most of the time, so floating without any real direction and existing in a state of bridled energy was something she hadn't had enough time to master. "Besides, I'm still angry with Mark. I need to talk to him. I need to know why he did this!" She felt so helpless as she searched the angel's face. "I need to forgive him," she pleaded, letting go of the anger she felt. This event with Rain had exhausted her spirit.

Regan still struggled with being dead. She'd been taken from her last life without warning, missing everything she could have looked forward to—and now she hovered above the earth watching her dearest loved one struggle with whether to live or not.

"I think you already have forgiven Mark." The angel's voice was like a soothing balm over her tattered soul. Regan moved the wind around her, pushing it toward the angel. She refused to go, and she used the air to ground herself to this world.

"If you refuse to go this time, Luna, there will be no way home. Part of dying is accepting what we have not finished, the things we leave behind."

"My name's Regan. My mother named me that. It means popular or little ruler." Regan snorted with sarcastic humor. "I think she may have regretted that choice." Regan was trying to stretch the moment, weighing out the possibilities. "Look, Angel, Rain and my mom aren't things. It's not like I'm asking to stay to be me again. I want to make sure they're okay."

"The creator has a plan, but alas, as I said before, there have been mistakes." The angel's gaze turned back to Rain, who now sat on the beach, tangled in the remnants of her half-shed jacket. Sobs poured from her and she stood, taking off her clothes with clumsy, shaking hands. In her underwear, she stalked back into the water and didn't try to swim as the current began sweeping her away.

"Stop her! What do you mean he has a plan? She's going to drown. That's not okay. You said she was on the right path," Regan screamed.

The angel extended one luminous arm, showing Regan the palm of her hand. A golden star burned in the center of her palm, draining the emotions that burned within Regan. She felt hypnotized. "As I said, she's on her life's path. Rain has chosen to end this journey. She will fall into the pool of souls and rejoin you again in another life. Calm yourself. You will be reunited."

A slight pause and a brief glance at the water distracted Regan from the trance. The angel's eyes engaged her once more. Everything around them came to a sharp halt. Time stood still. As if caught in a magnetic field, Regan reached out and touched the angel's magical hand looming toward her. Light shards burst all around them and she heard the angel's voice in her inner core. "With death comes life and a chance for renewal." Regan saw the angel in another life as a man. She had long golden hair, tied into a loose braid down her back. She held a baby in her arms. The baby morphed into a grown man. It was Chase, and he was suddenly standing at the entrance of the French Quarter bar. Regan stood next to Mark's BMW. It was the night Regan died. She recognized the clothes they wore and the location. As she got into the vehicle, the angel looked off in Chase's direction. Regan saw herself get into the car, and Mark peel out of the parking space leaving skid marks on the pavement. This was exactly what happened, so why did the angel replay the events? Regan felt herself physically pulled backward as the events rewound like a silent film. The same scene unfolded, but this time the angel cloaked Regan with her wings spread wide and her arms wrapped around Regan's shoulders as she fervently channeled energy through Regan for protection. Regan slammed the door and screamed at Mark to leave. He peeled out and Regan returned to the bar. Now, inside the car, her luminous spirit watched as different events unfolded. Rain was still tucked behind the passenger seat. Mark drove, choking back a sob. Rain sat up, touching a finger to Mark's cheek, wiping away a tear.

Her voice was soft as she whispered to him. "Don't cry. I love you."

Mark's eyes widened in surprise. A sharp jerk of the wheel sent the car careening over the guardrail. An eruption of bubbles gurgled at the surface, and then the water stilled with a slight lapping wave that could have been a passing boat. There was no evidence of the car's disappearance, just the blackness of night and the cicadas singing in the distance. In a sudden flash, the vision ended.

The angel had failed in her duty to protect Regan. Because of the soul watcher's derelict actions, Regan was dead. Now, Rain would die too. Regan struggled from the angel's shared vision and felt herself float a few feet away. Time ticked again as it had before, sending Rain further downstream and deeper into the water's current.

The angel's voice was a shaking force. "Decide now, Regan. You will not have this opportunity again. I made a mistake, and in this one moment, I give you the chance to right the past. I cannot make you Regan again, but if you accept this life, you will be Rain for the rest of your days, and if you choose to do so, you may never speak of what I am about to share with a living soul. Breaking this promise could lead to terrible events."

"Help her," Regan screamed as she surfaced to reality. She didn't know how much time had passed, but Rain was being swept away by the water at an alarming speed. She would surely drown.

The angel looked ashamed as she formed the words. "I can't. It was meant to be. It was always meant to be." She raised her hands as if summoning an event. "Luna. I made a mistake in not protecting you that night. You were not supposed to meet your end. I was distracted by something I wasn't expecting to encounter. I cannot bring back the life of Regan, but I have agreed to make a sacrifice. You have been awarded a second chance in this life, and it is up to you to take it. Once you accept, you will be transformed, and there can be no escape. Do you agree to this offer?"

Rain's hand came crashing from the water and disappeared again. Regan blanched, giving the angel an incredulous look. "Do you mean—?" Realization hit her with a powerful sense of loss. This was really happening and there was nothing she could do about it. Her soul was being ripped in two. The love she felt for Rain and the inability to save her was pure anguish. "No! Why? This isn't the way it's supposed to be!" Desperation flooded her. There had to be another way. "I can't. This isn't fair. She doesn't know what she's doing. You can save her. Please! Save her!"

The angel shook her head, but Regan didn't know if it was because she denied the plea, or if her guardian pitied her desperation. "Rain has taken her own life. She will not exist on this plane no matter what you choose, but if you truly desire to stay and help your mother, this life can be yours."

It was the only thing the angel had said that tempted her sanity to react. Rain would die, and her mother would be totally alone. The image of their mother's limp body lying in bed sobbing flashed through her consciousness. The only way to help Rona was to take Rain's body and to be Rain for the rest of her life.

How can I agree to take Rain's life?

What felt like forever was surely only a matter of seconds. The angel's expression breathed empathy, but she didn't relent in her prediction of what was to come. Regan knew there wasn't time to weigh out the morality of her actions. An image of Rain laughing as she twirled in ballet shoes flickered through her mind, followed by her mother sipping a glass of iced tea on their dusty porch, and finally, Chase singing her song. Her answer was clear. There was still much to live for.

"Yes."

Her answer burst forth, and in an instant, she found herself thrashing with all her might, fighting the current that threatened to take her. Regan swallowed great gulps of muddy water as she tried to swim.

Was this some sort of sick joke? The angel made a mistake, so to save her ass, she dunked Regan back into the world just to drown her again. Regan felt her energy draining as she swallowed too much water. Choking, coughing and sputtering to the surface, she almost gave up. It was all too painful, and Regan didn't know if she could fight the current any longer.

Strong arms wrapped around her, dragging her through the water. She tried to remain calm so she didn't take them both down, but it was difficult to relax when she was struggling to breathe. After a few gasping moments, she lay prone on the bank, rolling to one side as she threw up all the creek water she'd swallowed. She could hear the guy shouting at her. "Are you crazy, kid? You could have drowned. What are you doing swimming in this part of the river?"

Regan ignored him, still gasping for air. Finally, his words sank in and she responded. "I'm not a kid."

Delila stood on the bank of the river, watching the water rush over her ward. Had Regan waited too long to accept the gift? Was Rain's body a chance at a new reality for her ward or would it be a casket for an all-new horror? She watched Regan flail against the current, but the brown water swirled around her like a great drain, sucking her farther into its depths. A ray of light broke through the canopy of the trees and shined down upon a dark figure that emerged from the leafy shadows. With one quick motion, he dove in, splitting the surface of the water with a great splash. It was mere seconds until he emerged, gripping Regan's chest. Delila pushed wind at the water to help speed the current to the shore. The two sputtered and gagged as they lay on the muddy riverbank. The young man finally found his feet, and he bent over, trying to catch his breath.

She didn't know if it was a gift from Rodanian, God, or pure coincidence, but she thanked her stars for the stranger coming to her ward's rescue. A soul could suffer only so much in such a short amount of time. Already the collateral damage was too great. Her ward would struggle with issues and grapple to find her footing in this new life, but now there was a chance to make things right.

CHAPTER 17

The young man who had helped her from the water was probably about her age. Correction, Regan's age. It would take some time to get used to the idea that she was alive, breathing air and now in Rain's body. Tears of loss ran down her face. She'd never had the chance to mourn the loss of her life as Regan, but it seemed less sad than the knowledge that Rain was lost forever to her. Regan would look in the mirror for the rest of her life and see the little sister she could never be with again. Could she pull it together and help her mother? Rona had been through too much grief to suffer once more, so the news about Rain would have to be buried with Regan's guilt about usurping her sister's body. How she would live with the choice she'd made was to be seen. Regan took a deep breath, trying to steady her emotions. *One thing at a time, Regan.*

The guy who saved her life introduced himself as Jorge. She'd floated too far downstream, so he drove her back to the spot where she'd left her clothes on the bank. He'd given her a large hoody from his back seat, which she'd put on, pulling the zipper up with great speed. It was almost a full-length dress on Rain's slight form. They stood, overlooking the scene where it had all begun.

"So, you thought you'd go swimming after the train almost ran you over and crushed your backpack?" He pointed to the scraps of material littering the area.

It would have made more sense if Rain hadn't taken off her clothes. Then she could say she fell from the tracks. It would look less intentional. Regan shrugged. "It was a stupid idea." What else could she say? She wasn't fooling him. "Look, I know it was crazy, and I promise I'll never do it again, so please don't tell anyone."

He frowned at her as she shimmied back into Rain's clothes under the hoody. When she was finished, she tossed his jacket back to him.

He inspected the scene a bit longer in silence then turned to her. "I know who you are. You go to school with my little sister." He paused uncomfortably. "Hey, I'm sorry to hear about your sister. She was a year behind me. I graduated last spring."

Regan squinted, vaguely remembering the guy. He used to be a lanky, dark-haired boy from the swim team. It made sense that he could save her, and she was thankful for it. Jorge had changed a lot since she'd seen him last. Now muscular with wide shoulders, he had a more manly presence, though his face was still as smooth as a baby. She guessed it was his Hispanic background.

Regan nodded coolly. "Yeah, I remember you." He was probably onto the mystery of her swim, but there was no way he could really know Rain had tried to take her life.

He seemed surprised. "You were in junior high, right?"

Regan reminded herself that she wasn't Regan anymore. She was in Rain's body and she had to play the part. She wanted to lay down on the bank and sob with the unfairness of it all, but she needed to hold it together in front of Jorge. She didn't need him telling anyone about this, mainly her mother. It did feel good to breathe air, walk, to exist in the physical world. She sat down to tie her tennis shoes, thinking about the sequence of events. "Do you believe in angels, Jorge?"

He paused, watching her as if she might be insane. "Like, with feathery wings and golden halos?"

She smiled, nodding at his description. Was her angel still around, watching her now, or did she get released from her duties once Regan took up Rain's form?

He looked at the few white clouds dotting the light-blue sky. "I don't know. I'm Catholic. I still go to church with my mom and sisters most of the time." He shot her a sheepish grin. "I do it for my mom. She worries about my soul." He said it like it was something to be embarrassed about. Knowing what she'd seen and experienced in the afterlife and after meeting the devil, she didn't think it was silly at all.

He picked up a rock and threw it into the water. "Are you wondering if Regan went to heaven?"

He was predicting the reason for her question, and in truth, she wasn't sure why she'd brought it up, except she was thankful to him for saving her life.

She gave him a broad smile. "No, I was thinking you are an angel for saving me. I'm thinking of calling you St. George." Standing, she brushed off her wet jeans and winced. Wet clothes were the worst on a windy day. "Can you give me a ride?"

CHAPTER 18

J orge had been reluctant to leave her at her house alone. She had to promise to call him later to let him know she was okay. A hot shower helped revive her senses. She stood in her towel at the refrigerator door studying the contents with despair. After being dead, all she could think of at this moment was one thing. She slammed the refrigerator door and looked out the front window. The Mustang was still there. Her keys sat in a basket on the kitchen counter next to the phone. Bingo!

Regan felt overwhelmed by her awakening senses. Putting on a pair of Rain's dry jeans and a cotton T-shirt was wonderful and devastating all at once. Rain's scent clung to the clothing, but Regan pushed all feelings and thoughts aside for the moment. Things felt different in her sister's more petite form. She adjusted the driver's seat but avoided looking in the rearview mirror or any mirror that would show her the repercussions of recent events.

Consoling herself, she spoke aloud. "You had no choice. Mom couldn't have handled losing both of you. You had to do it." A hot tear rolled down one cheek. She blinked her eyes rapidly, forcing the flood back. Taking a deep breath, she promised herself that she would sort out her emotions later. She couldn't do it right now without losing her mind. Her grief was too great and her emotions were already jagged shards of glass. If she touched them, she would bleed out her sanity. She turned into Coot's parking lot, watching gravel spray in the rearview mirror. Chalky-white rock bounced and arced up behind the bright orange trunk of the Mustang.

The police officer walking to his car changed directions and waved for her to stay put. Looking next to her for her purse, she realized it was Rain's. "Shit!"

There wasn't time to run now, and the last thing she wanted to do was get Rain in trouble. Wait, she *was* Rain. This new existence wasn't going to be easy.

The officer in the starched uniform motioned for her to roll down her window. "Young lady, do you often speed into parking lots filled with cars and other possible pedestrians?" Regan tried to look mature. Rain never wore makeup but could pass for sixteen with her lean dancer's body.

She pushed her shoulders back, hoping her small bit of cleavage was visible under the V-neck t-shirt. "Sorry, officer. No, sir. This is my sister's car, and I wasn't used to the gas pedal being so sensitive. I drive my mom's station wagon most of the time, but—" It wasn't hard to turn on the water-works. Tears welled up in her eyes and she found herself blubbering. "I just wanted a Coke. My sister passed away, and she and I always drank soda together when I had a problem, and I just wanted to feel close to her, but she's not here anymore, and now I have to deal with things all alone."

The officer walked the short distance to his patrol car and returned with a tissue box. "Here, darlin'. It's okay. I was just reminding you to be more careful. Poor thing, come on in and I'll buy you a Coke." He nodded to her kindly and she sniffed, nodding back.

The officer didn't stay to chat. He told the waitress to bring Rain whatever she wanted and to put it on his tab. The reckless driving incident was forgotten as he patted her on the shoulder and asked her if she needed to call someone. When she assured him she would be fine, he said good-bye. Regan was starving. She wasn't sure if it was that Rain hadn't eaten in a while, or if she was having real-world withdrawals. She ate two burgers, an order of fries, a chocolate sundae with all the trimmings, and three full glasses of soda throughout the meal. A large belch escaped her when the waitress took away the dessert bowl. Regan sighed with satisfaction and relief. She'd escaped getting a ticket and being arrested for underage driving. The comfort food had distracted her from the harsh reality of her new existence.

Regan found three crumpled bills in Rain's purse and left them on the table for the waitress. Where did Rain stash her allowance? She was sure that the sum total of what their mom gave them every payday didn't add up to the three dollars in Rain's cloth purse. It was a mess inside, and it sported multicolored marker stains at the corners. Regan would do a room inventory when she got home. She'd saved money over the summer and had a hundred dollars in an old shoebox at the back of her closet.

The keys jangled in her palm as she made her way back to the car. Regan carefully drove the three miles back home then sprinted from the car into the house. Her mother was in the kitchen sitting at the table, smoking a cigarette. Rona hadn't smoked before the accident. Guilt washed over

Regan—so many of her choices had caused negative implications on her family. She wanted to rail at the stupid angel who'd messed everything up, but then she remembered the other outcome of the angel's story. If it wasn't Rain's physical form standing here, it would be Regan's. She wasn't supposed to die in the first place. Either way, she was at fault for going to see Chase that night and using Mark to do it. If she'd just stayed home, would everything still be the same? Would her sister still be here?

"Rain, come sit. We need to talk." Her mother's voice was calm and low. It was her heart-to-heart tone, like the time Regan had fallen from grace, and half the town was talking about her and the football captain.

Regan held the door frame, glancing back at the car and wondering what excuse she could use to get out of this. On the other hand, she wanted to hug her mother to her and never let go. She hadn't seen her in forever, and the depths of Rona's heartbreak needed to be released. But Regan was supposed to be Rain. If she grabbed her mother in a bear hug and started crying, her mother would be alarmed, to say the least. Regan needed to stay in character, but she was a singer, not an actress, damn it!

Rona pushed the metal chair away from the table with her foot. The loud, scraping noise woke Regan from her meandering thoughts. She crept toward the vinyl seat covered with big yellow daisies. Her eyes were wary as she inspected her mother's lined features.

Rona crushed her cigarette in the butt-littered ashtray, blowing out a billow of smoke in the other direction before assessing Regan. "Now I know you miss your sister, but we can't change what the Lord has ordered. So when you grab your sister's keys and go runnin' off to God knows where, I understand that you miss her and that maybe you need to rebel a bit to feel like her, but Rain, honey, you're not." Her mother sniffed, looking up at the ceiling as if there would be some sort of divine intervention. "Rain, you are all I have left in this world, and like it or not, I'm all you got, so we're just gonna have to get along. I know it may not be cool to mind your momma, but I trust that you won't try to break my heart after all I've been through." Rona paused again to choke back a small sob that half escaped. "I promised myself I wouldn't cry." Her mother blinked rapidly, reminding Regan of herself. If this were any normal set-down she'd gotten in the past, she would have been laughing at her mother's tactics to bond, but things had changed since she was in her old body last and her perspective in the new body now was very different. Regan finally realized what was most important after she died, and her previous, silly teen aspirations were last on the list.

She looked down, staring at her dirty sneakers and mismatched socks. She hadn't noticed the fashion mistake before now. It made her grin.

Her mother took her smile as a truce. "Okay then, off you go to your room for the night. I'm not grounding you for long, but driving without a license deserves some punishment or what kind of mother would I be."

Regan couldn't help herself. She embraced her mother and took in a deep breath of her. She smelled like strawberry-scented shampoo and cigarettes. Rona pulled back to look at her. "You okay?"

Regan sniffed, trying to look more casual than she felt. "I'm just relieved you aren't grounding me for the week." Rona stood, nodding, then pulled another cigarette from her pack as she walked to the porch. Regan turned toward her room, then realized she should go to Rain's room instead. Her mother called through the screen door. "Did you eat, or do you need me to make you something? There's leftover meatloaf from last night if you want it."

Regan smiled. Her mother, the hard-ass. What a joke. Her soft nature and inability to be tough was half the reason Regan had become so willful.

Let it be a lesson to all mothers—Spare the rod, spoil the child—

Look where it had gotten Regan. She'd been cocky and sure of herself. She thought she was above her mother's rules and so she broke them often enough until she was broken. Mark was another spoiled kid that thought he should be able to have whatever he wanted, and he'd wanted Regan. What would he do now that Regan was Rain? Would he stalk her forever? Would he haunt Rain on the other side?

The phone rang just after nine and Regan answered it before her mother could pick up.

"Hey, you never called me to say you were okay."

"Saint George, is that you?"

"Yeah, it's Jorge. I was worried about you. You didn't seem all that good when we met today."

A click was heard and then Rona's voice came over the line. "Rain, you are grounded from the phone tonight. Tell your friend to call back tomorrow."

She heard another click, and then her heart raced with fear. "Hey, sorry about that. I'm kind of grounded for driving without permission. I'll call you tomorrow." Regan hung up quickly before her mother picked up the phone again or Jorge started talking about the incident. She lay in bed with her hand over her thudding heart, contemplating each beat. The blood in her veins wasn't hers. The veins weren't hers, none of this body belonged to Regan, but it was her existence right now. She began to sob at the thought. Rain was gone, and yet Regan would remember her every time she looked in the mirror. Crawling out of bed, she made her way to the bathroom and grabbed a wad of toilet paper, blowing her nose. She dared to look at her reflection. A very disastrous-looking Rain stared back at her, but something was different, besides the unkempt hair and wrinkled clothes. It was her eyes. They were Regan's eyes. As sisters, they had both shared the same green eyes of their father. It was the only thing they had in common, but now the light in hers was not the glint usually reflected in Rain's eyes. Regan was inside, and it showed.

"I'm still here," Regan reminded herself. If she hadn't said yes to the angel, no one would help their mother in this life. Regan needed to be Rain. She needed to patch up the past and make their mother happy again, somehow, someway. People said that time healed all wounds. Regan had to believe she could do this. She would heal their lives and find happiness for them both. Returning to her bed, she switched off the overhead light and crept under the blankets. They smelled of lilac body spray and Rain's after-ballet sweat. She wrapped herself deep in her sister's scent and wept. No matter how strong she must be tomorrow, she allowed herself to be vulnerable tonight.

CHAPTER 19

One of the worst things about becoming Rain was that Regan was now a freshman in high school again. At almost but not quite fifteen, she couldn't drive, so she was back to riding the bus. She'd always hated riding public transportation, and Rain's friends were losers. Apparently, they had assigned bus seating and she was stuck next to a kid who picked his nose. *Gross.* The two seniors opposite her kept looking her way, then giggling. She wanted to punch their smiling faces. Who did they think they were, laughing at anyone? Sure, they came from money, but one's dad had run off with his secretary, and the other's brother was in rehab. Another glance was followed by more laughter, drawing out more of Regan's ire.

Regan's eyes narrowed. "How's your dad, Mandy?" She paused and waited, smiling at their blank faces. "How about your brother on his *vacation* in Florida?" Regan made air quotes to the other girl. They murmured something inaudible and turned to the front of the bus. Regan smiled. "Yeah, that's what I thought."

The rest of the way to school was uneventful. She'd been following Rain around in her ghostly state for a while, so she knew her locker combination, classes, and routine. It wasn't so hard to pass off being Rain. Homework would be easy since she'd already taken the courses. Regan retrieved the first two hours' textbooks and slammed the locker door. Cold air assailed her in a whoosh, and she turned to see Mark's faded image. Anger wrinkled his luminous features and his fists lay clenched at his sides. Regan watched as other students filed passed them, leaving the hall empty as the bell finally rang.

"Mark?" Her voice was low for fear of being overheard.

A horrid sound pierced her ears. There weren't any words, just the ear-splitting anguish of a tortured soul. Another gust of cool air assailed her, sending the tendrils of her hair back from her forehead and leftover pages of homework swirling across the polished green and white checked tiles. A door slammed at the end of the corridor, breaking the spell. The principal's large form darkened the doorway. Sun streamed in behind him, shadowing his features, but she knew the suit he usually wore and his massive shoulders from the years he spent coaching football before becoming their principal.

"Young lady, what's the holdup? First period bell has already rung."

Regan hitched the books closer to her chest and nodded. "Yes, sir. Sorry—I had a spider in my locker, and I was afraid to get my books. I didn't know what to do." It wasn't entirely a lie. She had seen a small spider run along the outside of the locker when she opened it. She didn't have a fear of insects like most girls her age, but why offer free information.

He approached her, staring down at her books. His expression was stern. "Do you need a hall pass to get into class?"

"No, sir, I'll be all right if I go now."

He nodded. "How's your momma, Rain?"

He knew her. She breathed a sigh. Oh, shit! She skipped detention. Would he haul her off to his office now? Regan decided to play it cool. "She's all right."

"Good. Tell her I said hello. Now off to class and no more stories about spiders."

Regan sighed. He knew. She smiled meekly, turned on her heel and marched toward class.

"Oh, and Rain," his sharp voice echoed along the corridor. "Don't forget about detention today. I'll be expecting you at three-fifteen sharp."

Mark's tortured soul couldn't harm her ward in a physical manner, but his spirit was growing more anguished, and Delila could only assume it was Regan's reappearance amongst the living. Why else would he seek her out? He had done it before, at the restaurant with Chase, but it wasn't Rain he was after. It was her ward's soul he was set on torturing. As a soul watcher, she was bound to help only one soul and forbidden to interfere with another's journey. She had to be careful how she navigated these turbulent tides of emotion. No one really walked on water.

Regan wasn't sure how she would communicate with Mark in her new form, but somehow she could still see him and hear his caustic screams. He was obviously a tortured soul, and she needed to figure out a way to close the door between them. She was still angry that his jealousy had ruined her previous life, and now he was trying to ruin Rain's as well. Things were so screwed up in her reality, but she had to own some of the responsibility. Regan wasn't sure how she would get over losing her sister, but she could at least be with their mother. She had to make peace with her destiny, accept her past, and move toward a better future. Forgiveness was the key, but how did she communicate with Mark to bequeath that clemency and clear her own slate in the bargain? An idea suddenly occurred. She needed to go to New Orleans. The problem was she was fourteen again and not allowed to drive. She also had detention. Maybe if she asked around, she could get a ride home without having to call her mom to pick her up after her shift at the Piggly Wiggly. It was possible that Regan wouldn't have to tell Rona about the skirmish at the locker and getting detention. It wasn't really her fault. Rain hadn't done anything wrong, but the squabble had landed her in trouble at school just the same. If she got home before her mother, she might be able to call in a favor.

The light blinked on the answering machine as Regan entered the house. She pushed the button and heard her mother inform her there was chicken pot pie in the freezer and that she wouldn't make it home from work until ten that evening. The teacher's aide on detention duty gave her and three other students a ride home. On the way to the parking lot, Regan had stared at the cheerleader with loathing. It was all her fault they were both being punished. The girl had sneered back before getting into her mom's fancy car and speeding away. Regan really hated being a freshman again.

The house was empty, and she was home free. There was no one there to monitor her actions, and she had five hours to make it into the city and back without anyone knowing. She grabbed the keys from the kitchen junk drawer and raced to her Mustang. The engine roared. Checking the gas gauge, she frowned. She needed gas and Rain was flat broke. Regan ran back into the house to find her hidden shoebox. Luckily, Rain hadn't found it. She might need money when she got to the city. The three crumpled bills from the glovebox bought gas at the corner station. It would be enough to get her there and back. She didn't like the idea of walking on the interstate at night, not in Rain's petite body.

Taking the Vieux Carre exit, she made her way to the Quarter and found street parking a few blocks from Bourbon. She knew the area well and quickly made her way to the seer's home. Passing through the courtyard, she admired the pretty pink flowers that hadn't been there before. Spring was magic to landscape. Regan knocked tentatively on the door. No one answered, so she knocked louder. The light of a cloudless afternoon still lingered, casting tangerine rays of sunlight through the cracks between brick buildings and wrought-iron railings. Regan was about to give up. With a heavy sigh, she looked at her scuffed tennis shoes and felt the remaining folded bills in her jeans pocket. She turned and surveyed the long row of shotgun houses through the passage of the courtyard gate. Maybe the seer was at a neighbor's borrowing sugar. Walking back to the fountain, she heard the door finally scrape open.

"Yes. Can I help you?" The seer's tone was laced with annoyance.

Regan wavered, wondering why the woman didn't recognize her, then remembered she was now Rain. "I—I need your help."

The seer looked her up and down, then looked beyond her through the courtyard gate. "Is that so? Did *someone* send you? How'd you find *me*?" Suspicion dripped from each question as she emphasized random syllables.

Regan inspected the area where the seer stood waiting. "I heard of you from my sister. You told her fortune, and I need to talk to her. Can you help me? Please." The sincerity in Regan's voice must have lifted the feeling of distrust. Was it her age that made the woman search for a prank? "There's no hoax to my being here. My sister saw you before she died, and now I need to reach her."

The older woman nodded and led Regan into the house. It was dark inside since most of the curtains were pulled shut. She followed the seer to the small room that they'd sat in before. With a roll of her head, the seer closed her eyes and murmured something inaudible to the heavens. Regan wondered if she was praying. After a moment of silence, the older woman studied Regan closer. "I remembers you, chile." She made a noise with her tongue then shook her head. "Um-um-um. I tried to tell you, but young people only hears what they wants to. I can't fix what's already done. You is you, and that's a fact, Jack."

Regan shook her head. "But that's the problem." After a pause, the lady pointed to a chair on the opposite side of the purple satin-covered table.

The seer sat and waited for Regan to join her. "You want me to contact the sister I saw, but the problem is, she's right here."

Regan's heart thudded in her chest. "She is? Rain, are you here? Can she hear me?"

The seer held her hand out for silence. "First things first. You come bearing gifts?" Her other palm shot out and Regan stared at the deep contrast. Her milky white palms were in conflict with the rest of her chocolate veined hands.

Regan dug into her pocket and pulled out a twenty, a five, and two ones. The seer arched an eyebrow. Regan didn't know if the old woman doubted the amount was real, wondered where she'd gotten the money, or was considering if it was enough. "It's all I have, at least for now." Regan used Rain's soft, youthful voice to appeal to the woman's sense of pity.

The seer grinned. "All right, all right. But I ain't no fool, so don't be trying to be sly. Tell me what you's here for."

Regan stammered. "I—I did already. I want to talk to my sister. She recently drowned."

The old woman nodded, making an um-hm sound. "You both did."

That grabbed Regan's attention. The woman's eyes widened like she surprised herself with the declaration. The light in the room flickered, and the old woman's eyes rolled back in her head. She hummed like a refrigerator compressor about to give out. She rocked back and forth for a few minutes, then a light, lilting voice came through.

"Regan, Regan."

It was Rain's voice that mirrored Regan's plea. "Rain!"

"I'm sorry. I'm so, so sorry." The small voice crackled, then sobbed. "It's dark, so dark and all this water. Where is it coming from?" Regan surged with panic. Was her sister still drowning?

"It's okay, Rain. It's okay." Heavy tears dripped down her cheeks, and she reached out to touch the seer's hand. In an instant, her energy flashed from her small form and collided with the old woman. A vortex sucked her into the dark world where she'd been the night she drowned. The cave's surrounding was inky black and dripping water to the stone below them. She felt cold, but certainly not alone. She looked at the wispy silhouette of her sister. "Why, Rain? Why did you do it?"

Her sister's filmy existence wouldn't look at her, but after a long pause, her voice trickled through the dripping water all around them. "It was past my time. I couldn't think straight. I somehow didn't belong there anymore, and I sensed it was time to leave. Something pulled at my spirit until I saw only the end of my journey. I didn't mean to hurt anyone. I didn't want to live in pain, but now I'm nowhere and I'm so lost, Regan. I don't understand. It wasn't supposed to be this way. It was you I was going to, but I couldn't find you." Confusion mottled her words.

Regan focused on the energy between them, feeling the warmth coming from Rain's existence, an ember of light in a cave of darkness. "Rain, have you seen a light? When you crossed over into the darkness, did you see anyone, hear anything?"

Rain's luminous form shook as if she were weeping, but no tears fell from her ghostly face. Crying was a luxury for the living. "No. I don't know. I'm scared."

Regan felt an uncoiling of energy, and she knew she was being forced out. The connection she had with Rain was ending. "Find the light, Rain. Don't stay here. An angel will find you and invite you in. Don't wait for me. I will come and join you eventually. Now keep moving until you find it. Don't worry about Mom. I'll take care of her. You go, go to where the angel waits, and we'll all be together again—one day." Their connection ended abruptly, and Regan fell back in the chair. Exhaustion and hunger claimed her all at once. Her shaky hands splayed out on the lavender silk, grasping for something steady.

The seer's hand shot out and unexpectedly grasped her cold, white hands between hers. "Regan!" She yelled, but again, the voice was not her own. This time she recognized Mark's deep tone filled with anguish and jealousy. "Regan!" the seer shouted again in his voice.

Regan tried to pull away, but the seer held her hands in a death clutch. "You live." It was an accusation. The grip at her wrist was squeezing the blood from her hands. "I killed you. I killed you. I killed you." His voice rumbled with rage and fell over a precipice as terror released itself from the seer in a hollow cry. Regan stared blankly at the woman who suddenly slumped forward. Did Mark kill her too?

She was afraid to touch the old woman but shook one upturned palm. "Hey, lady." She repeated the shake several times until the woman awoke with a start.

The seer seemed confused. "What are you doing here?" The words were an accusation.

Regan fumbled to stand. "I came here to speak to my sister. You don't remember?"

"No, I mean, *why* are you here? You were dead. You both are dead. Yet here you stand." The woman's brow furrowed with fear and awe. She skittered away from Regan, tipping her chair over in the rush. "I've seen ghosts, I've even talked to demons and tortured spirits, but I've never seen a soul return from the dead unless it has reincarnated or—snatched a body." The look of disdain scorched Regan.

"I didn't take my sister's body. I'm not a thief." She paused, thinking of the best way to explain it. Tears rolled down her face as she thought of Rain's last moments. Regan was tired. Her spirit felt drained from the interaction with Rain and Mark. "I didn't ask for this. I never wanted my sister to leave this world, and never in the way she chose to leave it. I think it was all an accident." Regan swiped her cheeks and ran a finger under each eye. She'd made a promise to the angel, but the seer already knew she wasn't Rain. Wariness still graced the older woman's lined face. "This may seem unbelievable, but an angel gave me her body. There was a mistake."

The older woman shook her head in disbelief. She made a tsking sound and muttered an expletive under her breath. "I'm not about to ask why an angel would do that, but more important, why would you say yes?"

It wasn't tough to explain that Rain would be dead either way and that their mother would be broken. Rona's life would be over if such an event occurred. What was tough was explaining how she would live with her choice. Every time she looked in the mirror, she would see her own loss, two-fold.

"It happened so fast. The angel told me that Rain was destined to pass. My choice made no difference to her soul's existence. I'm not sure that I want to live her life, but it's clear that my life as Regan is gone. I guess I did it for my mom." Though, Regan felt a tinge of guilt as the image of Chase flashed through her thoughts.

The old woman nodded, looking at her with new-found sympathy as if she'd connected the pieces of the puzzle and now understood Regan's trap. "Dear chile," was the only thing she uttered, but her eyes said more.

Regan confided. "I saw her just now through you, but she's lost. She hasn't found the light."

The seer took a moment then softly placed her hand on Regan's. "She's a suicide, chile. She may never find the light."

It was true. Rain had chosen to take her life. "But it's not fair," Regan protested. "She—" Regan trailed off, remembering her promise in her exchange with the angel. She vowed never to tell a living soul about the vision the angel shared—about how things should have gone. It had all been her guardian's mistake. Had Regan already said too much? "I can't explain it. I promised the angel, but trust me, it wasn't supposed to be this way." Regan motioned toward herself.

The seer chuffed. "Obviously, but now it is, so what will you do about it? That boy's soul who visited you. He was awful angry. What's his part of the story?"

Regan shuffled her feet, leaning onto her other hip as she touched the back of the chair. "I don't know exactly. I mean, he was my boyfriend, but we broke up. He killed us both out of his own jealousy, and Rain swam away—that time." She took a deep breath then pushed the air out of her lungs slowly, stretching her spine. "He has no reason to be angry at me any longer. He won. I looked at someone else, and he killed us over it. I don't know why he won't go away."

The seer's brows were high arches of surprise. "You mean you've seen him since the drowning, before now?"

"Yes. A few times. He never speaks, though I've spoken to him in the in-between world, and he only responds with that horrible scream. I don't know if he can hear me, but he's never said a word — until today."

The old woman nodded in understanding. "He's stuck in darkness, and he's angry because you still live."

Regan leaned forward, gripping harder on the chair. "He was angry even before I took Rain's form, but he has no right to be," she protested.

The seer nodded. "Some souls have a deeper past than this life, and I think you and he have had a few go-rounds before. You somehow cheated his purpose, and now he is trying to defeat you from the other side."

Regan scoffed. "I don't fear him. He's just a ghost. I've been one, and I can tell you he has no power. He's just pushing a little hot air around. Unless I'm standing on a tightrope, he can't hurt me—it's just annoying that I keep seeing him." She paused, combing her fingers through her hair. "Hey, can you get rid of him, work a spell or something?"

The seer crossed her arms over her chest. "This ain't no charity psychic agency I'm running."

Regan tilted her head to the side, placing one hand on her hip. "I guess you want more money. How much?"

"These things take time. Let me think on it and I'll get back to you. Now go on home, chile. I've got thangs to do." Her words weren't unkind, just tired. The energy used for the connection with Rain had shaken them both. Regan felt beat, as if she were a rug on a Sunday morning cleaning.

Regan nodded and turned toward the door. When she grasped the handle, she turned to the woman. "Thanks. I'm not sure what I'm supposed to do next, but I'll be back. We have unfinished business."

The woman smiled. "I think you need to just be you, chile, the real you. The rest will come as it may. Lord only knows what plan he has for us small folk."

Regan let the screen door close softly and she thought she heard the woman say, "Be safe, chile."

Had her ward betrayed her? Delila fretted. She spoke of the promise she'd vowed to keep. Reviewing the conversation, she admitted the seer had a gift and knew that Regan's soul was different than young Rain's. She would have to allow that Regan felt she needed answers, and in her embodied state, she could no longer communicate directly with Delila. She had, however, contacted Rain. Delila worried for Rain's young soul. She'd been lost in the world of the living after missing her true destiny. It was all Delila's mistake. It was her fault that Rain felt pulled toward meeting her end. Destiny was a powerful force that threaded itself through the eye of the soul, pulling energy through the fabric of time, and making a pattern in its web-like quilt. When Delila missed a stitch, the unraveling spread like a wayward spool of thread, dancing across eternity and sewing an entirely new pattern across the heavens. Souls were not tethered wholly to this intricate knitting of the universe. Each entity—embodied, unembodied, or soul watcher—could choose. Every action set off a synapse of reactions that constantly changed the structure of reality.

Delila thought about Mark railing at Regan in the school hallway and again, just now, through the seer. On both occasions, she'd wrapped her wings around her ward so that he would not leach happiness from her soul. Regan was wrong. The dead could harm the living. Humans were made up of energy and so were souls. It was the sustenance of all embodied and non-embodied entities. Spirits could leach energy from each other in any state. Many beings didn't even realize it was happening to them. A visit with a family member or friend that left them feeling drained or sad. Maybe they couldn't define the words that provoked such weary feelings.

After such encounters, they just felt a sickness in the pits of their stomachs and craved solace.

Delila had her work cut out for her. She wasn't sure how powerful Mark's energy had become. Anger for the dead was like gasoline in a grassfire, unpredictable.

CHAPTER 20

It was eight o'clock, and it would take fifty minutes to drive home, but she couldn't pass up a chance to see Chase. She was angry at him for rejecting Rain, though she should be happy he hadn't been a sleaze. He did the right thing, but it was his rebuff of Rain that sent her spiraling to her death. Regan corrected her thoughts. It wasn't Chase's fault. It was no one's fault that Rain made the choice. People had free will, didn't they? She remembered the angel's mistake and how the repercussions affected her life. Regan was alive, and she should somehow appreciate some of the sacrifices that brought her to this point. After all, she'd had a hand in her destiny. She may not have chosen to die, but Mark did, and she needed to forgive herself for the actions that led up to that event. What had happened that night was his destiny, and she was just along for the ride.

The sun made its way below the horizon and the city twinkled in an array of streetlights and neon signs. Horses clomped through the streets and vendors hawked their wares. Regan thought about the devilish spirit she'd encountered and wondered if he was watching her now. Would he know she had cheated death, that she had even cheated the light? A shiver danced down her spine, and she moved a little faster through the square. She stood outside the bar, watching the band play for a bit. It was a different band, and disappointment covered her like a damp blanket, but she also felt relief. She needed to make her curfew.

Guidry spotted her from a barstool and waved. She held up her palm, then noticed Chase's broad shoulders wedged in next to him. A young woman was draped over half his body as they laughed together. He raised his hand to the bartender, occupied with getting another round. The music came to a halt and the trio stood up from the bar and moved to the stage with their beverages. They took a moment to tune their instruments and then the blonde turned to the microphone as the band struck up. Emily, her fake friend from Mark's entourage, was now crushing on another one of Regan's interests. The brassy blonde belted out the lyrics to "Walk on Water," and Regan wanted to fall to the stone walkway and scream. She hated to admit it, but her former nemesis had been practicing, and she didn't sound half bad. In fact, Regan conceded that Emily's enhanced voice, long blonde hair, and barely there shiny black crop-top drew the attention of everyone in the room. Her voice was a bit more polished than Regan's had been, which made the song more mainstream and less unique, but she had a feeling it wouldn't stop its success. How was Chase able to use her song for his band? It was hers! He'd never met her mom, Rona, and gotten permission. Didn't he need her approval? Regan wrote the song when she was living. It was part of her estate or something. He couldn't just steal it. She wouldn't let him.

Without thinking, she pushed through the throng of patrons to the stage. When the song came to an end, she pointed to Chase, then to herself, giving the come-now signal. He tossed the guitar to Guidry, who stepped into his place as they picked through a slow ballad that Emily crooned.

His face was flushed with color and his hair stuck to his forehead from sweat. "Rain, I haven't got time for kid stuff. You're not supposed to be here." He leaned one hand against the hallway outside of the restrooms.

Regan flinched. "That's my song. I mean, Regan's song, and now we own it, not you!"

Chase's mouth tugged at one corner like he was trying not to laugh. "Rain, anybody can sing any song they want. We just can't record it to make money without your *mother's* permission, not yours."

Regan cooled a bit. He was right. She'd sung other bands' music in public and she hadn't asked for permission. "Well, why are you letting Emily sing it? She's all wrong."

Chase sighed and rolled his head back, thumping it on the wall. "I haven't got time for this. Rain, you're a nice kid, but you're too young to be in a bar this time of night or any time. Now go home and stay there. If we decide to record the song, we'll get the proper permission first, I promise."

On the wall, just above his right ear was ink graffiti that caught her attention. *Chase the Moon, Capture the Moon, Love the Moon.* It threw her off balance. The angel called her Luna. His name was Chase. Was there a message in it for her? Was it some kind of sign that she wasn't supposed to give up? That they might still have a chance? She was Rain now, and he wouldn't know she was still Regan, trapped inside her almost fifteen-year-old sister's body. There was eleven years difference between them. It would be a long time before society would let that slide, even in Louisiana. She had a thirteen-year-old friend who married a twenty-eight-year-old man, but her parents had to sign papers to allow it. Napoleonic law was different than the other states. It should be called Neanderthal law, but it could lend some flexibility if the stars aligned. Rona would never agree. She would call Chase a pedophile and then press charges. No matter how attracted Regan was to the sandy-haired guitarist, she wouldn't see him put behind bars just to have him for herself.

"Rain, I'm sorry, kid. I know you're hurting from losing your sister. I—I can't even imagine the pain, but life goes on, and one day you will grow up and find a nice boy your own age. Stick to those ballet shoes and they will lead you to your next step. I bet you have talent. Everybody has somethin' they can cling to in times like this. Stick to your art. You'll survive it. I promise." He squeezed her shoulder as he moved past her, leaving her staring after him. He disappeared down the corridor and back to the stage. She looked at the olive-painted wall once more. Like confetti thrown at a party on New Year's Eve, graffiti covered every inch of the wall. She couldn't find the words she'd seen before, and she prodded herself to move toward the exit. It was late and she needed to get home.

CHAPTER 21

The seer's place was only a few blocks away, and the car was a half block from there. Still, it was dark now and the party crowd was out. Regan was alone and carried nothing but the keys to her Mustang. The hair at the nape of her neck prickled and she felt gooseflesh rise on her arms. Looking over one shoulder, she saw three men behind her. They were a distance away but picking up their pace. She accelerated her stride as well. The problem was, she was getting farther away from the crowd in the square, and she was alone. Regan darted around a corner and cursed. Most of the streetlights were out. She could turn back, but then she would have to pass the guys directly.

The car was only twenty feet away. If she ran and got the keys in the driver's door and it opened before they reached her, she could get inside and push the locks before they arrived. It was her only choice. Gripping her keys hard, she bolted. Her focus was on the door, and she slid the key in on the first try. The lock almost turned, but something thumped behind her and she turned with a scream. It was a tennis shoe. A shoeless young male in a fraternity t-shirt leered at her as his cronies chortled. They were drunk. She could tell by their vacant eyes and swaying torsos as they jostled toward her. Probably college sophomores. Freshmen wouldn't have the confidence, and seniors would be too busy picking up girls to harass a kid like her. She tried to calm herself. They looked like a trio of thirsty bloodhounds on a fox hunt, and if she panicked, the pack mentality would ensue.

Rain bent down and picked up the shoe. "Did you lose something, ass-hole?" It was better to show confidence rather than fear. She smiled, lifting her head as she straightened her shoulders. Her voice dripped with a tone of sarcasm she didn't feel. "Size ten. Same as my friend Joe. He'll be here in a minute. Maybe you should give me the other one, so he can have a pair."

She would have thought the guy with one shoe was handsome if he wasn't creeping her out. He had chiseled features with a cool haircut that fell softly onto his forehead in just the right way. She couldn't see the color of his eyes yet, but the shape was exotic with thick lashes. *Was he wearing mascara?*

"Joel, huh?" He laughed as he bent down to take off his other shoe. After he straightened, he held it over his shoulder for a minute like he was making a game play, then he tossed it at her feet.

"Joe, J-O-E. He plays football, you dork, and he's a linebacker," she added as she searched for a strong position. Football player would convey big and scary, right? It didn't work. They all bent over with great guffaws. Regan fumbled behind her for the key to turn in the lock as they started to close the distance. She gripped the door and pulled it open, but the leader of the trio reached around her and slammed it shut.

"Where are you rushing off to, sweetheart? The evening's just begun." His eyes were like whiskey, dark and potent. He had a mole above the corner of his full lips. He looked like a work of art. Perfectly chiseled, but something demonic settled around his irises. The one streetlight over her parked car illuminated his lurid intent. "Don't you wanna have fun?" He gripped her wrist, pulling her away from the door.

His cronies chortled and one chimed in. "She wants to ride the wild pig, ya'll."

Her captor jerked her to him. His mouth was on hers in seconds. His arms were like vise grips around her middle, and his body pushed against her pelvis. Regan struggled with all of her might to pull away. She tried to lift her knee to his groin, but he pushed her back onto the cold metal of the car. He fumbled to open the backdoor as he held her locked in his grasp. One of his buddies stepped up to help. The door opened with a whine, brushing against her hip. He pushed her in, and she skittered to the other side to escape, but the third guy was holding the door. Wind kicked up, and as the shoeless assailant straightened and turned to see where the hurricane gale had come from, the door slammed shut. Regan acted quickly and pushed all the locks. It was like playing a game of Whack-a-mole. The key was still in the driver's side door. She hadn't had a chance to pull it out. Every time she pushed the lock down, her attacker turned the key and the lock popped up. He was doing it slow, then fast, laughing as she panicked. His laughter echoed against the window as he relished teasing her. The game of cat and mouse was making her heart thump dangerously. She was too afraid to cry. Fear was like a cold layer of ice, freezing her in an alert stance. She had to think of what to do next. Hurdling the console into the driver's seat, she punched the locks again and hit the horn intermittently. A light came on, and Regan recognized the seer as she emerged from the courtyard gate. Inside the car, with her blood pounding inside her ears, she couldn't hear what the older woman said, but she heard the gunshots as the seer fired the weapon into the air. Like birds taking flight, the lurid prince of evil and his devil dogs took to the darkness.

Regan was afraid to open the door even after the guys had fled. The seer stood in front of her car for a few moments, then walked up to her window and tapped lightly on the glass. Regan took a deep breath and rolled it down.

"Honey, you okay?" Her voice was gravely like she'd been sleeping.

Regan took a deep breath and gripped the steering wheel for support. "No." She shook her head as tears tumbled down her cheeks for a second time that night. Her shoulders crumpled and she shook with the fear she had tried to manage for what felt like a lifetime.

The seer reached through the window and stroked her hair. "Hush now, chile. It'll be okay. Did they..." Her voice trailed off with the unasked question.

"No, he kissed me. That's all. Maybe bruised my arms a little pushing me into the car." She looked up at the seer and opened the door, slowly stepping from the vehicle. "Did you shoot him?"

The seer shook her head and chuckled. "No, but I should have. Damn bastards."

Regan didn't know why she laughed at that, but she guessed it was nerves.

"Come on in, chile and I'll make you a nice cup of tea."

Regan didn't hesitate, nodding and following the older woman. Her young nerves were too frazzled to drive.

The seer's home was becoming a familiar place. Before the older woman could invite her to sit down, Regan sat at the kitchen table. Her legs were shaking too bad to continue standing. As she watched the woman move about the kitchen, boiling water in a small soup pan over the gas stove, she remembered the visit in her ghostly state. The seer had powers. She'd sensed Regan's presence without being told. When the water was ready, the seer poured it into two mismatched cups and plopped tea bags in each.

"Sugar?" she asked Regan.

Regan nodded. The woman put two heaping teaspoons in and stirred each. The tea was sweeter than Regan might have usually liked, but it was just what she needed to settle her stomach. She felt like throwing up. Nothing happened, but it could have, and that's what scared her. It was getting late and her mother would be worried, but Regan would just have to take the heat when she got home. After tonight, it would be a long time before she'd want to drive anywhere.

Some time passed as they sat quietly, Regan looked at the woman and asked, "You heard the horn?"

She studied Regan for a moment, sucking her teeth. "The window in my bedroom opened…" she paused, setting her cup down. "Then I heard your horn."

Regan looked at her with confusion. "Someone was breaking into your house. Is that why you had the gun?"

"That window has been stuck for twenty years. When it slammed open, I knew something was wrong. I heard the horn and grabbed Jacques here." She tapped the revolver she'd placed on the table. Regan had no idea what kind it was, but it looked like a sizable caliber that would have graced a bank robber's holster from the old wild west.

Regan leaned her head forward, studying the antique metal. "Your gun's named Jock? Why?"

"Jacques. The name's French. The revolver belonged to my great grandpa and he called it Jacques. I inherited the gun, and she's been the best security I ever needed. No monthly charge." Hearty laughter poured from the woman as she slapped the top of the pistol. Regan moved back. It was probably still loaded.

She liked the old woman's rusty voice and the way she cackled when she found something funny. "Jacques sounds like a man's name."

"Well, this here pistol is a lady. Women are powerful, chile, and don't you forget it."

Regan nodded with a slight smile. She liked this old woman and her candid way of speaking. "If you don't mind me asking, it seems we might be seeing each other more than expected. What's your name?"

The woman arched a brow, obviously surprised that Regan didn't know her given name. After a pause, she must have decided to indulge her guest. "Zada Mae Auclair."

Regan smiled. "That's pretty."

Zada chuckled. "It all depends how you say it. My momma used to yell it out across the hood." The seer cupped her hands around her mouth and made a shrill call, "Zada Mae—. Now that ain't so pretty, is it?" They both laughed and Regan shook her head. "You ain't so bad, chile. I might even take a shine to you if you keep buttering me up."

Zada rose and collected the cups, placing them in the sink. "You think you ready to drive where you gotta go?"

Regan nodded. "I feel better now." There were more questions she wanted to ask, but she limited it to one. "Where did the wind come from? It was like a hurricane. Did you do that?" Regan wasn't sure of the seer's abilities, but she knew the woman talked to spirits. Ghosts moved air, sometimes with force if they were desperate. Hadn't Regan moved air so violently that she made Rain roll off the tracks?

Zada shook her head. "No chile. I think that was someone you know. Someone was looking out for you, and I don't think it was that wack-job who came into my head screaming at you when you were here before. But I did feel a male presence lingering in the area after those goons scattered. You gotta a great grand-daddy or someone who watches over you?"

Regan's mouth opened, then shut as she thought of her decisively female guardian angel.

Zada licked her lips as her gaze rose to the ceiling. "I smelled fresh soap and something sweet, like home-baked cinnamon rolls."

Regan's eyes lit up. Abruptly, she stood and rushed to the front door. "Gustave," she called out. "Are you here, Gustave?" She called out into the night several more times then returned, shutting the door.

"Zada, I know it's late, but can we do a short séance?"

Delila wasn't sure what more she could do. She'd pushed at the air, chanted for her ward not to go toward the car, but some things must unravel themselves for the living. It made sense that Regan would return to her car. She needed to go home, yet Regan was aware of the men who followed her. As a soul watcher, Delila had limited ability to affect others, but she could call to the spirit world if necessary.

In desperation, Delila pushed wind in the direction of an overflowing bar, hoping to inspire some of its inebriated patrons to walk the street for some fresh air and hopefully stumble in Regan's direction. She was surprised when a spirit from the in-between world caught her energy and floated out. He could not see her wide-winged presence, but she knew he had spotted Regan's spirit. His spirit had lurked in the French Quarter for many hundreds of years, and Delila knew this soul favored Regan. His energy force was lost and his presence was waning. He'd spend eternity hiding and then searching for the hidden light. In an indirect way, Delila might lend him a hand.

Regan sat at the lavender silk-covered table where a thick crystal ball graced the center. Zada, who had looked weary, now showed vibrant energy. It had taken a few minutes to coax the older woman into granting Regan's request. In exchange, she told the seer about her experience with death and meeting Gustave in the Quarter. She kept her promise to the angel and left out that peculiar meeting where the angel divulged her lapse in guardianship. When Zada had said she smelled cinnamon rolls, Regan knew the seer sensed Gustave's presence. Surely, he was still floating around somewhere nearby.

Zada ran her fingertips over the ball, stroking it like a beloved pet. She started the familiar humming, then her eyes closed as her head lolled back. Zada cleared her throat.

"Gustave," Regan half-whispered.

"Sh, not yet. I have to open the pathway." She continued mumbling words that were indistinguishable.

"Sorry," Regan whispered. It sounded like a lot of hocus pocus to her, but she shrugged her shoulders and remained quiet.

"There, there, cherie. No reason to be sorry. It was those despicable young souls who have no honor." The decisively French male voice that came through Zada confirmed that Gustave was with them. She'd never told her about his accent.

"Gustave! Did you see what happened? Were you there? Did you cause the wind?" Regan's questions were like bullet marks on a chalkboard.

"Oui, oui, and oui. They angered me. Such weak spirits, but strong bodies to prey on one so petite." Zada's fingers went to her chin, stroking the skin there as if it were a groomed beard. "Sorry. You are not weak, but your current form is rather slight. Do you care to tell me how you made the switch?" The seer's voice was deeper now and filled with interest.

"You recognize me?" Regan asked with excitement.

"I knew it was you when you approached the bar. I felt your lovely energy. I followed you trying to engage in conversation, but you didn't stop when I hailed you. You were too involved with the guitarist, so I gave up and went into another bar where I saw the three young men. The handsome one was called a faggot by another patron. He got in a fight over it, but I could tell he was internally excited by the suggestion. His friends started bragging about the fight as they left the area, and unfortunately, they must have seen you. I was bored by their youthful idiocy and had no interest in following them, but then a breeze blew through the bar, and I felt compelled to leave. I think you were supposed to be the proof the oaf needed to show he was heterosexual, but *I* think it was evidence he was a coward." Gustave's indignation straightened Zada's shoulders and lifted her chin. "Tell me. You really didn't hear me?"

Regan frowned. "No, I've lost my ability to see or hear the dead."

"How did you get this body?" His voice rose with interest.

"It's a long story, Gustave, and Zada Mae is tired. I wanted to thank you for your help. I don't know if we will meet again in my current form." Sadness tinged her words. She hadn't known Gustave in the physical world. Maybe he wasn't a saintly spirit, but he had helped her, and maybe that would mean something to the angel that kept score for good deeds.

"You are jesting, of course. I am sure we could arrange a mutual friendship with Madam Zada Mae. Say, what if I bring her business? I'll find needy souls, and you bring their living counterparts. She would make money and we could stay in touch. I am desperate to hear more of this body procurement."

Regan wasn't sure if the smile Zada wore was her own or Gustave's. Either way, it sounded like the perfect solution.

"Great idea, Gustave, but how can we do it?"

"I've been around the block a few hundred years. I'll manage my end." He paused and made a few murmuring noises followed by an "Um-hm and yes, perfect." Zada finally spread her hands out on the table. In Gustave's voice, she said, "Time to go. Toodles."

With a deep intake of breath, Zada's head dropped, then slowly rolled back up again. She shook her head as if shaking off the effects of a strong narcotic. "Jesus Christ. That man smells like fresh-baked shepherd's pie and smudged sage on a frosty winter morning. I don't know who he is, but dead or alive, he can enter my body anytime." Her eyes were wide as saucers and full of bewilderment. "Damn, now I'm hungry. It must be eleven o'clock." She swore softly as she stood up, her knees creaking in protest. "You want some grits?"

Regan shook her head no. "I better get home before my mom calls the police."

"Come on, then. Jacques and I'll walk you to your car."

CHAPTER 22

If Regan were in her old body, she wouldn't be nervous about entering the house. As it was, she was her fourteen-year-old sister, Rain, and as such, she was in for a bigger scolding. Rightly so, as she was probably pushing her mother over the edge. Regan put her key in the rusted lock and pushed the heavy wood door. The hinges screamed her arrival, and even if her mother had been deep in slumber, the door would have woken the dead. As it was, Rona sat at the kitchen table, smoking the last inch of her cigarette. The crumpled pack of Virginia Slims next to the ashtray spoke volumes. Rona had let herself run out of her favorite vice to wait for her wayward, disobeying daughter. Watery eyes and tangled hair told the tale of the night Rona was having. Regan felt a twist in her gut, knowing she was the cause of her mother's distress. Her first death destroyed any peace of mind her mother might have had, and now her existence as Rain was a constant worry. Regan vowed to herself that she would make this right. Somehow, her wandering around trying to clutch onto the past and solve the puzzles of her existence had consumed her common sense. Finding Rain a safe entrance to the beyond had become her priority, and she'd momentarily forgotten her mother's frail existence. Regan had to try harder. She doubted she could stay out of trouble for long, but she would try for their mother's sake.

"Hi, Mom. Sorry I'm late." Her voice squeaked on sorry.

Rona stubbed her cigarette out angrily, not considering that the pack was empty, and the corner store was closed.

"Rain Grace, you had better have the best reason in the world to make me wait here wondering if you were out there in Regan's Mustang somewhere dead on the side of the road." Tears broke through the anger and her shoulders shook with grief as she wiped the back of her hand across her nose.

Regan's heart clenched as she watched her mother's slight form shudder. It was all her fault. She ran to her mother and wrapped her arms around her. "I'm so, so sorry, Momma. I didn't mean to be gone long. I know I shouldn't have left, but…" What was she supposed to say, that she needed to fix this thing with Mark, and she went looking for a fortune teller in the French Quarter — that she needed to talk to the guy who killed her so she could put the past behind her?

She hated to lie to her mother. Maybe she could use some portion of the truth. "I went to New Orleans where Regan met that guy who wanted to produce her song."

Rona shook her head with disbelief. "You girls." She paused as if remembering there was only one girl now. "Rain, you are fourteen years old. You don't have a driver's license. If you got caught, they'd probably put me in jail. And you went to a bar? Are you kidding me? You are grounded for the rest of your life!"

Regan shook her head, rolling her eyes in exasperation. "Mom, I'm almost fifteen. Regan taught me to drive. It's not a license I need. We need money. Just look at you." She rubbed her hand over her mother's tousled hair. "I just need to be careful. You need to meet Chase. He's the guy who wants to record Regan's song. It could mean big money, Momma. I know you work a lot to keep things going around here. This could be something. It would help you pay the bills, and Regan would want that." She felt her mother's deep intake of breath as she reached out a hand for the crumpled pack of cigarettes.

"Damn, I'm out of smokes."

Regan piped up. "I can run to Hammond to get some. There's an open 7-Eleven that sells your brand."

Rona shook her head, wiping her eyes. The stress was getting to her, and she looked ten years older than her thirty-eight years. "Put the keys back in the drawer, Rain. I don't care if you know how to drive or not. You won't be doing it without a license. Now go to your room before I…"

Her mother was at a loss for words, and Regan knew she couldn't find any words to comfort her mother without tumbling both their worlds. She'd made an agreement with the angel that she wouldn't expose the truth, that she was Regan, and she supposed no one would believe her anyway. Telling her mother such news would surely land Regan in an institution. And it would devastate Rona to know that Rain had taken her own life.

Regan fell into Rain's bed, tugging the blankets over her tired body. She hugged the pillow close as she fell asleep. Rain's scent wafted up from the cotton sheets, tormenting her. Regan's eyes grew heavy despite her restless mood. Melting into the folds of night, she smelled damp foliage and the metallic scent of rock. Trickling water prodded the outer fields of her existence. Bright light poured down through darkness, illuminating a small circle around her. She was in the cave. The place she'd stood after drowning in the car with Mark. Rain's luminous figure floated to her, and wind whipped at them both.

"Let me in," Rain's spirit cried. She charged at Regan, forcing her to topple onto the hard ground. Regan was breathless, and it was moments before she realized what her sister was trying to do. She was trying to meld with her physical body again.

Scrambling to her feet, she held her hands up. "Rain, stop. This wasn't my choice."

"You—can't—have—"The sound of her sister's voice was like great gusts of breathlessness. Long pauses punctuated her efforts.

Regan's shoulders fell in defeat. There was nothing she could say to defend her decision, just the truth of Rain's actions. "You gave up your life. I didn't want it, but for Mom…."

Rain's shadowy white figure rippled like a watery reflection. The only hint of color was her strawberry blonde tendrils. "Not yours!"

The image of Rain waved and faded, and Regan suddenly stood in front of a mirror, staring at her own ghostly reflection. She looked like she did when they pulled her body from the lake, pale, chalky-gray tinted skin, black lips and hair. Her eyes were milky white over greyish irises. Regan opened her mouth to scream, but nothing happened. She was trapped in this place of darkness with so much anger, hurt, and regret. Mad at Mark for stealing what was supposed to be hers, mad at the angel for giving her what was supposed to be Rain's, and now the truth stared back at her. She was a soul trapped inside someone else's identity, but without it, she was trapped somewhere she didn't want to be. Had there been another option?

Delila gazed at the night sky. She wandered a distance from Regan as she slept. Time was something she could not gauge in the solitude of her soul-watching state. She had a better grip on her task now than she had many other soul-watching lives ago. As a young guardian, she often disappeared from her wards in a narcoleptic sleep. She was here and there, bouncing throughout her ward's timeline without knowing how to ground herself. If she made too many mistakes, she was removed and assigned someone less complicated. She had watched over countless animals in the beginning of her existence, lost and unwilling to bend to God's rules. She might have been lost to that reality if it hadn't been for Rodanian. He'd called out for her attendance to guide a spirit he said was born of purity and love. He assured her the task would be easy, and it truly was. His beloved soul complement was nearing the end stages of her existence as an embodied soul. The experience was for Delila. She learned the warmth of love for guiding and the fulfillment of success. It had changed her very presence. Rodanian's spiritual partner had been almost ready to join him. Delila wondered if they spent time together now, or if in their new enlightened state, they no longer needed a connection.

Before Delila's existence as a soul watcher, she'd experienced a spattering of enlightenment here and there. Blindly guiding and pushing energy at her assigned ward. Then, over time, she'd risen to a state of near perfection, growing long feathery wings and a bit more energy to wield among the living. She was forever present with her charge now, and that may have been her downfall with Regan. Had she failed because she'd become bored with the tedious activities of embodied life? Young love—so trivial in the grand scheme of soul-purpose that she'd been fooled by its frivolous design? She'd thought nothing of it. Now, this mistake would haunt her for many lives to come. Set back in her own spiritual journey, she was no longer near perfect and would not obtain the moment she'd aspired to, to omit living again, and instead exist in peace in the afterlife, like Rodanian.

A cry of distress drew Delila back to her ward. She flew through the bedroom wall. A dark, shadowy figure cloaked Regan, its energy source bent over, drinking from the lips of her sleeping form. Delila had seen these despicable entities leach from old, sick, and young souls, but never the likes of a healthy spirit like Regan's. Pushing energy at the dastardly thing, it reared its head and screeched like a banshee. Delila batted her wings with great force, pushing energy at the evil shadow harder than she ever had tried to move anything before. Without flinching, the black culprit resumed.

Regan cried out in a muffled voice. "Rain, stop! It wasn't my choice." Her head thrashed. Moisture beaded on her forehead as she fought with the darkness leaching her soul. Delila didn't have to be in the darkness in-between to know that Rain's young spirit was imploring her sister to give back her body. Regan's guilt was a palpable thing. Delila knew she wasn't strong enough to resist the call. The monster's stealthy hunt for weary souls might actually succeed if she didn't do something quick. With a loud thwack, Delila drew the window open and pushed at the door until it flew against the wall, banging on its hinges. Her only chance to save her ward was to wake Rona so that she could rouse Regan from this ghostly nightmare. Physical intervention was her only defense.

CHAPTER 23

"Rain, Rain, honey. Wake up. Wake up. It's just a dream."

Someone was shaking her. Regan woke with a start. Light filtered in through the sheer blue drapes, telling her that the sun had pierced the horizon. A breeze blew the drapes inward toward her mother's sleep-lined face. "Why is my window open? What time is it?"

Her mother shut the window with a click and pushed the levers to lock it. "It's a bad idea to sleep with your window open, Rain. It's almost seven. You still have time to sleep, but I heard you moaning. It sounded like you were in pain."

Regan sat up, pushing away a lock of hair from her forehead. "I had a nightmare." She scrubbed her hands over her face, trying to snuff out the images of her sister begging for her body back. "No, no more sleep." Regan stood on unsteady legs.

Her mother followed her to the long, antique vanity mirror. She stood behind Regan, watching her. "You okay?"

Regan took a deep breath, placing both hands on the mirror, staring hard at Rain's reflection. There was something different about it. She turned to her mother. "Do I look different to you?"

Her mother gave her a quizzical stare, then tilted her head as she walked toward her. Placing both hands on each of Regan's arms, she smiled. "You look like Rain. My baby girl. Always."

Regan pressed her lips together, forming a tight smile as her mother embraced her. "You don't think my eyes look different?"

Her mother stood back, looking at her a second time. "Maybe a bit darker green? Mine changed, too, when I was about your age. They'll change again when you get to be older."

It was true. Her mother's eyes had lightened over the years and now looked like green glass or waves on the ocean when the tide came in. She called them sea-foam-green.

Regan bit the inside of her cheek, nodding in thought. The brown ring around her irises seemed thicker, like when she'd been Regan. Even the white dot graced the two o'clock position just above her right pupil. It wasn't something that her mom would notice, but it certainly piqued Regan's interest. Had it been in Rain's eyes all along and she had just never seen it? Was it true that the eyes were the window to the soul? She was inside Rain now. Could the body change with the spirit? She'd never taken the time to look hard at her little sister. Most of the time, she tried to ditch Rain to go somewhere alone. She regretted it now that Rain was gone.

Her mother left so she could get ready for school, so Regan tried to remember as much about her dream as possible. Was it really Rain she'd seen, trapped on the other side, or was it just her guilt taking her on a night terror ride? Either way, it was unsettling. How long would she have her own identity before her memories blended with Rain's and the Regan she'd been was lost in the maze of her mind? Even now, Rain's memories melded with her own, causing confusion in the wake of a different perspective.

The shrill ring of the phone broke the silence as Regan and her mother ate their TV dinners. Rona cooked most nights that she was off, but they'd both fallen into different life patterns since the event. Now, they found themselves eating whatever was easiest and sometimes avoiding the laundry until there was nothing left to wear. Rain normally would have leaped to answer the phone, but Regan couldn't find any reason she should be excited about a call.

Rona rose to answer it. "Hello. Yes, she's here. Oh, yes, I'm sorry. Um-hm, well…" Rona listened for a minute, then continued. "I think she just needs a break right now and…" Rona twirled the cord around one finger and turned toward the living room.

Regan heard her hushed voice. Something about money, time, and transportation. She knew then it was Mrs. Landeaux from the ballet studio. Rain hadn't been to class lately, and the instructor was concerned. Regan couldn't solve the issue now that her mother had clamped down on driving without a license. She should just tell her mother she wanted to quit. What did Regan know about dancing, anyway? She wasn't really Rain. But she did have Rain's memories and her body. Suddenly, Regan was interested to know if she could dance. Springing to her feet, she stood on her tiptoes and did a pirouette. It felt graceful, considering she was still in her sneakers. She supposed she could dance if their mother still wanted it. She realized she was still thinking of *their* mother, rather than just *her* mother. It was like Rain was entwined with Regan in the same existence, but she knew Rain was trapped somewhere else. There was no resistance to accessing her sister's memories or actions. In fact, Regan was having a harder time finding her own recollections. She wasn't sure how many remembrances were hers versus Rain's.

The angel never mentioned how this body acquisition would work. She'd only made Regan promise not to tell anyone. That was pretty easy since people would think she was seriously crazy if she started spouting off that she was Regan. Would she soon forget who she really was, or would she always retain the instant she stole her sister's body? Was it a sin to take what was offered to you by an angel? Had it been a test from God, and she'd failed? Just because the woman looked heavenly didn't mean she couldn't have been a minion of the devil in disguise. Regan thought she'd met Satan. Beautiful and alluring, he could have done anything he wanted to her and she wouldn't have protested under his spell. Had she been bewitched by the angel on the trestles?

Her mother returned to the kitchen, placing the phone back on the receiver with a small sigh. "That was Mrs. Danskin. She wants you back in class ASAP." Her mother knew the instructor's name but always called her after the popular clothing brand because of Mrs. Landeaux's sleek ballet outfits that enhanced her elegant beauty. The petite, brunette woman was a stark contrast to Regan's mother. Rona's shoulders slumped as her wiry form sank to the kitchen chair with tired, sore movements that spoke of a long shift at the grocery standing on her feet.

"Momma, I don't want to go back. It's expensive, and I don't have a way to get there." Regan looked longingly at the junk drawer that held the Mustang's keys.

Her mother nodded as she chewed a split fingernail on one thumb. "I know, but money's not for you to worry about. I can pick up another shift or get a part-time job if I have to. Mrs. Danskin thinks you have talent. I don't want to kill your dreams just because…" the catch in her voice stopped her words and her eyes glimmered with unshed tears. "We'll figure something out. Your birthday is next week, and I'll take you down for your learner's permit. Maybe there's some appeal we can make for a special license or something."

As they cleared the table, tossing the metal containers for their dinners away and wiping the table clean of crumbs, Regan smiled. She'd be able to drive again soon. Her mother went to the TV room and clicked on the television. They didn't have a VCR or cable, but the news was on and her mother would spend an hour smoking her cigarettes and catching up on the daily sorrows of the world. Regan didn't know how Rona could stand it. The media never shared anything upbeat.

The evening was temperate, and a moderate breeze made her grab a sweater before settling onto the porch to gloss over her reading homework. She might not enjoy the extra years of high school that she would have to endure, but at least it would be easy. As she flipped open her textbook and began to read, a car pulled up the drive. Tires crunched on gravel before the engine shut off, and the familiar face she longed to see emerged from the small hatchback. *Chase.* The last time she saw him at the bar, she'd longed to be Regan again. He'd talked to her like she was a toddler, then told her to grow up. Hell, she *was* a kid now. Fifteen might be next week, but to a twenty-something guy, she was jailbait. Besides, he'd liked Regan, and now she was Rain.

He moved toward the porch where she sat, book in her lap. "Hey." He greeted her with a guilty smile. Was he thinking about that night at the bar too? She'd been angry with him.

"Hey is for horses," she returned. She wouldn't make this easy, whatever this was.

"I thought about what you said the other night, and I feel a little guilty."

She sat up straighter, giving him an, I don't give a shit, look. "For what?"

He looked uncomfortable. He stood at the rail of the porch, grasping the banister, staring off at the pink haze of the setting sun. The days were getting longer, and soon she'd be free from the toil of school for the summer. What would she do with all of her time? She was suddenly limited by her age again.

He avoided looking at her directly. "Look, I wanted to talk to you and your mom. Is she here?"

Regan stood up. "Sure, come on in." Worried about the state of the house, she rifled through her mind to think if she'd left the TV room a mess. When was the last time anyone had vacuumed, and what did it smell like?

After being outside, her sense of smell was clear. She entered the front door, holding it open for Chase to come in. It smelled like turkey pot pie, coffee, and cool air-conditioning. As she stood in the foyer, she called out to her mother. "Momma, we have company." She paused a minute, giving her mother time to prepare. She walked around the short wall separating the entry hall from the living room. Her mother stood looking at them curiously as her lit cigarette dangled from two long fingers. Rona's bony elbow stuck out as she took a drag. Her hip jutted to one side, and her free hand held her shoulder as if it pained her.

A worried look crossed her mother's face, and Regan knew she thought Rain was about to introduce a love interest. She was, but her mother didn't need to know that part.

"Chase, this is my mother, Rona. Mom, this is Chase. He's the guy who wants permission to sing Regan's song." Regan waited for a heartbeat as she watched her mother's shoulders relax. Rona stubbed out her cigarette and moved toward them.

"Hi there. Nice to meet you, Chase. How'd you know Regan?" She waved to the loveseat on the other side of the coffee table. Chase nodded and took a seat. Regan hung back, not wanting to sit close.

"Ms. Landry, your daughter sang with my band once." He saw Rona's concern and immediately rushed on. "Not professionally. It was just one time. It was during the day, and we were just practicing is all." He spread his hands to ward off any untoward thoughts. "It was just one song. One really amazing song." His words were filled with awe, and he studied Rona, waiting for some reaction.

She lit another cigarette and sat back as she took in a long drag. "Regan had a beautiful voice. I never told her that." She blinked rapidly as she looked out the window, then flicked an ash into the glass tray on the end table. "I wasn't trying to be mean when I told her she'd never be a singer like she wanted. I just know it's not reality for most people. It was a nice dream, but…" Rona's voice trailed off.

"Yes, ma'am, but I think she would have made it," Chase said. His words were a soothing balm over Regan's soul. Like touching the strings of his guitar, he played a tune so sweet that her heart clenched with sad longing. She'd wanted to hear that she was good enough by someone who mattered. Chase mattered. Her mother had never encouraged her singing.

Chase rambled on. "Her voice was amazing. So much so, that we'll never be able to make the song sound as good as Regan could have, but…." He smiled, clasping his hands together, twisting them inside out. The movement made Regan think of the church, the steeple, and all of the people her mother had shown them when they were children. She had done it over and over again with her hands. Rain had loved it.

"You're going to try." Regan's voice lilted with hope as she finished his sentence.

Chase's broad smile set off sparks in the depths of his hazel eyes. He nodded to Regan but directed his answer to her mother. "Yes ma'am, we think it will be a hit. I don't need permission to sing it in the bar. Music is free that way, but I do need permission to produce it with a record label and make money off it. We'll give Regan all the credit for writing it, and of course, we'll give you and Rain a cut of the profit." He watched Rona as if he was trying to discern her feelings toward the offer. "Or we can pay you one check outright. I brought papers for either way, but I think you stand to make a higher percentage of the profit if you go with a net royalty. I believe in this song, Ms. Landry. I really hope you'll consider letting us make your daughter's memory famous."

A tear slid down her mother's cheek as she made an awkward facial movement, half yawn, half grieving pain. Regan felt her mother's emotions. She missed her old body and she missed Rain. She was so excited about the music, but it was anticlimactic after all she'd been through to get where she was now. What she'd hoped and dreamed of as Regan was now coming to fruition, but she wasn't herself. Was there any hope for her as Rain?

Without thinking, she blurted out, "Can I sing it?" She didn't try to support her request with any reasoning that could be shot down by her mother. She wanted to hear Chase's answer.

Her mother's head jerked up in surprise. "Rain, darlin', you can't sing."

Rain glared at her. "That's what you told Regan." It was a short, punctuated response that packed a wallop. Her mother looked pained. She blinked rapidly, looking up at the ceiling as if trying to compose her emotions.

Chase looked at Rain. "If that's what it takes to get you and your mother to sign off on this deal, I'm willing to give you an audition."

Rona's head tilted to the side in consideration, and she chewed her bottom lip. Regan was sure that her mother wasn't thinking about the possibility as much as she was thinking of how to let Rain down gently. Finally, she spoke. "I don't think it's a good idea."

Chase faltered, "Ma'am, we can do it any way you want. It's up to you, Ms. Landry, but please, don't let this song die with Regan. I didn't know her for long, but what short time I did, she was a spitfire. She would have wanted this song to make it, even if she couldn't." His eyes shone with something that Regan was afraid to think about. Was it sadness, his own desperation and ambition, or was it irritation at Rona for being so small minded?

She crushed out another cigarette as she exhaled a long stream of white smoke. She stood and walked in the direction of the kitchen. "Go get your papers. Let's get this over with."

There was a lot of legal jargon that confused both Regan and her mother. Chase tried to read through it all with Rona but eventually suggested that they come and meet Rodney Long, the producer, the following day. Rona agreed, and Regan couldn't help but jump up and down a few times when he told her she could audition at the same time. Her mother didn't disagree, which was even bigger news than her consenting to sign the papers. Timing was everything, and tomorrow was her mother's only day off. Regan would take a sick day from school.

Rona agreed to the audition, but only if it wasn't in a bar. Chase said he'd call the house in the morning to give them a place and a time to meet.

After Chase said goodnight to Rona, Regan walked him out onto the porch to say goodbye. The excitement was such that she could almost forgive him for treating her like a kid before, but he *should* be hands-off with her. Technically, she *was* too young for him.

The sun had set while they were talking about Regan's song. Chase's sandy hair blew in the slight breeze and Regan breathed deep, taking in the scent of fresh shampoo and maybe a hint of cologne. This deal was important to him. He wanted to make a good impression with her mother, and he had. Full of, "Yes, ma'ams." Chase was the perfect gentleman, and she could tell her mother longed to be close to any memory of Regan's past. It was too bad Rona hadn't felt this way when Regan was in her old body. She could have used her mother's support. It was baffling, but as Rain, she would finally have the encouragement she'd always longed for.

Regan watched Chase step off the porch and head toward his car. He turned and started to wave, and then as if just remembering something, he held up a hand for her to wait. He stooped inside his car and retrieved something from the floorboard. Returning with a paper bag, he handed it to her. Inside was a silk pouch with something hard inside.

"What's this?" She looked up at him, studying his lopsided grin.

"It's a peace offering. I know the past few weeks have been hard for you, and I probably sounded like a dick the other night, but I was in a hurry to get back on stage. Anyway, I saw this, and for some reason, I thought about you. You were wearing something that I thought matched it when you came to the bar."

Regan pulled a silver and turquoise bracelet out of the pouch. It was the same one she had wanted to buy for Rain in the French Market when she belonged to the world of the dead. She smiled. It had to be a sign, just like the graffiti in the bar. The bracelet matched the post earrings her sister always wore. Her hand touched the small stone at one ear. "You noticed." It would have flattered her if she were still Regan. What did it mean that he noticed something so personal about Rain?

"I uh—" his voice caught, and she watched his Adam's apple dip and pitch. The slight stubble sparkled across his golden skin. She wanted to reach out and run her fingers over the fine hairs to see how they felt against her hand. "It's just that you seemed so upset that night at the bar and the last time I dropped you off. I just need you to understand that I wasn't rejecting you. You are a very pretty young lady, and one day you will make some guy really happy." He paused as if waiting for her to nod or something. She waited him out, seeing how deep of a hole he would dig. She liked watching him squirm, but then she chided herself. The depth of his chivalry was adorable, and he didn't owe Rain anything. All parties would make money from his band producing the song.

She smiled with a small nod to smooth out the moment. "Thanks. It's pretty."

Clearly, at a loss for further explanation, he backed toward his car. "Anyway, I just thought you would like it. See you tomorrow." Stretching one arm up, he saluted goodbye and slipped into his hatchback. She wondered if fame would change him. He was too gorgeous not to become famous, and she was confident that her song would hit the charts. Would he trade his rusted Honda for a sleek BMW or Trans Am? Would he cut his hair and use mousse? She liked the way the sandy tendrils turned up at the ends and brushed the back of his long neck above his t-shirt. His hair was too long, but she had a hard time imagining him any other way. He was an artist like her, and she longed for him to look at her the way he had when she was Regan.

She let the screen door slam behind her as she took off to the bathroom to take a shower. If she was still in her old body, she might have taken the five extra minutes to pleasure herself after seeing Chase. She still reacted to his presence, but any type of sexual release was just gross as long as she was Rain. Ugh, she may have to become a nun. Maybe one day she would forget about her old identity or the fact that she was now in her sister's body, but as long as she felt the way she did today, boyfriends were off the list. She wanted to shower so she could listen to herself in the acoustics of the tiled walls. Water was a conductive source. As she belted out the lyrics of "Walk on Water," she expected pure beauty in the sound of her voice. She tried once, then started again. Over and over, she concentrated on letting all the air out of her diaphragm and loosening her shoulders. She opened her mouth and let the hot water fill her throat as she gargled, hoping to relax her larynx. Nothing worked. In her excitement to audition, she forgot that she wasn't Regan. She was Rain, and their mother was right, Rain couldn't sing. Tears mingled with the rivulets of water cascading down her skin. How could she quit when she'd come so far? She had died and been given life again. Success tasted bitter, and she felt like a failure, but how could she give up? *This is my destiny.*

Part of Delila's duties as a guardian was to know what was best for her ward. Though Regan was destined to have some part in the music business, Delila needed to make sure that following Chase down this road was to her ward's benefit. It was true that Chase and Regan were drawn to each other, even in Rain's young form. The two spirits were probably more than soul complements. She had no doubt that they were meant to spend eternity together in some capacity, but Regan's loss of form and the exchange for Rain's younger existence put a cap on romantic prospects for now.

Regan's new voice may never have the capability of her former self. She would also never have the grace Rain had. Souls were given a gift upon their creation. They carried it through all their lives in some varied capacity, even if only as a hobby. A simple bank teller might have once been a printer of money or a money lender. If the teller had been a famous artist before, then there were sure to be sketches on paper or paint on canvas somewhere in the bank teller's life. If things that were connected to one's gift went horribly wrong, then there might be a suppression of that talent for several lifetimes, but the ability was always there, just under the surface, waiting to be tapped.

Regan was musical. Her creative writing ability was her true gift, but the ability to hear music inside her head and touch the words to the notes in a seamless variety of instruments was stupendous. There were souls more gifted than Regan, but not many. Music was her destiny.

Delila wanted to follow Chase for a bit and see what kind of life he led in this existence. She told herself it had nothing to do with her previous connections to him. Venery was a strong soul complement to Delila, but he was not her soulmate. Early on in her existence, she'd wondered if they were meant to be connected, but after so many lives, she'd finally been granted an existence with her true soulmate, Languish. Being with him was like no other reality she'd ever known. Secure, warm, filled with joy until they'd met their great sorrow of separation. She'd known her counterpart's love a few times, enough for her to know what true perfection was. Yet, this connection she had to Venery was special. A warm current of energy encompassed her when he was near. It was true she desired Venery's presence, but she assured herself that she was just ensuring her ward's security for a better future.

CHAPTER 24

Chase called in the morning. Her mother carefully wrote down the address where they were supposed to meet. She made a detailed list of which roads to take and how many lights were in between each turn. Rona hardly ever left Bonne Fete. She worked too many hours to go anywhere far, and Regan wondered if her mother had a fear of getting lost. Her hand shook as she took a cigarette out of the half-empty pack. She held the butt pressed between her thin lips and recited the directions, erasing a blunder and correcting the street name. Standing up straight, she lit the end and inhaled as she muttered the directions over again to herself.

Regan waved a paper map she'd fished out of the Mustang's glove box. "Don't worry, Momma. I'll make sure we can find our way back."

Rona rolled her eyes and let out a breath she'd been holding. "Thank God."

The trip was just under an hour and they only made one wrong turn. Pulling into a convenience store to get directions, they righted their course and arrived at the studio on time. Regan tapped her fingers on her knees as she flexed and unflexed her toes in her tennis shoes. It was a studio, so not a lot of reason to dress up. Besides, she didn't own anything except jeans and t-shirts. Correction, she owned some ballet clothes, but somehow, she didn't think that would get her the gig.

It only took a few minutes to go over the contract, and Rona signed on the dotted line without any coercing. Then it was Regan's turn. She'd thought about skipping the whole thing. Why embarrass herself? Rain didn't have the talent, and it wouldn't do the song any favors if they accepted her for the part. She wanted "Walk on Water" to be a hit even if it meant letting Emily sing with Chase.

The band members tuned their instruments behind the glass window of the sound room. They played a couple of songs, and Regan was impressed.

Even her mother, who only liked country music, swayed her head back and forth to the melody.

Chase released the strap of his guitar from around his neck and came out of the recording area. He smiled at Rain. "You ready?"

Regan flinched. "Um, yeah. Maybe a little nervous." She could do this, she reminded herself. She might be in Rain's body, but she wrote this song. Regan could be anything she wanted to be, even Rain. She would belt out the first lyrics but bring it down an octave to shorten her range a bit. Chase tossed her a set of headphones and the music piped through the small, closed-in room. She missed her cue the first several times and apologized. Her mother's worried look and hand wringing didn't help her confidence. Regan had to get it together and at least try.

The drums were too loud. It was drowning out her voice, and she could barely hear the guitar. Something was wrong, but she couldn't put her finger on it. Regan had never been in this situation before. It was a new experience that had nothing to do with being in Rain's body. She'd heard that studios could alter or enhance the singer's voice and she was counting on it to get her through the take.

She held up her hand, stopping the lead-in. "It doesn't sound right. There's too much drums, not enough bass, and I can barely hear my own voice."

The recording engineer nodded, adjusting some levers and turning a few knobs. The producer leaned into the microphone. "Let's take it again from the top."

The band started, and the music piped in clean. It was just like she remembered it, and this time, she didn't hesitate to meet her cue. Washed with emotion and a deep-rooted desire to be Regan once more, she felt a tear trickle down her cheek as she reached the chorus. She knew she wasn't good enough. She could hear her voice tremble under the weight of her desire and the disappointment of her inability. The microphone to the box, where the producer and sound engineer sat, was turned off. She couldn't hear the conversation they were having, but she could see the wrinkled foreheads, fingers pointing at the keys on the boards, and knew it wasn't to their liking. Her mother was oblivious to the mechanics going on behind her. Rona sat in her chair smiling back at Regan with what looked like pleasant surprise.

The music lingered. Chase was giving her a creative moment to prove herself. She wanted to push Rain's abilities but knew from her constant trials in the shower that it wasn't going to happen. She pulled off the headphones and made a cut sign with her hand across her neck. The band ceased playing.

Chase's crestfallen expression washed over her heart. He set his guitar in the stand and made a motion to the producer and sound engineer, telling them he'd be there shortly.

Regan tried to smile as he approached her. "Not too bad, Rain. I didn't know you could sing."

She snorted. "Obviously, I can't, but it took coming here to find that out."

Chase placed a hand on her shoulder. He didn't say anything until she looked up and met his eyes. "Everything sounds different here in the studio. Given time and with a little practice—"

Regan didn't give him time to finish. "It's okay. You don't have to patronize me. I can handle it." It was a lie. She was shattering inside. The physical pain in her heart, combined with her rumbling stomach, was enough to send her running to the bathroom to throw up. She tried to stave off her feelings of failure for just a few more minutes. "Look, I appreciate you giving me a chance to try out. It would have been cool to sing it for the label, but I really want to see Regan's song make it, and I know I don't have what it takes."

"Chase, can you step in here for a minute." The speaker crackled as the producer held down a button in the sound control room.

Regan picked up her bag and started to leave the sound booth to meet her mother, who was already standing. It was time to admit defeat and go home to lick her wounds. When her hand touched the door, the music piped in with a boom, startling her at first. It was Rain's voice that blared from the speakers. Her voice. Adjustments were made as the music came together. Chase's head was bent over the keys, moving levers and turning knobs. The voice was Rain's, but way better. She saw them all concentrating as the song continued and the tempo picked up. They were all nodding, and a smile as big as the neighboring state of Texas spread across Chase's face. He looked at her, nodding to the rhythm.

He held down a switch again. "What do you think?" The music was coming to an end where she might have crooned on if she'd thought there was half a chance.

The room fell silent and all eyes from the booth were looking at her.

She shrugged her shoulders. "It's better than I thought."

They all laughed and then the producer's voice piped through. "How old are you, sweetheart?"

Old enough to resent being called sweetheart, she thought, but instead, she responded with, "Fifteen in three days."

He flipped the switch and she was met with silence while she saw all of them deliberating. She went to see her mother, and Chase came out to meet them.

"It might take some time to make a decision. The track is great. I think we could sell it anywhere, but what happens after is the big question. Ms. Landry, Are you willing to let Rain travel to perform?"

Regan had never thought about any possibility past this moment, making her dream come true. The rest was lagniappe. However, Rain was just about to turn fifteen. She still had school to finish.

Her mother must have been thinking along the same lines. "What about school?"

"If this thing takes off like we hope, and we go on tour, the record lable provides a tutor. Probably better than the education she receives now. Louisiana is forty-ninth out of fifty ranked in the US for its education system." He chuckled, but it wasn't real humor. His face expressed the common shame that most residents showed when hearing the bayou state's statistical education deficit. All that oil money. Where did it go?

Her mother wasn't as quick to say no as Regan would have thought. Chase may have hit a motherly nerve. All parents wanted their children to do better in this world than they had. Rona's eyes reflected interest, and Regan could practically hear her ticking off the "if I had…" and "I should have…"

"Would she graduate on time?" Rona's voice warbled a little.

Regan thought she might have to sit down. She never thought her mother would consider her auditioning, let alone going on tour with the band—an all-male band. She forced herself to quell her excitement and stay quiet.

Chase smiled as if his dream were about to become true, but the real truth was that his dream would become a reality with or without her singing the song. What dog did he have in this fight? Did he have some sort of feelings for Rain after all? A bittersweet excitement pulsed through her as she thought about being on the road with Chase, alone, to sing with him on the same stage, sleep in the same hotel. She knew it was his lack of interest in Rain that pushed her sister over the edge, and she knew that she had mixed emotions about how he played that last hand with her sister. She reminded herself that he did the right thing and that no one was to blame but herself for starting this sequence of events. The angel and Mark had also played a part. If Regan analyzed the entire cast, everyone had to accept some of the blame, and yet, maybe it was all destiny. Here she was, standing in the presence of the man that was probably her soulmate, and she was in an entirely different body. Her mother, who always said no, was seriously considering the future of her daughter's musical career. Regan glanced up, wondering if she was about to be struck by lightning. Isn't this what happened to her before, standing on the brink of everything she desired and then swimming in a lake of despair?

"Absolutely, Mrs. Landry." The producer's voice boomed from behind Chase.

"Ms. Landry. I'm divorced." Her mother looked embarrassed. It was the eighties, but her mother was raised in a time where divorce was frowned upon. It wasn't Rona's fault she'd chosen a loser, and Regan didn't correct her by saying, "Separated, not divorced, since dad won't sign the papers." She thought about her father and his last gift to her, the bright orange Mustang. Had word caught up to him about her death yet? Would he find out in a year or two when he showed up to bring Rain a car? Would her mother take him back again?

"Of course, Ms. Landry." Rodney Long had introduced himself before the contract was signed earlier. His eyes held a certain look of interest in Rona now, and Regan wondered if it was about her mother's unveiled relationship status or his interest in Rain in this scenario. "Can I offer you a drink? We can talk about things in the office. Regan?" The producer's voice was that of a radio announcer, clear and warm with intelligence but obviously lost in his own thoughts. The room went silent, and she could see his eyes taking in their solemn expressions. "I'm sorry, forgive me. You're Rain. I'm truly sorry about that. It's just that Chase has said that name so much." He cleared his throat in discomfort. "My condolences to you both for your loss."

Her mother nodded quickly, and the producer took her hand, patting it, then led them to a separate room with an oval table in the center. The contracts to sign were simple and there wasn't much to haggle over.

Just when Regan thought she was home free, her mother folded the papers in front of her and stood up. "Gentlemen, I think I need some time to think things over. There are a lot of things to consider. Rain has a career in ballet to think about, school, and leaving home for so long." Rona's smile waned. "I think we need to go home and discuss the possibilities."

The producer, sound engineer, and Chase all stood, the scraping of their chairs like an exclamation point to her mother's sentiments, though Regan could see the concern in the producer's eyes. She was sure that it wasn't for her mother so much as for his contract that awaited a signature.

She was sure he could replace Rain in a New York minute, but time was everything to these people. He didn't look like the kind to wait, and Regan worried if this opportunity would still be on the table tomorrow. She looked at her mother with pleading eyes, but Rona was already headed toward the door.

It was a long drive home in silence. Regan wanted to beg her mother, but she figured it would just end up in a fight. Being mad and stuck in the car was never good. She gave her mother time to think, and in turn, she stared out at the depths of Lake Pontchartrain as they traveled the causeway. The murky brown water that claimed her young body when she was Regan was now flat and lifeless. Flashes of water flowing into the car, Rain's shrill yell and Mark's limp form in the seat next to her tortured her thoughts. She opened her eyes wide as if she could wake herself from the nightmare and erase those images, but they were the memories of two people tormenting one.

"Rain, you okay?"

Regan looked at her mother. "Yeah, Momma. I just..." She stopped herself from finishing. She didn't want her mother to think about the accident. It would depress her. The thought of losing another daughter to travel and fame might be too much. Regan hadn't thought about this before now. Rona would have an empty nest all too soon, but it would happen eventually anyway. Rain couldn't live at home forever, but her mother hadn't had the normal amount of time to prepare mentally.

Rona put her hand over Regan's. "You did good today. I may not have told you girls how proud I was over the years for all the things that you've accomplished, but it's not because I haven't felt it. I haven't forgotten what it's like to be young and to want." Her eyes had a far-off look of their own, and Rona looked like she might be thinking of some missed opportunity or wrong turn in her own life. It made Regan wonder what her mother had wanted to be when she was younger. Surely it wasn't a checkout lady at the Piggly Wiggly.

Deciding to brave the question, she asked, "Momma, what did you want to be when you grew up?"

Her mother looked surprised, and her lips parted as her eyebrows furrowed. "I don't know, maybe I thought of being an archeologist. I was good at science and social studies." She lit a cigarette and cracked the window. "No one ever asked me back then, and I guess I was supposed to get married and have kids, so I did."

"Didn't you ever want more in your life?" Regan felt disappointed for her mother. She wasn't sure if it was for her lack of ambition or the pressure of society, but she wished there could have been more for her.

"Ha!" Rona said, blowing a stream of smoke toward the crack in the window. "You will find out when you grow up that everything you see isn't dipped in gold and smells like roses. You think joining a rock band to sing your sister's song will make you happy and save her memory, so that's all you can think about right now. I get it. If I were your age, I would feel exactly the same.

"You see my life as a checkout lady with kids, bills, and a no-good ex-husband who never helps out, but I have seen things in my life that make me want more for you. This dream you suddenly have to sing isn't really what you want. You think it is, but all the time Regan was alive, you had no interest in singing. You love to dance, honey." Her mother looked at her with sincere confusion, and she was right. Rain hadn't ever wanted to sing, not at church, not in the school choir, not even in the shower.

"I didn't want to sing because Regan was better at it. It's like standing next to a tall girl when you're only five feet. She would have made me sound worse." It was a lame excuse, but she saw her mother contemplate her analogy. "I haven't felt like dancing since the accident," she confided. It was true, but she didn't confess to her mother that she'd never danced. Maybe she should try. In Rain's body, she might be better than she was before. Regan never thought she was a horrible dancer when boys asked her to dance, but there was a discomfort in not knowing if she was really any good at it.

"This thing." It was as if her mother couldn't actually talk about Regan's music. "It might not go anywhere, and then what? You've already given up dancing for who knows how long and then Juilliard isn't an option anymore. Then what?"

"I don't care about Juilliard. I'll just go to a regular college."

"And do what? Chemistry, English..."

Regan thought about it. She'd never thought about college as Regan. Now that she was Rain, there were more possibilities and expectations. Rain was a straight-A student. She could possibly get a scholarship from her grades. Rain was also good at art. "I could get an art scholarship, and then you wouldn't have to worry about paying for school."

Rona tossed her cigarette out the window as they turned down the last road toward home. She cranked up the window and looked at Rain. "Trust me. Money is the only reason I'm considering letting you do this."

Regan couldn't contain herself. She bobbed up and down in the seat, dancing with her hands like a child.

"Don't get excited, Rain. I'm just thinking about it and only because it could further your education, but it will really depend on the income because I'm not sending you on tour alone. I would have to quit my job and go with you."

Like ice water, the words washed over her with freezing clarity. Her dream world collided with reality as she imagined her mother sitting between her and Chase on a tour bus. "No way!" she spat out automatically.

Rona looked at her with parental anger simmering just below the surface of her eyes. Her nose tilted up a bit as she shoved the car into park and turned to look at Rain. "Then you have your answer. If you don't want me to chaperone, you need to wait until you're eighteen."

Regan rolled her eyes. This is exactly why she'd tried to wait until they got out of the car. She knew it would end in an argument. The Rona at the recording studio was reserved for strangers. This Rona was her mother. The woman slamming the door of the car and marching onto the porch. Regan grabbed her bag and followed her in, but the argument had been lost already. Her mother's bedroom door slammed shut and Regan heard the shower running in the master bath. She would have to wait to plead her case, and maybe it was for the best. Regan started preparing dinner. She'd make something from scratch. Real food might give Rona a better outlook on both their futures. Regan needed to call Chase for support. The phone rang as she put the meatloaf in the oven and cut the potatoes into a pot of water. She answered it before her mother could be disturbed.

"Hello."

"Hey, Rain. I just wanted to check on you and see how you were feeling."

It was the guy who rescued Rain from the river—rescued *her* from the river—she reminded herself. She wasn't sure she would ever get used to being called Rain.

"Yeah, I'm okay. You?"

Jorge was silent for a beat. "I'm good. Hey, listen, I won these tickets off the radio station, and I was wondering if you like Ratt."

Regan smiled at the catch in his voice. How cute was this? Jorge was asking her out. Did he have a crush on her, or was she his charity case to make sure she didn't slit her wrists?

"The kind with whiskers and pink swirly tails?" She teased.

Jorge chuckled, then took in a breath. Regan could tell he was nervous. "No, the kind with guitars. They're playing at the Superdome next weekend. You think your mom would let you go? There are four tickets. She could come if it's an issue."

Regan didn't know what to say. She liked Jorge. He was a good-looking guy, and if she were really Rain, he would be a great pick, but this whole body-switch thing was too strange. She didn't know how to separate what was her and what was her sister. She also still had feelings for Chase, and though she couldn't act on them, she couldn't lead Jorge on like she had Mark.

"Thanks, but I'm kinda going with someone right now." Her mother took that moment to come through the kitchen door, giving her a questioning look. Regan turned her back to her mother, lowering her voice. "I can't date yet, anyway."

"I—I didn't mean for it to be a date. I just thought you could use a friend."

She knew it! It was a charity date. When she'd been Regan, she loved Ratt. If Jorge wasn't into her, then why was she saying no to something she would love to do? Who cared if it was worry that prompted his call? She could use someone who cared about her as Rain. She needed to find some people she could bond with and start a new life as she melded into the blended role of sister-sister. She could think of it as research. If she was going to sing in a band, it would be great to actually see one in concert.

Regan put her hand over the mouthpiece of the phone. "Mom, my friend Jorge has tickets to see Ratt next week. Can I go?"

Rona looked frazzled. She could see her mother's worry. "I don't know, Rain. Is it a school night? Where do you know this boy from?"

"Call me back after dinner. I'll have an answer for you then." She didn't wait for him to say anything but hung up the phone and turned the pot on to boil. Turning to her mother, she wrung the dishtowel she held. "He's just a friend. He knew Regan. I think he feels sorry for me and is trying to cheer me up. It might be good to see a real band play in a huge stadium. Who knows, maybe I'll change my mind and trade fame for college."

Her mother laughed. "Yeah, right, and I was born yesterday."

They both laughed and Regan took a seat at the table. "It's okay. If you're too worried, I don't have to go. It won't break my heart."

Rona's eyebrows went up in suspicion. "Is this some sort of reverse psychology trick?"

Regan held up two fingers. "Scouts honor. I want to go, but my first inclination was to turn him down. I thought maybe he was asking me out, and I don't like him that way. Then he said it was a friend thing. So, I thought, why not." Regan felt like she was having her first adult conversation with her mom. She liked the way her mother looked at her and was listening for what seemed like the first time ever.

"I think it's okay if you think you can make it home before midnight. I mean it." She emphasized her words. "Go to the concert and then come straight home. Besides, your learner's permit is riding on your good behavior, so don't screw it up."

Regan stood up and leaned down to hug her mom. It wasn't the tight hug of excitement because she seemed to be getting her way. It was the tender hug of a silent promise not to break her mother's heart. She may be turning fifteen again, but her soul felt like it had led a multitude of lives. She remembered speaking to the angel about some of those existences, but they were becoming a blur to her now. Things were slowly blending and changing. Her world as Regan was mixed with her reality as Rain, and somewhere in between, she was finding her true spirit. She wondered about the fate of her little sister's soul, where Rain was now, and how she could help her. As soon as Regan got her license, she needed to get back to the city and see Zada. Besides the dream she'd had of Rain, she had no idea what was happening in the in-between world. If Regan got to live out this life trying to fulfill her dreams, then the least she could do was help Rain find her way into the light.

Delila watched Chase hold Emily's hand. She hadn't meant to be here. Yet, like the narcoleptic days of old, she was now watching this romantic encounter unfold. The couple looked out over Lake Pontchartrain in silence, both seeming to linger in their own thoughts. Delila didn't know why she was here or where Regan was at this very moment. The last thing she remembered was walking out of the room when Regan went to shower.

Though she was supposed to guard and guide her ward, Delila had followed Chase before to see his living arrangements. She was curious how he lived and if he was a good match for her ward. If Chase and Regan found themselves tethered by friendship long enough, their age difference would rectify itself over time. Both souls had a lot of living to do, and much could happen with the passing of years. Chase could marry someone else and have children before Regan was old enough to consider having a relationship. Nothing was certain in any spirit or embodied state. He could die in a plane crash, develop cancer, or get hit by a bus. Life was a subtle mix of triumph, tragedy, and the unexpected. Not knowing the future was essential for peace of mind. Delila fretted for a moment, then reminded herself that the happiest of lives bore loss and pain.

She watched as the young couple kissed, and she was thankful Regan didn't share her sight. Chase was a simple soul with a warm heart, and many women were drawn to him. Though he was full of life, music and love, he was still lonely. Delila could feel his energy in this moment. Though he lifted Emily's skirt and his hand fondled her beneath, his act was one of physical hunger and lacking any true connection. The same went for Emily, though Delila' was sure the girl's young heart thought she was in love. Chase would later curl into his bed with his golden retriever Zack and forget about the titillation he'd shared. It wasn't that Delila knew the young girl's spirit, but she felt her energy. If Emily had a watcher, they were nowhere in sight, and Delila was sure it was why the girl wandered about aimlessly looking for conquests in vain. A band, a boy, a starlit life. Delila didn't understand why everyone wasn't gifted a soul watcher in every existence, but the rules of the afterlife weren't fully understood. Emily hadn't realized yet that all that glittered wasn't gold. Delila learned long ago that precious metals held no value for the soul.

She shook herself from the negativity she felt in Emily's presence. There were too many souls failing at life to count, and she couldn't worry for them all. They were not hers to account for. Time was ticking by, and she felt the pull of energy tugging her back to her ward.

The coupling was quickly concluded on the hood of the car, where no one would see them in the early rays of dawn. Most were still at home in slumber, or just having their coffee to seize the day. Only an old fisherman on his boat scoped them out, using his binoculars to see just what sordid business was happening. Delila watched the man shake his head and set the binos on the ledge of the boat. As he cast his line, she pushed a gale of wind that rocked the boat and tipped the binoculars into the water.

"Think about it as a small favor. It'll be one less sin you have to account for when you have that coronary."

CHAPTER 25

Getting her learner's permit was a breeze. Now Regan could drive as long as there was an adult in the car, and only during daylight hours. She needed a ride, and she wanted to talk to Chase. Dialing his number, she waited to see if he would pick up the phone.

Three rings and then a voice husky with sleep greeted her. "Yeah?"

It was a woman's voice. Regan quickly hung up. Could it be his mom, maybe his sister, or Emily? She didn't know him well, and she didn't have a claim on him. They barely knew each other. It was the electricity in the connection she felt that made irrational emotions eat away at her sanity. Deciding her behavior was ridiculous, she dialed the number again.

The same voice answered, more awake now. "Hello."

"Is Chase there?"

"Who's calling?"

"Reg—Rain."

She heard a clattering as the phone was tossed on a hard surface and heard a bellowing, "Chase."

Well, at least she knew the woman wasn't lying in the same bed. It gave her some relief. A few moments passed before she heard another line pick up and a "Got it" from the other end.

Regan jumped right in before he could say hello. "Hey. Sorry to bother you, but I was wondering if you would give me a ride today. I've got my learner's permit, but I need an adult in the car."

"Whoa, wait. Are you asking to drive my car?"

Regan hurried to explain. "No, I just need a lift, and it's a little far to call a cab. Besides, I wanted to talk with you about the contract." It was a lie. She understood everything the producer had said to them. Her mother still hadn't given her consent, and Regan just needed to see the seer. At least that's what she told herself. Thoughts of Chase filled her every waking moment. It was a farfetched request, but her only other choice was Jorge. She didn't know who Rain's friends were, if she even had any, to bum a ride.

"Yeah, okay. Rehearsal isn't until three today. I can be there in an hour."

Her mother had an early shift, leaving her to prowl the house alone. Their neighbors were a mile away, so no one to report her coming or going. If her mother called the house, she'd say she was outside. Chase pulled up exactly one hour after their conversation, and she made a note of his punctual personality. Most people in the music industry couldn't be counted on for the same promptness. She could tell he had ambition, and she believed he was the sort who could make things happen.

Regan opened the passenger door and got in.

He glanced at her with a raised brow. "Where to?"

She stared back at him. "Nice to see you too," she smirked.

Chase shook his head. "Always on guard. What's with that chip on your shoulder? I saw it in your sister, and it seems to have been passed down to you as well."

She preened from his recognition of her similar traits to her old self, even though it was a part of her old self that she probably needed to change. She'd have to work on that.

She ignored responding to the dig. "I'm going to the Quarter."

"I thought I told you you're too young to be hanging out there. I don't care if it's late morning or early evening. There are always deviant types that wouldn't think twice about selling you into slavery."

"Get out of here. Slavery?" She laughed.

The lines in his forehead and flat expression on his face said he was serious. "Sex slavery—particularly abducting young, good-looking girls is very much a thriving business. Murder, rape, or just taking you into the bayou to marry you off to some swamp Cajun that will never let you see the light of day again. Don't be naïve, Rain. The French Quarter is dangerous. It always has been." He paused to glance at her as they hit the ramp to the interstate. "I won't keep harping on it but promise me you won't go alone."

"I'm not alone," she retorted. "I'm with you." Her smile was infectious as he gave in and grinned back at her.

Chase nodded slowly as he let out a sigh. "All right, then. I can't promise to be your chauffeur always, but if I have the time, you can call me. I'm starting to feel like you're that rascally kid sister I never had." He reached over and tousled her hair.

Great, just what she wanted, for him to think of her in a forever off-limits sort of way. She pushed his hand away and rolled her eyes.

"Don't tell me you're one of those 'Don't-mess-up-my-hair' girls?" He laughed.

Regan arched a brow, tilting her head to the side. "So, what if I am?"

"My advice is that life's too short. Besides, you have long hair, and it's in a ponytail. You can't mess it up."

"Hmph." She crossed her arms over her chest.

Chase turned on the radio, and a Ratt song came on. "You like heavy metal?"

Regan smiled. "I love all music except country. Ratt's coming to the Superdome, and I'm going to see them in concert."

"Cool. Got an extra ticket?"

She shrugged one shoulder. "My friend, Jorge, asked me. He has four tickets, but I don't know who else is going."

Chase looked surprised. "Your mother lets you date?"

Regan stared at his profile, inspecting his concern. Was he interested in her? "I'm fifteen! I'm not a baby."

He put a hand up to ward off any further argument. "Okay, you're right. Happy birthday, by the way."

"Thanks."

She heard her own disappointment and wasn't surprised when he said, "Don't wish it all away. After eighteen, it flies by."

He stared straight ahead, and she could tell by the look in his eyes that he was contemplating his own years.

"How old are you, old man?"

He looked like someone had yanked his chain. His brows furrowed as he swung around to face her. "What? I'm not old. I'm twenty-six."

"So, you're saying the next couple years will crawl and then I'll be as old as you in a blink of an eye." Her tone was mischievous. She smiled to herself as she looked out the window at the many cypress and pine trees whizzing by.

Chase nodded. "Something like that. Look, twenty-six isn't old. My life has just begun. When I look at things, they're just starting to get good, but don't throw away the teen years. It's gonna be great, and you are going to have the time of your life. I'm sure you must be popular at school." He gave her that kid-sister smile again, and Regan just turned and looked out the window. "Any word from your mom about the contract?"

Regan sighed. "No, she said she'll let me know by the weekend. We're going to have my birthday then, so hopefully, there is something to actually celebrate."

Chase bobbed his head to the music slightly as he tapped the wheel. There was a moment of silence then, "You said you have some questions?"

Regan remembered her original request for him to pick her up so they could talk. She spat out the first question she could think of. "Is the tour bus really big? Does it have a bathroom inside and everything?"

Chase laughed. "Really, that's what you wanted to ask?"

Regan felt heat radiate to her face as she laughed nervously. When he glanced at her again, she confessed her biggest worry. "Am I really good enough to pull it off?"

Chase's features turned serious. "Do you want me to be honest or sugar coat it?"

Regan felt her heart pound harder in her chest. "Be honest. I don't think sugar-coating it will help either of us."

"You have raw talent. You could even be as good as your sister, maybe better. You're young, and you have time to grow, but you'll need practice and lots of it. The sound booth can make a cat squalling sound good." His fingers flexed, then fanned out as he turned the car steering wheel.

They'd just reached Metairie and there wasn't a lot of time left on their drive. Maybe that was good, considering he was leveling with her. Inside she was still Regan. The loss of her former talent hurt. But he was right. Rain had never sung before. Her vocal cords hadn't developed the ability to hit the notes Regan pushed them to produce.

"Don't be upset. There are a lot of things the sound guys can do if we go on the road. They won't let you flop. I'm just thinking about the gig at the bar. Emily will have to continue for now. You're not old enough, and… you aren't good enough to sing live." Regan noticed him wince as he said it. His face turned toward the passenger seat to see how she was taking his bluntness.

Regan nodded, sure that she looked stricken. Years of pretending she was tough had made her a good actress, and maybe she was tougher than she thought, but Rain's hormones were a little more volatile. She swiped her eyes, trying to keep from embarrassing herself.

"Hey, kid. Don't. I'm sorry. It's just…"

Regan held up a hand to stop him. "You gave me the truth, and I know it's a fact. I just… need some time to process what I already know." They sat in silence as he turned off the exit toward the Superdome. "Tell me this. If I'm so bad, why are they using me? Why not someone with more talent?"

Chase bit his bottom lip and glanced at her. "Because I asked them to."

CHAPTER 26

Chase parked near the bar and came around to open Regan's door. She was still sulking. He stood in front of her blocking her exit as if he knew she was about to bolt.

"Rain, they liked the way the track sounded, and they see your raw talent. They are also looking at promotions and marketing. You're a pretty young girl, and that will sell records and tickets. You have a lot to bring to the table." He paused, lifting her chin to meet his gaze. "Hey, I didn't mean to be so harsh. You'll be great one day. I just don't want you to get comfortable and think that day is now. There is a hard road ahead, and it won't be fun and games. You need to practice. It needs to be your biggest priority, and I wonder if you're giving up something you might regret later."

Regan felt a mixture of hurt, confusion and inspiration to work harder. She was a fighter. She liked a challenge and there was no way she was giving up. "Like what?"

He put a hand on her shoulder, giving her a playful shake. "Your scholarship to Juilliard."

"Oh, that." Regan scoffed. Rain would have been devastated. Maybe she should go back to class and give it a chance. He was right. This body was wired for a different talent. What if singing flopped? Should she waste the chance to excel at something in her life? "I—I don't know anymore."

"Maybe you should think about it. Signing this contract will seal your fate. You will probably be famous, just for a while. There aren't any guarantees we'll make it, and there won't be time for ballet lessons on tour. Think about what comes afterward. What do you want to do with your life, Rain?"

Regan made her way to the seer's, promising to meet Chase back at the car in an hour. Zada took her sweet time opening the door. Regan had been about to leave when she heard the older woman's gravelly voice.

"I'm comin'. Hold your horses." The door swung wide. "Hey sugar, what are you doing here? Nice surprise." Zada turned without further conversation. She headed toward the kitchen, and Regan followed her.

The room was dark. The shades were down, and the cracks only let in a few slivers of light. Zada flipped the switch, and the fluorescent light above hummed before blinking to life.

"I came to see about Rain."

"Rain? You are Rain, chile."

Regan cocked her hip to one side and tilted her head. "Come on, Zada. You know who I really am."

The seer looked at her with keen eyes then made a *pssht* sound. "Honey, you own that body now, and to call yourself anything else is only going to be confusing."

"Well, regardless, I want to check on my sister. I think she's like Gustave. Rain's stuck in the dark and can't find the light."

"And what makes you think you can help her?" Zada waved a hand up and down, indicating Regan's present embodied state.

"I don't know, but we have to try."

Zada scoffed. "We?" She made a *hmph* sound.

Regan's tone turned to pleading. "Please, Zada, I thought you wanted to help. And I need to talk to Gustave. He's supposed to drum up business for you."

Zada brought two cups to the kitchen table and waved for Regan to sit down. "I do want to help. I just don't know if I can. Lord knows I sure could use the business." She looked around her dilapidated kitchen with its peeling paint and rusted toaster. "Last time I went under to find your friend, Gustave, things got ugly. I have seen some stuff in my time, but that Mark kid scared me. There is a dark side to this world. It may lie between here and God. I don't know, but—" Zada shook her head, not finishing the sentence. She was silent a moment as if contemplating how to explain. "I have a gift," she said with wide, assessing eyes. "But I worry about my own soul using it. I go to church on Sundays, even though all that jibber-jabber doesn't sound real to me. Fire and brimstone, pearly gates. Pssht." She tilted her head back in disbelief. Her stony stare returned to Regan. In a hushed, but clear voice, Zada asked, "Chile, do you believe?"

Thunder boomed in the distance and Regan jumped. The lights flickered, and Regan suppressed the urge to go look out the window. It had been bright sunlight when she entered Zada's home.

"Spring showers bring May flowers," Zada sang as she patted Regan's hand. After a moment, Zada's smile faded, and her head rolled back. Regan could see the whites of her eyes and realized things were moving too quickly. They weren't at the seer's usual workspace with the silk lavender cloth and crystal ball. It was obvious she hadn't planned this unexpected pitch from consciousness.

"Regan, Rain, the Regan in Rain falls mainly on the plain." The laughter that followed wasn't Zada's. She had heard the sultry voice before, and it wasn't Gustave's. "I've been looking for you," the spirit's voice purred through the gravely tones of the seer.

"Who are you?" Regan pulled back, but Zada's hand wouldn't let go of her hand. The old woman massaged Regan's fingers and studied her palm. Creeped out didn't begin to describe the way Regan felt.

Zada finally let go of Regan's hand, then startled her by pounding her fist on the table. "You're not supposed to be here! We had a date, you and I," the spirit growled.

Regan repeated, "Who are you?"

"You were warned to find the light, and now you are here, and she is where?" The voice bit out each word with venom.

Definite recognition washed over her as fear sped through her body, pulsing at the wrist he'd just stroked. "I was going to the light." She stopped, reminding herself that she needn't give him any information. If the demon spirit she'd met in the square was searching for her and angry at the change in her appearance, then he might be looking for Rain's soul in her stead.

"Cat got your tongue?" It was odd to see Zada arch just one brow and then run her tongue around her lips in a leering gesture. Regan knew Zada was a nice woman with no interest in her of a sexual nature, but this wasn't Zada she was speaking to.

"I don't know what you want. I don't know how I got here."

"Liar," he scoffed. "I'll find her. I always do. Until then, there is apparently a queue waiting to hold court with the new Regan."

In an instant, Zada's features changed, and Gustave's voice came through. Zada's arms rose, and her hands waved about like great fans. "Darling—. Where have you been? I've been waiting forever, and there a dozen souls who want Madame Zada's attention."

"Gustave, thank God." Regan couldn't suppress her relief.

"Oh, but first, someone is here to see you."

Zada's face relaxed, then a small voice came through. "Regan, I'm okay. I'm not afraid anymore. I've found others here. I'm—I'm okay for now."

Fear raced through Regan's extremities. The devil was just here, searching for her sister. He said there were souls waiting to speak through the seer. How could he not see Rain? Regan took a deep breath. Rain said she was safe. She had to accept that one blessing. "Why are you still here? You should've gone into the light."

"I haven't seen a light, Regan. I'm not sure what's supposed to happen next, but I met Gustave after I talked to you. He said he knows you and he brought me here. I promise, I tried to find the light, but I haven't yet. Don't worry. There are lots of others here lost like me. I'm safe."

"Rain, this whole thing is messed up and I don't know how long I will remember being me. I think my memories are fading and I'm not sure how long I will be able to help you." She paused, waiting for Rain's response. There wasn't one. "Rain, Gustave has been in the in-between world a long time. Listen to him. He wants to find the light, but he can't."

"I know. He told me. He was murdered in a duel, isn't that awesome? I haven't seen the light. Do you think it's because I'm a suicide? Even Gustave saw the light." There was a great sigh from Zada, and Regan worried she was becoming too drained. "I'm afraid, Regan. What if I go to Hell? What's waiting for me when I do find the light? Gustave said his experience wasn't good."

Regan contemplated that too. She had spoken to the angel and had the memory of multiple lives. Maybe Rain had never lived before or couldn't remember her past existences. That would be scary. Hell, after talking to the devil, Regan could see Rain's point. Suicide or not, Rain was still a good person. Surely, she wouldn't be banished to Hell for eternity, but Regan didn't truly know. A question was burning at the back of her mind, but she was afraid to ask. Zada looked tired, and Regan was anxious.

She braved her fear. The time she had with Rain was limited. "Have you seen Mark?"

Her query was greeted with silence then a great boom as Zada's fists raised and hit the table with a thud. "I am here!" There was a pause. Regan gripped the table, preparing herself for some assault. "How are you there, Regan? Why is Rain here?"

Regan tried to calm her nerves. She wanted to bolt, but she couldn't leave Zada in his hands. Mark hadn't been evil in life. He was just a teen-age kid who made a stupid mistake. She recognized this and was ready to forgive him, but in this state of anger, it didn't seem possible.

"Mark, I don't know how to explain it, but I *am* here, and you are there with Rain. What is it that you want?"

"I want you to suffer the way I have suffered." The great boom of his voice shocked the quietness of the small room. Zada's deeper tone echoed off the close walls covered in yellow wallpaper.

"You've taken both of our lives—all of our lives. I am no longer truly Regan. And Rain is lost in a world that terrifies me to even think about. You are trapped there as well. What more do you want? Isn't that enough torture to appease your tarnished soul?"

Zada studied the table, a forlorn expression on her face. "I want you, Regan. It was always you that I wanted, and now we are separated." Zada shook her head, weary lines creasing her face with grief. "I love you, Regan. All I wanted was for us to be together."

Regan leaned forward, her voice slowly emphasizing the words as if she were explaining punishment to a child. "Mark, even in death, you haunted me. You didn't seek peace or absolution. You wanted to scare me. You took Rain's life!" her voice rose as her fist hit the table.

"No, no! I didn't. She swam out of the car. I saw her. My soul hovered over the lake. I saw everything before I departed."

Regan sucked in a breath, thinking carefully about her words. "You're right. She survived the accident, but she didn't survive the depression of losing a sister, of losing you. Did you know she was in love with you… or thought she was?"

"I feel tortured about it. I didn't mean for any of this to happen. In my body, I couldn't control my anger, then without a body, my anger was set loose into the atmosphere. It seemed to pick up wind, and I couldn't release it. Like a tornado, it's been spinning inside me, and I don't know how to stop it. Regan, I heard you talk to Rain about the light. Like her, I never saw it. Am I doomed?"

Again, she didn't know. She realized she wasn't angry anymore for the turn of events. She knew he wouldn't have come to such an end if the angel hadn't made her own mistake. Was that why he wandered without light?

Would he, too, be offered another body to fulfill this life? Regan thought about her vision provided by the angel. Mark and Rain would have died anyway, so why hadn't Rain seen the light? She was mostly innocent in either scenario. She committed suicide, trying to right her path from events that never should have happened, and the universe knew her body should have recycled. Mark, on the other hand, had committed a murder in the altered event. Maybe there were legalities to the hierarchy of the afterlife.

"I'm not sure. I think punishment waits for all our sins, but from what I saw in my own passing, I've lived and made mistakes before. I'm still here, so my thoughts are, you will live again. You will probably have to pay for your mistake, Mark, but if you truly let go, your soul may be able to move forward."

Thunder cracked the silence and Regan heard the tapping of rain on the roof.

"Paper and pen, please." Zada's voice was thin. She didn't recognize anyone coming through. Regan grabbed a telephone bill and a pen from the counter by the phone. The seer's shaking hands scribbled something on the back of the envelope.

Zada then stood up, giving directions to Regan. "Go there and bring them here in a few days. Lock the door on your way out. I need sleep." The older woman shuffled down the hallway like a drunken sailor.

Regan grasped the coffee-stained envelope and tore off the bit with the address written on it. She stood staring down the hallway, wondering if she should go to Zada to make sure she was okay. It had been a long session and it clearly exhausted the older woman. Regan decided she didn't know Zada well enough to invite herself to the bedroom, so she went to the door and let herself out. *There is work to do.*

Delila held her energy close. She tried to maintain a distance when the seer performed her talents. Like other souls, she understood that Zada carried her gift through all lifetimes. The clairvoyant had once been an emperor's wife and had predicted he would die. Before he rode off into battle, he tethered his wife to the battlements so that she'd be the first to see him return. When her vision came true, and the emperor did not return, his illegitimate son gave orders to leave her there until she died. Zada didn't remember that life, and it was a blessing. Now, she helped those around her in need to make peace between the darkness and the light. For many, she helped them to find closure in what had passed before. Her main business was curing people of their fears, habits, or addictions. When she walked their minds into the unconscious state, she often planted positive messages to enhance their existence.

Mark's presence didn't surprise Delila since he always lurked in the shadows around her ward, following her every move and sometimes trying to lie beside her while she slept. Delila used her great wingspan to cover Regan most nights, like a dome. She was ever watchful of the black demon who preyed on Regan's vulnerability while she slumbered. Mark and Regan needed to have this conversation, so Delila stood aside to allow Mark through. She couldn't afford to make more mistakes. Until Rain crossed over to the light, there wouldn't be any real security for Regan in this world.

CHAPTER 27

Chase held two glass Coke bottles by the neck in one hand as he leaned back against his battered Honda. "Everything work out okay?" He called to her as she approached.

Regan's heart skipped a beat as she studied his sun-bronzed face. His sandy hair fell past his eye on one side and he reached his free hand up to push it out of the way. Regan had never noticed the bright green flecks in his hazel eyes before, but she did now. The days were growing hotter and his hair shone with streaks of gold. There was more to her attraction than just his physical appearance. She'd known several handsome guys, but never this constant pulling on her senses. It had been there since the moment they'd first met. She wondered if he felt it too. She studied his eyes, searching for the same recognition. His Adam's apple bobbed under her assessing gaze. He fidgeted, looking down at the drinks in his hand.

Regan looked down at the Cokes. "Yeah, it's all good." She took the offered bottle and drained a third of it in one gulp. She smiled, savoring the cold bubbles dancing on her tongue. "God, I was thirsty. Thanks, Chase. Hey, do you know where this address is?" she showed him the scrap of paper and he nodded.

"It's not too far."

She smiled. Squinting at the sun. Would he grant her another favor?

"What? You want me to drive you now?" he laughed. "I don't know, Rain. I gotta drop you off and be back here for practice."

She hopped up and down a little. Using Rain's innocent youth as a crutch. "Please!"

He laughed again, nodding. "Okay, okay, but we need to make it quick." He pointed to the Honda and they both got in the car. As promised, the address wasn't far, but it wasn't in the best area.

He stopped the car in front of the house. She grasped the door handle and he caught her arm. "Rain, what is this about? I don't like the idea of you going in there."

She looked at the row of shotgun houses with dilapidated porches and peeling paint. "I just need to tell them where to go and when. I promise I won't go inside." She stood on the pavement and then leaned her head back inside the car. "But it may take a few minutes to convince," she looked at the crumpled paper in her hand, "Elsa."

Regan was excited about the prospect of bringing Zada business. The seer had helped her connect with her sister and even did a little therapy to find closure with Mark. Who knew if that thread had ended? She wasn't sure if she could be any more help to Mark, Rain, or Gustave at this point. And, what about the Diablo spirit? Was he really the devil? She didn't have time to think about his sudden appearance right now.

Regan stood on the porch, wondering if anyone was home. She grasped the shield-shaped metal door knocker and rapped it against the wood door. When no one answered, she pushed the small white doorbell button on the matching black metal plate. She heard a shuffling sound, then an old woman cracked the door without releasing the chain.

"What do you want?" The woman's pink rollers waved behind the crack.

"Mrs. Elsa Corporon?" Regan waited.

"Who wants to know?" Regan was about to answer, then the lady supplied, "She ain't here. She moved."

Regan blinked. She doubted the lady had moved and knew that the old woman was probably Elsa, but she didn't argue.

"Okay, well, if she ever comes back, will you tell her Willard wants to see her. He's got money for her." She headed back to the car. The last part was a lie, but Regan knew by the look of the place that the old woman would bite. She only felt partially guilty since the act of getting her to see Zada was to earn money for the seer. It might not be something Elsa could afford.

"H-How…?" the woman stammered. "Willard Corporon is dead!" The chain jangled as the woman released it. The old woman opened the door wide, accusation in her eyes.

Regan turned back, smiling. "I know."

After explaining that a spirit beyond the grave was organizing the meeting between Elsa and her late husband, Regan gave the old woman the seer's address and told her to meet her at Zada's *Tell-All Salon* in two days at noon. She mentioned there would be a flat fee of twenty dollars for the séance. If the woman didn't have it, perhaps she wouldn't go, no harm done. Who knew, maybe old Willard had stashed some money somewhere and was anxious to tell Elsa. If not, a twenty-dollar bill couldn't make or break anyone.

On the ride home, Chase asked her about her mysterious business in the quarter, and Regan wondered what he might say if she told him the truth, all of it. She knew she was sworn to secrecy for some of the past events, but she didn't mind shocking him a little.

"I went to see a fortune teller."

Chase laughed, turning to her and waiting to hear the truth.

"No, really. I went to Zada's *Tell-All Salon*. She's for real, and she's a friend of mine."

"Mm-hm," he said, nodding, then tilting his head to the side in silent question. "So, what did she tell you? Are you going to be a superstar?" he chuckled.

"She told Regan that she saw lots of water in her future."

Her words were like ice water thrown in his face. His mouth opened, but nothing came out as he looked at her, wide-eyed. "Really?" his voice squeaked.

Regan nodded.

"What did she tell you?"

Regan could tell she'd grabbed his interest and she smiled slightly, laying her head against the cool glass of the passenger-side window. Gazing at the solid white highway line as it flickered in the bottom of her field of vision, she wondered how much she should say. What could she say that sounded halfway believable? She couldn't tell him how she met Gustave or about Mark and the devil spirit. He'd think she was nuts.

"I went to her after Regan died. I wanted to reconnect, but—" she trailed off.

"Did you talk to Regan?" He looked like he half-believed the possibility.

Should she tell him? "No, but I talked to her ex-boyfriend, Mark."

"The guy who killed her?"

Regan swallowed. She hated that Mark would always be remembered that way. She had hated him for what he'd done, but now it was different. Life went on for the living. For the dead, memories were set and couldn't be changed.

"Yeah, him, but he wasn't like that. I mean, not always."

"Wait a minute. Are you standing up for your sister's murderer? This guy almost killed you. Is this like some Patty Hearst thing? Do you feel sorry for him?" Chase's voice sounded incredulous, angry.

"Yes—no. It's complicated. Look, all I know is that he wasn't a bad guy. He just..." she bit her bottom lip, trying to think of the right words. "He loved Regan too much to let her go."

Chase rolled his eyes, muttering, "That's utter crap, Rain."

Regan rushed on, "He's sorry for what he's done, and he's scared. He's trapped in the in-between world and can't find the light."

Chase scoffed. "What? You mean limbo? You don't really believe any of that hocus pocus. What's this lady charging you? Don't listen to her. She's a hack, for sure. Don't waste any more of your hard-earned allowance, kid." He shook his head in disbelief.

"She's not charging me anything." Regan tried to explain.

Chase gave her a look of pity. "Then what's with this Elsa lady? You get her to go see the fortune teller, and she doesn't pay either?"

Regan knew where he was leading her, and anything she said would only be incriminating. "Zada isn't like that. She didn't want anything to do with me, but she saved my life."

"Really? I don't believe it," he scoffed.

"The night you were angry at me for showing up and I left the bar...a group of guys followed me to my car, and she kept them from..." She didn't know what exactly, but she didn't want to say it. She knew Chase would only be angry at her for risking her life.

His brow furrowed, and he reached out a hand and touched her shoulder. "Did they touch you? Were you hurt?" He darted concerned looks at her as he drove. A look of anger was simmering beneath the surface of his inquisitive gaze. She watched his chest rise and fall as he downshifted and took the exit to her home.

"No. Zada came out just in time and shot her pistol in the air. They all scattered and there wasn't any real harm done. They just scared me is all."

Chase let out a breath he'd been holding with obvious relief. "That's good. Okay, so maybe Zada isn't a total flake, but she sounds like she's using you."

"She's not," Regan assured him.

"I want to meet her." Chase's voice was stern, like a parent.

Regan giggled. "I'm not a kid, Chase. Geez, just let it go." Then it occurred to her that she would need transportation to meet Elsa in two days. "Wait a minute. Okay. You can pick me up day after tomorrow and we'll go there at noon. I can introduce her, and you can get your palm read."

"What, and give her twenty bucks? No way."

Regan frowned, "Okay, then, don't meet her."

"All right, all right." He waved his hands above the wheel as they turned into her driveway. "I'll pay for a reading, but it better be good." He pointed at her as she stepped out of the car and turned to say good-bye. She didn't linger like Rain once had. She didn't trust herself not to make a fool of herself over him, too. The energy between them was too vibrant, and it crackled with forbidden feelings. Did he sense it too? There was no reason to ponder the question. She didn't want him to get into trouble with her. There were bigger plans at stake. In the future, they would both grow older. Twenty-six and fifteen might be out of reach now, but she would be eighteen again one day. Would he find her too young then?

CHAPTER 28

They made arrangements to go to Zada's, then to the bar. They would run through a few sets of music lessons-slash-practice and then he would take her to lunch before bringing her home. Regan was on cloud nine, counting away the hours and minutes until their date. Wait, it wasn't a date. It was just friends doing casual run-around things and band practice. She was really looking forward to training her voice, and since she'd been practicing, it felt like her range was growing. When Regan was Rain's age, her voice had been different than at eighteen, so she knew there were possibilities. Vocal cords were muscles, so they could be exercised and improved. She'd sung all of her existence and created the sound of her voice as Regan through many years of practice. There was still time for her as Rain. Who knew, maybe she could sound like her old self again one day.

The ride to the city flew by as they talked about the band and their first-ever practice. If things went well, they planned to record in the coming weeks and then she would work with Chase on some of the songs he was writing. One of the things Regan had forgotten was that she was first and foremost a songwriter. That was internal, and she inherently knew she still possessed that gift. As Chase sang a few of the verses he was working on, ideas gathered in her brain, and she took out a notebook to start taking notes. She'd have to hear what he'd created with music to know if her ideas would work, but creativity was crackling in the right side of her brain, and it was impossible to stymie the flow.

High on life, they turned up the radio as they belted out verses, singing the popular rock songs they both loved. Full of laughter and teasing remarks, they practically fell out of the car when they reached Zada's.

"Yeah, like you'd catch me at a Cindy Lauper concert. Not on your life."

"Well, if you have to be dead, then who cares?" Regan retorted over her shoulder as she made her way to Zada's door.

"Hey, seriously Rain, be careful at that concert. Sometimes people drink too much and get too rowdy. I don't need my lead singer getting crushed in a mob at the stage."

She arched an eyebrow. "Your singer?"

He held up his hands in surrender. "The Cat's Quarter's new singer."

She winced. "That reminds me. We really need to come up with a better name for the band if we're going international."

Chase pressed his lips together, squinting at the sun. "Yeah, the producer said as much. What do you suggest?"

Zada opened the door with a flare. Her deep purple silk dressing gown swirled around her as she threw up her arms in greetings. All smiles and excitement, she waved for them to come inside. Regan liked that the old woman had warmed to her. Their friendship was growing, and it didn't hurt that she brought the seer business.

"So, tell me who your handsome young man is?" Zada placed her glasses—attached to a set of Mardi Gras beads that she wore around her neck—on her nose. She peered closer. "Oh, chile, I hope he's your cousin, cuz he is too old for a young'un like you."

That put Chase on the defensive. "No, hey, we're just friends. I'm Chase. Rain and I are *friends*," he emphasized. "And that's all." He spread his hands out in front of him to demonstrate his platonic intentions.

Zada smiled. "I know that, but there is something else goin' on here." She reached out, touching his shoulder and then touched Rain's hand with her other hand. She closed her eyes and breathed in deep. Regan expected her to fall into her usual trance and was glad when she didn't. Zada sat down in her gold-painted metal chair, opened her eyes and stared up at the two of them. She motioned for them to join her in the sea of mystic colors. The room was like a purple rainbow, with her as the deep violet night sky in the middle of the splashes of lavender, lilac, plum and periwinkle.

Chase was silent. He'd asked her not to mention him to Zada or tell the seer anything about him. He wanted to see for himself if she had any talent or not. Regan couldn't deny the thumping in her chest at Zada's proclamation that there was more to their relationship.

The seer's voice was low and gravelly as she started a low chant. Her words sounded foreign to Regan, and she thought the cadence might be a mixture of French and Latin. Zada took a clump of sage branches bound by a red string and waved them in the air, around the table. Finally, she took one leaf from the bunch and burnt it in a small tray made of colorful stone. Its blackened belly revealed the many leaves that had been smudged before. Zada was cleansing the air of spirits that lurked. She'd explained to Regan that she needed a clean atmosphere for seeing. Chase sat still and didn't engage in nervous conversation like others probably did. He waited patiently. Zada reached for his hand and he gave it to her slowly.

"Hm," she said, running a finger down the center of his palm." She looked up, locking eyes with Chase. "You're an old soul. You have a guardian angel who watches over you in this world. Wait, no. She is not yours, but she has known you before, in other lives. You know Regan, too. Many lives you have been together and many more you have been apart. You are soulmates, but then I guess you knew that when you first met." She smiled knowingly at Rain. "There is an energy that separates you throughout all lives. You always find yourselves together then severed apart. A soul that is lost and bitter without reward. It stalks you and tries to make its brand, stamping out your happiness.

"Regan was burned at the stake because she wouldn't be with this soul. She is forever yours, Chase, but forever trapped by his curse. The angel has given her a chance to escape the wrath of this meddling spirit and find happiness in this life, but it will not be without its trials. Success awaits you, but there will be loss, too. Your angel is not your own in this existence and has only given this one chance to Regan. The path will be difficult. Don't waste this gift." Zada's stare never wavered. Regan watched Chase's beautiful unblinking face. He looked at Zada like he was entranced, broken only when she let go of his hand and slumped back in her chair.

He tilted his chin, looking at Zada skeptically. "Regan's dead."

Regan could tell he didn't believe the seer. She was still in shock that Zada had somehow seen the angel and made a connection to Chase. Mark must be the soul separating them throughout eternity, and her greatest question for Zada was why. Why was Mark dogging them?

Regan butted in before Zada could answer Chase. "Doesn't this attacking spirit have his own soulmate?"

Zada looked relieved since she probably hadn't meant to mention Regan in the reading, knowing that Regan was inside of Rain.

"All souls have soulmates, and some have such strong links to their soul-companions that they can be confused when they haven't seen their own mate in so many lives. His tortured soul has made so many blunders that time and destiny have separated him from his true soulmate for too long to remember. He's drowning in a sea of darkness." The seer looked from Regan to Chase and back again. "The connection he has with Regan is a bitter, black form, but Regan is his only life raft. If he snares her spirit and tears her away from you, it will be like a drowning person latching onto its only savior, pulling her into the darkness of his existence. Even now, he doesn't want to let go. Without Regan to go into his next life with, he won't return to the Guff—the hall of souls."

"Wait, Regan's dead," Chase complained again with a chuff. His disbelief was evident to them both, but Zada didn't contradict him. She obviously understood his confusion.

"Not all is black and white in this world like you and me, young man. There is more to it than what you see. Your angel gave you a gift. Now trust in me and don't waste this chance. You've been given a reprieve and an opportunity to break the curse that haunts the one you love. Be bright and shine."

Chase's smile looked forced and sarcastic, but his nod was polite as he rose. "Alrighty then. Thank you very much." He pulled out a crumpled twenty he had stashed in his front jeans pocket and slapped it on the table, nodding at Regan and Zada before turning to leave. "Sorry, Rain. We gotta go."

Zada chuckled. Taking no offense, she winked at Regan. Voices were heard from the entrance as Chase let himself out and Elsa in.

"Do you need me to stay?" Regan's voice held a hint of apprehension.

Zada looked past her at Elsa and a burly younger man who accompanied her. "Yes, if you can. I might need your energy to contact Gustave."

Regan ran out to ask Chase to wait for her a little longer. She sat through Elsa's reading, and to her great relief, Willard told his wife where a jar of money was hidden at the base of the live oak in their back yard. The amount wasn't disclosed, but after the reading, Gustave gave Elsa another address to search out. The woman folded the paper with Malva Bea Bouchard's address on Esplanade and put it in her purse. Regan was relieved. If Gustave could give each living soul another soul to petition, then Regan wouldn't have to worry about every appointment scheduled.

Zada was tired at the end of the reading. There weren't any spirits waiting to speak with Regan, and she felt guilty for feeling relieved. She was still excited about returning to Chase and going to the bar for band practice.

Before she left, she looked back at Zada's brilliant smile.

"You did good, kid. Elsa promised to bring me back a fat tip, and she's off to invite more business, thanks to your friend, Gustave." Her hand lay loose against the kitchen door frame. "You don't look so thrilled, though. You wanna share a Coke and tell me all about it?"

"I'll pass on the Coke this time." But Regan actually did need to confide in someone. She moved away from the front door, dropping her purse on the small entryway table. "Zada, I'm supposed to go to practice with the band right now and…" Regan found herself at a loss for where to start. "Rain can't sing. Well, that's not totally true. I mean, they want me to sing for the recording of my song."

"Wait a minute. You're talking about Regan's song, the one about water?"

"Yeah, but when I was Regan, I had a great voice, and I wrote that song for myself." She felt her eyes pool with unshed emotion. Her loss was great. She mourned herself in so many different ways, and standing there in Rain's body, she felt like a hypocrite, a traitor of the worst sort to cry about her loss of talent. "I know, I know." She put up her hand to Zada, knowing the seer must think she was a terrible little shit. "How can I complain when I'm standing here, right? I should be thankful to have any chance at all, but when Chase told me…" The tears splashed over her lower lids, and she felt her shoulders rock with suppressed grief. It was more than the loss of her voice that tormented her. It was the loss of her sister, Mark, the chance at happiness with her soulmate. She was still just a kid—again.

Zada approached Regan, wrapping her long, lean arms around her in a strong embrace, which only made her feel weaker. "Now, chile, there ain't no reason to cry right now. If you couldn't sing, that boy wouldn't be waitin' out there for you to practice with his band."

Regan hiccupped. "He's twenty-six and he was supposed to be my soulmate." She moaned with grief and let her shoulders shake once more. It felt good to tell someone how much this new existence could hurt.

"And he still is. Regan, Rain, you are who you are inside, not outside. Speaking of which, your voice is your own. I knew who you was the moment you walked through that door. This body just carries your spirit, and the music you make comes from within, chile. Muscles can be trained, and they can also be pulled and strained, but if you believe in the gift that God gave you, then you must believe in yourself." She stepped back, grabbing both of Regan's arms, smiling broadly. "Now go on to the washroom and dry them eyes. Time will fly by before you know it, and eleven years won't be such a difference anymore. You just have to be patient is all. Now off with you, so I can get back to my soaps. Luke and Laura are splittin' up again and I think it might be for good this time."

Regan smiled at the seer. "Don't you already know what happens on the soap opera? I mean, you know the future, right?"

Zada shook her head at Regan. "Some things are best left unknown, chile, or how will you ever delight in surprise. Now go on with yourself."

If Chase noticed she'd been crying, he didn't say. They walked in virtual silence the short distance to the bar. They left his car in Zada's neighborhood since it had free street parking. Chase seemed to be lost in his own thoughts and so was Regan. She studied his profile as they made their way to Jackson Square, thinking about the lives she had spent with him before. She wished she could remember them all. Guidry and the other guys in the band were tuning up. They greeted Regan and Chase with hellos and waves as they entered the cool air conditioning.

"Our Mona Lisa is here," Guidry smiled.

The bartender, Mac, screwed up his face. "I don't think that's a compliment, Guidry."

"Well, I would have said Phoebe Cates, but then there might be a stampede."

The few people on shift and the band members laughed heartily as the bartender tossed Guidry a can of beer. He caught it with one hand, popped the top and guzzled half of it. "Ah, breakfast."

"It's almost one-thirty, Guidry," Chase retorted.

"It's breakfast for me, Dawg."

Butterflies danced in her stomach. Regan didn't feel like jumping right in. Really, she didn't know where to start, but supposed they would lead her. Chase took the stage first, inviting her up.

She lagged for a minute, then dug in her shoulder bag for her notepad. "Can I just watch you guys a bit? I think I'd like to hear the new stuff you're working on. I had some ideas, and maybe if I get a feel for the music, I can ease into the sound."

The band members looked at each other, nodding and shrugging their shoulders. Regan found herself wondering if they accepted her or not. Did they dump Emily or was she still singing nights?

The drummer led in and Chase followed him, strumming the guitar. The music warmed up and Chase's voice joined the instruments, making her heart swell in her chest. He was an artful songwriter, but his voice was like warm buttered toast with hot tea on a frosty morning. Regan felt the cozy lyrics of love found, surrendered, and lost. She knew he had everything to look forward to in his career, and she wanted to jump in as he crooned, adding in bits of back-up. The only thing holding her back was her lack of confidence in her voice. She made notes in her notebook of the additions she thought would work. One part seemed a bit too structured and lingered for too long. The chorus changed beats entirely and should have been elongated with a faster tempo. They were into the third song before she couldn't take it anymore. Regan left her bag and notebook at the bar side table. She grabbed the microphone off the stand next to Chase. It was too tall for her short frame. Like a conductor, she motioned to the keyboardist to bring it up a bit, then drew out her hand as she joined Chase in the chorus. When his voice dropped off, she lingered on, taking more air into her diaphragm and belting out the last line again. Chase looked shocked, but Guidry was smiling, and the keyboard player nodded to the beat of the drummer, who now picked up the pace, hitting the snare and repeating the whole verse with Regan. Chase didn't lose more than a few beats. He was smiling too, now, and tossing his head as he lifted the guitar higher onto his thighs.

When it was time for a break, Regan was slick with sweat. Mac met her across the bar and placed a glass with ice in front of her. "What'll be, Phoebe?" he smiled, winking at her as she grinned.

"Coke, please." Mac knew she was underage, so there wasn't a chance of anything else besides water. She didn't like the taste of beer anyway. It was getting close to time for the bar to open, so she knew this was the end of her day. Chase needed time to drop her back at the house, and he'd said he wanted to talk to her mother. They needed an answer and Regan was half dreading what Rona would say.

She enjoyed the cold soda as it fizzed and hissed from the top of her glass. The spray tickled her nose in a delicious bubbly aroma. If she was addicted to anything in this life, it was music, Chase, and soda, not necessarily in that order. She wondered if she had to choose what it would be. She laughed as the hazy memory of her former self surfaced. The Coke bottle rolling into the bin and her inability to grasp it reminded her to be thankful for the small pleasures in life.

Chase joined her at the bar and ordered a soda for himself, drinking it all in one tilt of his glass. She was mesmerized by the strong angle of his jaw and the tight cords in his neck. He let out a breath and smiled at her when he finished. Regan knew she was in love with Chase the first time she met him, and the seer had confirmed he was her soulmate. She believed Zada. Music was still inside her, but was it always with her?

"That was truly amazing! You've been holding out on me, little ballerina. You've got a lot of talent inside that young heart of yours." His energy was almost tangible, and she couldn't hold back the smile as she listened to his praise.

Chase told her to wait. He went to talk to the band. Jangling his keys, he said goodbye to them and turned to her, smiling again. His sandy hair fell recklessly across his forehead, and he swiped it back as he strolled toward the bar. Without a doubt, Chase was her first addiction.

CHAPTER 29

Regan asked Chase to drop her off at the ballet studio on the way home.
"Did you bring your stuff?" he asked.

"We have lockers. Besides, I promised my mom I would go at least once this week, and I'm not sure if I can stand it if she tells you no about the contract."

"You think she will?" He frowned, and that made Regan smile. He wanted her in the band. Her cheeks hurt from biting the insides to keep from smiling like a damned fool.

Releasing the sensitive insides of her mouth, she gave him a worried glance. "I really don't know. My mom is difficult to understand, and since Regan passed, she's even harder to read. If you tell her I'm at ballet it might help put her in a good mood. However, it could sway her toward Juilliard."

"Rain, forget what I said earlier about your voice. You were a hundred percent better today. If we can expect this kind of improvement every practice, then there is a chance you'll exceed Regan's talent."

His sincerity shocked her and struck a chord of jealousy within her inner ego. She knew she was being ridiculous. Isn't this what she wanted? "Are you sure it's not because my songwriting abilities are better than yours? I think you need me most to patch up all your bad lyrics," she teased.

He chuckled. "Ha, ha. Are you sure you're not Regan? You and that chip, Rain." His features sobered. "Hey, I'm sorry. That was totally inappropriate. I didn't know Regan long enough to even say that, and I shouldn't have even brought her up. It's just that her first impression was a lot like... She was such a firecracker." He smiled at her and tapped the steering wheel as they pulled into the dance studio parking lot. "I guess it just runs in the family, and so does great musical talent. Don't ever let some dope like me tell you that you can't sing, Rain. You were awesome today."

Regan didn't comment on his compliment, just got out of the car, biting her cheeks again as she tried to suppress her permanent grin. She gave him a wave. "Good luck with Rona!"

Delila wasn't surprised by Regan's improvement. Her soul had sung throughout many lives. Even when her voice wasn't the best, people surrounded her for soul-soothing music. She sang once as a priestess beneath tall gray stones as the moonlight poured in through a dome above. Her voice was ordinary, but her spirit felt her words as she pored over the scriptures through song. The congregation followed her endlessly through the many prayers she sang, and no one ever criticized her talent.

Delila's heart expanded when Regan was with Venery. Her ward was special to her as any spirit was to their soul watcher, but Venery was also Delila's soul complement. Seeing him together with Regan was a special treat and she supposed it was why Rodanian assigned Regan to her. Long ago, she'd had a choice of who she would watch. She supposed that was part of the process of elevation. Knowing what soul to choose and giving them the right protection and guidance. It was all part of the task of a soul watcher. Delila was happy with her assignment except for her own failings. Regan was a much younger soul than her, but the two really couldn't be compared, so different were their journeys. She admired Regan's young brilliance and strong drive to succeed, her passion to protect her family at all costs, and finally, her love of Venery. It made Regan that much more special that she should love so deeply. Maybe in time, Delila's ward could find happiness in a life with her soul mate, but for now, it was time to see her ward with someone else.

It was a full day. Fortunes, band practice, ballet, and now a date with Ratt. After sorting it all out on the phone, Regan wouldn't call her night a date with Jorge. When he pulled up in the driveway, she grabbed her money, lipstick, and house key and headed toward the door.

"Rain," her mother called out. "I want you back here straight after the concert. I know it's a weekend, but you're only fifteen, not twenty!"

Regan would have cancelled seeing the concert if her mother had asked. Rona had come to pick her up after ballet and taken her to their favorite haunt, Taco Bell. They both devoured too many soft tacos with soda. When they were almost ready to go, her mother pulled out a copy of the signed contract from her purse. Rain wanted to cry for the second time that day.

"What? Really? What changed your mind?" Regan threw out all her excited questions at once.

Rona laughed. "Far be it from me to stand in the way of anyone's dream, especially yours, Rain." Her hand came up and stroked Regan's forehead, pushing back a stray strawberry-blonde curl. "You're all I have left. And your handsome band partner and the other music people were so convincing. They somehow make me feel like Regan's still with us." She swirled her straw around her cup. "They seem to think you have what it takes."

Regan ignored the pang in her heart. This was all so bittersweet. "I can't believe it." She said, stunned. After a few moments, she let the excitement wash over her and she hopped a few times in her seat. "Thank you, thank you, thank you!"

It wasn't nearly enough to express what she was feeling, but she thought she conveyed her appreciation by the one hundred hugs she bestowed upon her mother between the fast-food joint and Jorge arriving. She loved the way her mother smiled when she embraced her. Regan was starting to see a very shiny new future for them both.

Jorge walked onto the porch as Regan came out to meet him.

"Hey, Rain," he said, shoving his hands into his jeans' pockets. "I thought I'd come in and say hello to your mom. You know, that way she knows you're not going out with an ax murderer."

Regan laughed at his joke but didn't return inside. "It's all right. She knows you're a friend."

Jorge shifted his weight from one leg to another. His sheepish grin told her that he was interested in her for more than just friends.

As if she'd heard she was being summoned, Rona opened the door. "Hello there! I'm Rona, Rain's mom."

Jorge beamed. "Hello, Mrs. Landry. Nice to meet you." Jorge moved forward and held out his hand.

Rona smiled and shook the offered hand. She didn't correct the Mrs. "Rain tells me there are four of you going tonight to see—Ratt?"

Jorge chuckled. "Yeah, they're cool. I'll have Rain back right afterward, so don't worry, she's in good hands."

Rona nodded. "Okay. You kids have fun. Rain, I'll leave the light on for you."

Regan had to admit that Jorge wasn't hard to look at, and if it had been an official date, it would have been a good one. His dark complexion, white, straight teeth, and berry-colored lips were the stuff of Ralph Macchio. Rain would be drooling. The sudden thought sobered her. As they walked through the doors of the Superdome, handing their tickets to the attendant, the four of them made their way through the crowd and to their seats. Jorge's friends were his age, which she calculated to be around nineteen. They were nice, and she made some small talk with them on the ride, not discussing her most exciting news. She wondered if she might share it with Jorge at some point during the evening. Would he be excited for her? He loved music, but the way he was looking at her said he might miss her when she went on tour. Regan shook herself, freeing the daydream. Jorge might be interested, but he also found her trying to drown herself a few weeks ago. They had shared a couple of short phone calls, and that was it. Besides, she was still only fifteen, and she was waiting for Chase.

Her inner dialogue went on, taking in the ripped jeans and Ratt t-shirts of the other concert goers. She gawked at a pair of pink-haired twins and the many mohawks and punk cuts in the crowd. Jorge's elbow touched her arm as he returned with sodas for both of them. His friends were talking among themselves, and though it was loud as they waited for the opening band, it was like they sat in a bubble of silence. She fidgeted with the puffed sleeves of her shirt. Her hair was adorned with a feathered headband, and she wondered if it was out of style already. She didn't notice anyone else wearing them. Leg warmers had gone out the year after she bought them, but she still wore them at dance practice.

Mrs. Danskin wasn't pleased with Regan's total lack of knowledge about dancing. If it hadn't been for the hour-long class, her day might have been one of the best in her life. What had Rain seen in dancing? Not only was Mrs. Danskin uptight, but the other dancers were snobs. She could only imagine what Juilliard would be like. She'd lagged behind the other girls between the instructor's commands, falling seconds behind each bend, turn, and swirl. She had great flexibility, and she seemed to know what she was doing when she did it, but the language was all Greek to her, and so was the routine. She'd hoped she could just go in, and it would all come to her, but no such luck. When it came time to work on her routine for competition, she'd faked a hurt ankle. There were only ten minutes left of class anyway. The frowning Mrs. Danskin nodded her head toward the dressing room, indicating she should change. Lucky for her, her mother arrived before class let out, and she was spared the potential meeting between Rona and Mrs. Danskin. Her mother had looked relieved as well.

Regan now turned to look at Jorge's profile as the opening act took the stage. He smiled at her, standing with the crowd around them, clapping as the band took the stage. She was relieved for the lack of conversation, and she reminded herself that she was waiting to grow up for Chase. She wondered what he might think if he saw her now with Jorge, a handsome guy, and how very grown-up she looked tonight. Would Chase be jealous? Was he on a date as well, with Emily maybe? Would he wait another three years for her until she turned eighteen? Not likely. Now, when Jorge smiled at her and gripped her hip as they all did the bump in a line and rocked their hands in the air, she smiled back, giving him a different look than she had before. Why shouldn't she have fun? Eighteen was a long way away, and it was a concert. She shouldn't be thinking of Chase. She had to live for now, and she planned to enjoy every minute.

CHAPTER 30

Regan was allowed to drive without an adult, but only during the day. It was a relief to her mother, who didn't have to drive her to dance lessons between shifts or ask favors of friends to pick her daughter up. It also made it easier to catch band practice and sometimes meet Jorge for sodas or a movie, though he always wanted to drive. She guessed it was a guy thing. She hadn't told her mother about her friendship with Zada, and since the day Chase had his palm read, she hadn't included him in any business she did with the seer, either.

Today Zada wore the green outfit that she'd first met her in, and she sported white splotches of paint over her shirt, pants, and face. A few specks hung in her frizzy curls, and a large dab of paint ran across her palm where she'd obviously forgotten that the trim in the kitchen was still wet.

"Are you giving this place a facelift?" Regan laughed.

Zada swung her hips back and forth as she walked toward her. The radio blared from the kitchen. "Oh yeah, chile. This place is moving up, and it's all thanks to you and that handsome devil Gustave."

Regan quirked a brow with one hand on her hip. "How do you know he's handsome?"

"Um-um-um. Any soul that smells like homemade biscuits with honey butter must look like a Greek god. Apollo, hear my prayer and reincarnate that man so I can eat him alive."

Regan couldn't suppress her laughter. Zada's large personality was always a breath of fresh air.

"Oh, I'm sorry, chile. You is too young to be hearing all that. But trust me, one day you will know what I'm talkin' about. A woman has needs. Thank you, Jesus, for the invention of the shower massager."

Regan laughed some more, even though the statement made her turn a little pink. "Zada, isn't it blasphemous to pray to Apollo for Gustave to reincarnate and then to Jesus to fulfill your womanly needs?"

Zada huffed. "You know what? I think you done grown up on me. What will I do when you become rich and famous? I'm done used to you comin' all up in here sayin' what's what."

Regan shook her head. "If I become rich and famous, you will, too, because I will tell everyone that you told me about my fame. Then, there will be a line out the door and across the Louisiana–Mississippi state line. People will be wanting you to tell them that they're going to be rich, too."

Zada shook her head back at Regan. "Now see here, that's gonna be a problem, cause you know that not everybody can be rich and most of us fools lead a simple life if we're good 'n lucky. Most people don't know what to do with wealth. Folks think it's a cure to their problems, but the truth is, it's a blessing to very few. The fact that you would be so charitable to your old friend Zada means you is blessed, chile." She took a breath, wiping the peeling paint from her palm. "And don't we know it." She looked up suddenly, winking at Regan.

She supposed Zada was referring to the gift of her current living, breathing existence. Months had passed, and the band had recorded a few of the songs on the album. The music was coming along, but she hadn't had any contact with Rain, and Gustave hadn't shown himself except to send souls for new clients. She came to Zada today to see if she could make another contact.

"Do you have the energy to contact Rain and Gustave today?"

Zada looked concerned for a moment. "Gustave is here every time I do a reading. That should be easy enough, but Rain...I haven't felt her since the last time you spoke to her here."

Regan twisted the bracelet Chase gave her around her wrist. "I know. I'm worried."

"Maybe she found the light. You haven't seen that devil of a spirit, Mark, either, so that's something."

Regan hadn't told Zada about her meeting Diablo in Jackson Square and thinking he was the actual fallen angel himself. Zada didn't remember much of the conversation during that particular seance, but she'd known something evil had spoken through her. It was what made her hesitant about trying to find Rain or Mark again. He had been scary enough, but on the heels of the Diablo spirit, Mark was icing on the devil's food cake.

"I know we've tried before, and she hasn't surfaced in a while, but let's try one more time, please. I promise I won't ask you again if she doesn't show this time." Regan hated to say this, but if Rain was lurking about like Regan had in her in-between state, then maybe she would take it as an SOS. If communications were severed, then she couldn't pass messages from beyond or seek help.

"Okay, chile, but not today. My energy is low from all this paintin', and besides, the full moon's on Wednesday night. It's always best to hold a séance the night of the full moon. And, if your little sister's still lurking about, she'll be here then to speak."

Regan nodded. She knew that Zada's gift tired her and that painting was also exhausting work. She held out her hand to Zada. "Give me your brush, and you can make us a sandwich. Is there a Coke in the fridge?"

"There is indeed, and one of'em's got your name on it." Zada's wide lips spread in a beaming smile. Her gold eyetooth gleamed in the light that shined through the window. She'd taken down all the blinds and drapes, and the natural sunlight lit up the dust motes, giving the room an ethereal feel. Regan half expected a fairy to appear on one of the lamp shades. She wished a simple fae would zap itself into her presence. Then she could ask him to finish the rest of the painting for Zada.

Regan left Zada's and drove to Chase's apartment. He told her he lived with his mom and sister, but she'd never met them. She supposed it was because he'd never invited her. She wanted to show him her car now that she was allowed to drive it again, though he'd seen it the first day she'd ever met him. She knew his address because of Guidry. He'd casually mentioned the apartment complex being right off Causeway Boulevard, and she'd heard of the popular complex. It was nice, too nice for Chase to afford on his own. The problem was, she didn't know which building or apartment number, but she did know his car.

She found the building where he'd parked and braved a knock on one of the downstairs units. No one answered. Most people worked nine to five, so she wasn't surprised. There were only eight units in each building, but after going through seven of them with no luck, she would soon be forced to give up. It was starting to feel like a bad idea anyway. Music blared from the parking lot, and Regan saw the flash of a red car pulling up next to Chase's Honda. She moved down the open corridor until she could see who'd arrived.

Her heart dropped into her stomach. It was Emily's car. She was with Chase, and they were smiling at each other. Without any warning, they started making out. It was like a red flag waving in front of her, and she was hot to race after it. Regan wanted to bang on the glass and tell them to stop. She wanted to punch Emily. Chase was hers.

She took a deep breath, calming her initial anger. The Regan she'd been, long before she became Rain, knew chasing after him wasn't the answer. She would push the raw jealousy down and lock it away. Chase wasn't hers. She was a fifteen-year-old living a pipe dream of becoming a rock star. Sure, she had a contract, but probably because Chase felt sorry for her losing her sister. He had no idea of the life she'd truly lost. Even she wasn't sure anymore. Parts of her were becoming tangled inside, and she could no longer remember all the details of the past. Regan sometimes wondered if she'd dreamt the whole thing and if she might really be Rain. Was this some sort of sick mental breakdown? Was she only imagining she was Regan trapped in Rain's body?

Zada was her only true grip on reality. She knew who Regan had been and how she was now someone else, but they didn't talk about it much, and the details of how it all began were seeping into the gaps between memories. She remembered that Gustave brought her messages, but she couldn't remember how they'd become acquainted or exactly what had happened to her between her last moments as Regan and becoming Rain. It was probably best if she forgot everything, most of all that Chase was meant to be her soulmate. She was still half a child. In order for her to become the adult she wanted to be, she needed to let go of the past.

Slamming the door to her Mustang and revving the engine, Regan peeled out of the lot and headed to the nearest gas station. She needed to call a friend.

CHAPTER 31

Delila had watched Regan as she painted for Zada. The two laughed together while the music played popular songs from a small kitchen radio. Her ward was happy. Regan still worried about Rain's soul and Mark lurking in the shadows, but he wasn't there at present. Since Regan had spoken with him about her sister's death, he'd backed off. He was no longer raging at her ward but trying to share her energy. As if he were a sailor lost at sea, he longed for the warmth of what he thought was his lost love.

Delila let her energy sail forward and into the hazy gray sky. Raindrops spattered the hot pavement and steam rolled up off the streets as Delila left the crescent city to journey between worlds. She found herself floating above a field of wheat with ice-tipped mountains in the distance and a perfect blue sky overhead. It was Rodanian's existence, or what she perceived as his home. As she floated through stone walls and past billowing white curtains, she wondered why he kept up the pretense of a human life. Perhaps it grounded him or kept him in tune with his soul watchers and their living wards. She summoned Rodanian as she approached his domicile.

"You wanted to see me?" He asked from his intricately carved wooden chair. He wasn't ostentatious, but she remembered asking him about his presence on this plane and if he could, why didn't he surround himself with the best.

He'd returned her question with, "What is the best?"

She'd stopped asking insignificant questions after that and focused on the queries that mattered.

The problem she couldn't solve needed to be addressed. "Your Grace, I am trying to protect my ward, but her sister's soul still lingers. There's been no call to the light." Delila didn't know this as fact, but she waited for answers.

"She is not your ward. Why do you bother me with such inquiries?"

Delila worried she was pushing her spirit guide's patience, but she felt validated. "Some nights past, a demon loomed over Luna's form like a wolf drooling over an injured dove. She dreamed of her sister's soul trapped between worlds. If I hadn't interfered, she may have astral projected and been lost to us. Rain must find the light."

"I see," his tone was contemplative. "Is this all that concerns you?"

Delila decided to push the envelope. "The soul who drowned with Luna still loiters about. At first, I worried about his angry energy, but I have shielded her well. I feel like his unseen energy is leeching hers. How can I protect my ward and find her success with these beings lingering about?"

"There are always obstacles, Delila. Are you so weary of your soul watching time?" He sounded like a concerned father, and in a way, he was.

"No, I just ask that some solution is found for these souls who linger." She sounded like an embodied soul complaining about the homeless. Now that she was having this conversation, she felt selfish and petty. Who knew what reality Mark or Rain would fall into if Rodanian got involved? Sometimes, souls had to digress to elevate their energy. Even a soul as aged as Delila could make mistakes, but for those, she must pay.

"Yes, a solution. That is a grand idea for you to work on. Now go back to your ward. I sense she has need of you."

"But, Your Grace, I can't guide the souls in question, and no one knows how to entirely disengage the demons of that world. They're older than we are and don't have souls." In truth, Delila knew the demons served a purpose of sorts. Like vultures of carnage, they cleaned up the spirit world of too many souls. She didn't know exactly what happened when a body's energy was drained, but she believed the souls eventually returned to the Guff. The great hall was crowded with spirits waiting to return to the living. It might be that God needed a buffer between the living world, the Guff, and its many levels of the hereafter. Still, she would like to know a demon's purpose, black, evil things that they were.

Rodanian sighed. "Delila, all is as it's meant to be. Go forth and guide. Tend to your business so that your time with Luna is a fruitful one. Already she has grown and changed."

In a blink of an eye, Delila found herself sitting on a bench at the zoo. She watched Regan lean over the rail, tossing breadcrumbs into the bayou surrounding the crocodile enclosure. Jorge held onto her waist, but she had her foot wedged along the rungs of the gate she stood on. She slipped momentarily and Jorge caught her to him. Regan squealed, then laughed. The young couple stood facing one another now. Jorge leaned down to kiss Regan, and at the last minute, her ward turned her head and looked away, making a soft excuse. Delila felt her ward's energy, full of quelled excitement and regret. It was Chase she couldn't put away from her heart. It was stopping Regan from falling in love with Jorge.

Delila wanted her ward to be happy and grounded in this world. Letting go of something that couldn't happen and embracing something that could materialize was the first step in helping Regan. Delila pushed warm currents of loving thoughts, happiness in a solid future and the possibilities of love. A life with a soul complement could be very satisfying.

Jorge tilted Regan's chin up and made her look into his eyes. Delila heard the words, even though they were spoken softly and carried away on the wind. "I love you, Rain. I want to be with you. You don't have to sleep with me. That's not what I want from you. I want more for us. I want a future, and I'm willing to wait, but I need to hear you say you want me too."

Regan leaned into Jorge's taller figure, wrapping her hands around him and letting him kiss her. Delila felt a surge of hope, then as a cloud covered the sun, something dark and dank eclipsed her emotions. She smelled something burning, like eggs that had been left to boil too long.

"Ah, young love." The entity beside her purred with mischief.

Delila didn't turn to look, for fear she might be turned to stone, or greater yet, singed to a crisp. Had Rodanian turned her out? Was this to be her final mission? All those lives she'd endured to end like this.

"It's been an eternity since I've seen you. To what do I owe the not-so-pleasurable experience?" She wasn't sure why she baited him, but if this was her last sojourn, she wasn't going down without a fight. He wasn't taking her soul easily. Fear struck her core. Maybe he was here for Regan. Delila knew he was looking for Rain's soul when he crashed the séance. Regan was a good spirit and hadn't taken her own life. She was protected amongst the living. *This is all my fault.*

The devil purred, "Yes, it has been quite some time. How is my old friend Rodanian? He was never one to grant my requests. Do tell me, how's the old man treating you?"

Lucifer had somehow seen Delila's flight to the other world. She was sure there wasn't much that the devil missed, but why was he focused on her comings and goings?

She kept her features blank and tried to force her energy into a calm state. Demons were like wolves, instigated by the chase. "He's the same. Time does not change one of his status, nor yours."

"I do rather think we could help each other out here. You need to protect Luna, and I need to find Rain. We all need the same things to happen to accomplish our desired tasks. Why don't you give me Rain, and we can both go our separate ways?"

Delila looked at him incredulously. "Rain is not my soul to give, and even if she were, I'm a guardian, which you well know."

He arched a fine brow of the gorgeous face he'd glossed himself with for this appearance. A wicked smile spread at what must surely be the horror etched across her shadowy features.

"Come now. You gave her body to your ward. A power I did not know soul watchers of your stature possessed, but now that I see the possibilities, you and I could share quite an existence."

She was immune to his charms. Not many were, but as he slithered through the world of the living and the world in-between, souls couldn't resist his bidding. She could. The many lives that she'd soul-watched had granted her the keen ability to ward off evil, at least for her own soul.

"That was not my gift. That was my blunder, as I'm sure you well know." She paused as her spirit went on an internal search for answers. "Why are you here? Why don't you go and get the soul you seek without needling me? Better yet, why am I necessary in your scheme?"

"Ah, you do not know this little secret, but I will share it with you since we are such old acquaintances." He paused to chuckle at her distaste. "I cannot see the pure of heart. I can only see the souls who elude the light or are lit with wickedness."

"So, you could find Regan because she shunned the light of God, but you can't find Rain, who is a suicide and hasn't been offered guidance?"

The devil shrugged. "I'm not all-powerful. Rain may be a suicide, but she hasn't been offered the light. Until she rejects God, she is invisible to me."

This was good to know. Rain was safe as long as she avoided the light.

"What if she goes into the light?"

"As a child of God and tricked by an angel, she will spend a life repenting and be put back into the rotation. She is a young morsel of a soul, so malleable. You can see why I want her to reject the other team?"

Delila would have laughed if the topic wasn't so grim. She'd asked Rodanian to show Rain the light, not knowing the wolf of evil waited for his virgin prey.

"It's out of my hands. I've asked Rodanian, and he has refused."

"Has he?" The curious lilt in Lucifer's tone divulged his disbelief.

Delila could tell he wasn't buying any of it. She decided to divert his interest in Rain. "What about Mark, the boy who…"

"His soul is damned. Not for all eternity, since he, too, was duped by your blundering mess, but he will sit out several rotations with me. It's just a matter of time before he's offered a choice, and I think once he's found by my colleagues, he will scamper to the protection of God. It's my favorite part, dragging them screaming down to the bowels of Hell."

His grating laughter was unnerving. Before Regan's initial death, Delila had only seen his presence once before, long ago. She'd never seen him without his glamour and was thankful that she couldn't see his true evil presence now.

"Stay away from my ward. She's done nothing wrong and has been awarded this life by Rodanian. You wouldn't want to cross him."

The devil sneered at her warning, repeating her words in a mocking taunt. "Rodanian doesn't scare me." His eyes flashed brilliant orange-red embers, then cooled to pools of blackened tar. "Forget I asked," he purred. "I'll have her soul. I'll have all of their souls eventually, and possibly yours too. But I won't absorb you just now. I may have need of your powers later. My how the mighty have fallen."

Delila tried not to gasp as she saw Mark's spirit floating in their direction. He was eternally drawn to Regan's existence, and even as she held onto Jorge, Mark pursued her energy. Sorrow turned to anger, and Mark raged against the couple with all his might, but his rant was in vain. Exhausted, he hung his head in sorrow, beaten by the void between the unembodied and living. The sun took that moment to peer beneath the clouds, sparkling down upon his luminous spirit. He let out a harrowing wail of loss and defeat, then suddenly stopped, staring up into the white-hot sunlight. As if giving up his quest, he threw his arms up and soared into the light. As his soul began to disappear, black demons chased after him, biting at his heels and tearing at his limbs. As Lucifer had promised, they dragged him kicking and screeching into the watery depths of the crocodile preserve. Delila was sure that Mark's soul was now much deeper than the man-made bayou surrounding the enclosure, but she didn't allow herself to ponder his fate. She was guilty, but Mark had made the choice to take Regan's and his own life. Delila spread her wings protectively around the young couple holding hands against the railing of the bayou.

With a snap of his fingers, Lucifer's smiling beautiful face disappeared. Delila looked out across the brown surface of the murky water as a shiver ran through her core. Her attention whipped back to the railing. She'd been distracted, and her ward was suddenly elsewhere. The seasoned guardian used her energy to track Regan and Jorge. Luckily, after the heat they'd shared in their kiss, they weren't in the back of Jorge's car, and Delila hadn't missed an opportunity to guide. Instead, they had walked hand-in-hand a short distance away to the Imax theater. She remembered Jorge's promise to wait until Regan was ready, but he was mortal, and mortals made mistakes.

Mark's spirit was no longer present. The devil had taken care of one plight, but Delila would still have to find a way to protect Regan from the black demon who stalked her until Rain found the light. The devil was wrong. Delila didn't have the ability to offer up souls to anyone. She was summoned by the light to meet the departed, not the other way around, but she was sure the prince of darkness knew this. Why was he toying with her? Maybe it was all for his unearthly amusement since he knew where to find Regan and he probably knew Mark's soul was loitering nearby. He couldn't have known Regan was about to share her first kiss with Jorge, but knowing that the event would drive Mark to react in anger was central to his location and timing.

Delila couldn't hold back her gloomy energy, so she took a breather from Regan and lingered outside as the movie played inside of the booming Imax. The sweeping panoramas of the Grand Canyon were breathtaking, but her focus was somewhere else. She'd made a mistake, and Mark had to pay for the actions not taken to protect her ward, but that didn't excuse his alternate reaction. He had lived more than a few lives, making similar missteps over his fascination with Luna's spirit. Delila hoped that his absence from the living would separate their rotation and give her ward a reprieve from his stalking for at least a few life cycles.

She should be relieved that her ward discovered Chase with Emily. The blonde was still playing with the band at the bar, and there was talk that she might go on the road as a back-up singer. The guardian should be glad for any degree of separation between Regan and Chase. Didn't all men have a few life experiences before settling down? Chase's relationship with Emily was forcing Regan to look at other options for happiness. A life with a soulmate should be God's greatest gift, but it wasn't all there was to living, and there were complications with Regan being underage for the next three years. Delila sensed a greater cause inside of Emily's aspiring energy. The young woman knew the band was going somewhere, and she didn't want to be left behind. Chase might be using Emily as a buffer for his attraction to Rain, but even these small sins had their consequences.

CHAPTER 32

Zada opened the door for Regan, looking up at the full moon. Her eyes scanned the clear night sky then landed where Jorge stood.

"You didn't tell me you was bringing guests. Who's this handsome young man?"

Regan smiled at Zada. She loved the way she accepted Jorge right away. Louisiana was an odd place. There weren't a lot of Hispanics, and though times were changing, black and white people alike were sometimes hostile toward their budding friendship.

"This is Jorge. I wanted him to meet you."

"Is he joining us for the séance?"

Jorge held up his hands. "What? Séance? You gotta be kiddin' me." His smile didn't hide his comic interest. "Like ooh-ee-ooh?"

Regan rolled her eyes. "Act your age, Jorge. I told you Zada has a gift."

Jorge blanched, "I thought you meant she was a healer or something. I didn't know we were all going to hold hands and talk to the dead."

Regan looked at Zada apologetically then let out a breath, pointing to the couch, she said, "Sit. We'll be out in fifteen minutes. Watch Scooby-Doo and I'll come and get you when it's all over."

Jorge shrugged. "Sorry, I didn't mean to be rude. I was surprised, that's all." He sat down with a thud, looking over to Zada. "No disrespect, Ma'am."

Zada sniffed and lifted her chin. "None taken." She flipped on the television. "I ain't got no cable. You'll have to make do with the Family Feud."

"Ouch." Regan chuckled as she followed Zada down the hall. She looked back over her shoulder to see Jorge turning the old-style knob. Nothing but static buzzed across the screen.

Hopefully, they would make contact with Rain. Zada performed her usual ritual, brushing the sage at the empty air, then burning a solitary leaf in the smudge tray. Regan loved the smell. It reminded her of a cool fall day when the neighbors were burning leaves. It made her think of the new school year, new school clothes, and a chance at a new beginning. Fresh starts were usually thought about in spring, but she associated them with the fall. She watched as the leaf went from green to red to orange and then black as the edges curled and burnt to ash in the clay dish.

Zada placed her hands on the round crystal ball and instantly began to hum. Her head rolled back, and she called out to Rain.

"Something's not right. It feels empty. The room is vacant of voices. Usually, there are so many, but…" Zada hesitated. "There's one." Her eyes rolled up, and all Regan could see were the whites of the seer's eyes. "That's right, my lovely. Do you remember me? My how you have changed. I have someone with me you might remember."

A piercing scream rolled out of Zada that was not her own. "Regan, help me. Don't let him do this. It wasn't planned. I'm sorry." The voice cried. At first, she thought it was Rain, but as the words tumbled out, she realized with almost as much horror that it was Mark. "He has me, Regan. I found the light, but as I reached for it, his demons attacked me. Help me, please." His cry was jagged as he sobbed through Zada.

Regan was speechless. What could she say? There was no comforting dialogue for a soul pinched and taken to Hell.

The smooth voice of the devilish spirit returned. Zada's head turned to the side with a slow grin as she spoke to Mark's damned soul. "Now, now, Marcus. You'll fit in here so nicely. We love murder-suicides. They're one of our delicacies. So delicious."

"Why are you doing this?" Regan felt tears pool in her eyes. "Stop! He didn't mean to. It was half my fault that he did what he did."

Zada's head snapped toward her. "Indeed. I do believe man's fall from grace was at Eve's hand. What sweet piece of fruit did you offer?" Regan could see a smoky outline of Diablo as he fashioned himself over Zada's form. His gorgeous face was now visible to her, and she watched him tilt his head in delight. Her eyes focused on his handsome hologram.

"What do you want?" Regan hated the way her voice quivered.

"I want your eternal soul, but I will settle for Rain's. Suicides have a special place in my—" His hand went to his heart, but then slid lower grabbing at his crotch. "Oh, don't worry, my sweet. She will enjoy every minute of my ardent attention." He ran the tip of his pointed tongue over his full lips. "I remember how much you loved my touch."

Visions fluttered through her mind of another time and place. Dreams she'd forgotten exploded with illicit force, causing her nipples to harden and her breath to catch. She tried to stop the visions flickering through her head. She'd never done these things with anyone. She tried to remind herself these were just images he used to taunt and tease his victims. She had free will. He could not take what was not given, could he?

"Stop!" she yelled, standing tall.

"Come out, come out wherever you are. Rain Landry, you are hereby summoned to come and speak to your sister. The sister who has usurped your body and has illicit plans to trade you to the devil." His cackle was like that of the movies as he rocked back and forth, pointing his finger at her.

"So, you are the devil. You admit it!"

Lucifer cackled as he raised his arms. "Admit it? I writhe in it! I am king of the damned."

Regan began to panic. "Zada, call my guardian angel. I don't know if she is still with me, but I need her help. We need her help!"

Again, the devil shook with laughter, but then he straightened with a mischievous grin. "Fuck the rules. The angel had her way, now I will have mine. If I can't find Rain, I'll have you instead."

"No." Regan shook her head in confusion. Could he do that? Where was her angel? She needed Zada to snap out of it. The last thing she wanted was for Rain to appear now.

"Wait! I'm here," Rain's desperate voice chimed in. Zada's eyes were wide. She looked like a frightened child as her lower lip trembled. "If you have to take someone's soul, take mine. Regan is a good person. She's going to be someone and make a difference in the world, and she needs to care for our mother. I was weak. I gave it all up because I was too scared to live."

"No!" Regan screamed. "Rain, don't do this. You can have your body back. I'll ask the angel. She'll make it happen." Her hands grasped the silk-covered table, wrinkling its folds in her fist.

"It's too late, Regan. I don't want my life back. I want you to have it. You have so much talent, and I know now that you were meant to be with Chase."

Regan reached out to the seer and grabbed her hand. "Zada, call my angel, call God, call anyone. This can't happen to Rain!"

Zada's lips were moving as she chanted in another language. She'd told Regan on a previous occasion that she spoke in tongues, and there wasn't a way to learn its meaning. With a deep intake of breath, she straightened her shoulders and lifted her arms to the ceiling. A guttural wail escaped her as her black, weathered fingers fluttered above her head.

"Rodanian."

Regan wasn't sure whose voice came through Zada, but someone else was with them.

Regan's brow furrowed. "Who's Rodanian?"

Rain's voice lilted like wind chimes in the breeze of a summer's day. "Regan, I see the light. It's so beautiful. Do you see it?" Rain's voice was filled with awe. Tears dripped down Zada's cheeks. "It's like nothing I've ever seen, Regan. Do you see it?"

Regan felt her heart pound with adrenaline. "Rain, run to the light. Don't you dare run away. Go into the light, and I will find you again, in time. I promise."

"Regan, I'm scared."

"I know, Rain, but I can't take you. You have to do this by yourself. I need to stay here and take care of Mom, but I promise we will all be together again." She paused as images of her life with Rain flashed through her mind. Memories of them holding hands on Easter Sunday in their new dresses, opening gifts on Christmas morning, riding in the car, and singing to the radio together. With reluctance, she urged her sister. "Don't miss your ride, Rain. It'll be a great one." Zada wrung her hands together and chewed at her lower lip as Rain had always done when she was nervous. "Please, do it for me, Rain."

Delila watched as Rain ascended into the light, and her connection to the in-between and living world was severed. She even saw Mary Magdalene with her bright peach-colored wings embrace Rain's soul, hissing at Lucifer's minions as their sulfuric mists drew near.

Rodanian was a formidable presence. Bearing wings made of shining metal, he was armed for battle. To think that two young girls had almost brought about a war between Heaven and Hell today was significant. Both souls were young, living far fewer lives than Delila or Rodanian. Something about the relationship between them and the sacrifice they were willing to make bonded the young women with an energy unlike any other she'd ever known. Their love connected them to their mother, and each was committed to protecting the other. The three had cycled through lives together many times, and Delila was certain they would again. However, she admitted there was knowledge she did not possess. The workings of the soul's energy or how, threaded together, they could build kingdoms or tear through the fabric of existence to forge new destinies, was beyond her comprehension. Maybe a similar occasion split the fabric of paradise, thus changing the cycle of man's presence in the world forever.

Lucifer's handsome face crumpled as he hissed Rodanian's name.

Metal feathers raked against one another, sounding like a sword being drawn from its sheath. Rodanian looked fit for the task. "You know the rules." His energy flowed in a steady stream, thumping like the beat of a drum on the field before a medieval battle. Delila felt her own energy waver, then intensify. If it came to a test of wills, she knew what side she championed. Spreading her own wings, she flanked Rodanian. A trumpet sounded, and in a sudden flutter of guardian wings, the walls of the small home disappeared and there were angels standing at attention for miles.

The devil spread his massive, black, harrowing wings with a last, lingering hiss, then flapped them closed with a great clap of thunder. "Another day, boys."

He summoned his minions as they scrambled around him, howling their disappointment. As if a switch flipped on, there was bright light. Black ashes swirled around them and the smell of boiled eggs wafted in their wake.

"Rain was a suicide," Delila said, her voice quivering from the rush of energy that had come and gone so quickly. She tried to calm her inner power, assuring herself the danger was over.

"Not originally, but yes, when her fate was displaced, she sought to correct her own path," Rodanian replied.

Guilt for her one mistake still haunted Delila. "Still, it is a mortal sin, and we are given free will."

Rodanian cleared his throat as if he were a reverend getting ready to give a sermon to his wayward flock. She was his wayward lamb at the moment, trying to get back into his good graces. Like all souls, no matter what elevated level, she needed to learn to progress through the hierarchy of existence.

His eyes turned soft as he explained. "She was willing to sacrifice herself to save her sister. She accepted the light in the end, and that's all that matters for now. Besides, all souls have given up at one time. It's not a fair sentence to be damned for eternity. Suicide is the soul's struggle to find meaning. The only way Lucifer can snatch a soul is if the light is rejected, and only then if he is present at the time of the rejection."

"What is his interest in this pair of souls? They are young. They haven't lived enough lives."

"Not everything is known to me, Delila. We are special in our own tasks. My mission is to guide you as you protect your ward. Regan would have given her soul today, and if I had not come, I might have lost all of you. Don't discount your own value in this situation." And with the clattering of his wings snapping shut, he was gone.

Delila stood again in the seer's small room, charged with fear, anxiety, and relief. The guardian waved her hand before the seer's face, passing on a vision of Rain's assent so that she would remember that Rain was saved. The rest would be forgotten as soon as the trance was over. With a breath of wind, the seer's tears were dried, and she awoke with a radiant smile.

Regan gripped Zada's hand, shaking it. "Zada, Zada. What happened? Tell me what happened to Rain."

The doorknob rattled behind them and Jorge burst through. "What's wrong? I heard a scream and a man's voice." He looked confused when he only saw the two of them.

There had been a lot of voices in the small room, but all had come through Zada. Regan didn't want to explain right now. She wanted Zada to tell her what happened to Rain.

A bright smile spread across the seer's face. "Oh chile, it was the most beautiful vision I've ever had. I've heard of such occurrences, but I've never seen the light." Zada clapped her hands together, putting them both to her lips as she sighed expressively then shook her head. Fresh tears of joy slid down her cheeks. For a moment she was speechless, clearly overwhelmed.

Regan's heart stilled. Zada hadn't confirmed it yet, but with the look on her face and the few words she'd said, Regan was almost certain Rain had made it.

"Wait, who is Rodanian?" It was a foreign name to her, and she was sure it wasn't her angel. It sounded male, and her angel was decisively feminine.

Zada looked confused. "I don't remember a Rodanian, but in the light was a glorious young vision of yourself. She was embraced by an angel with peach wings. I could not see its face, but with such loving energy, I am sure it was the most beautiful angel in heaven." Leave it to Zada to conjure an angel with a bright color scheme.

Regan smiled, but could no longer hold back her tears. "She's safe." Collapsing back into the chair, her shoulders shook with relief.

Jorge ran his warm hand over her shoulders, assuring her that everything would be okay. Lost in the aftermath, she was impressed that he didn't solicit clarification of what had happened. Standing on wobbly legs, she approached Zada, who stood. Regan embraced her friend tightly.

"Thank you. I'm forever in your debt."

Zada squeezed her back, hard. "You don't owe me a thing, chile. That's what friends do. They help each other, and lord knows you and Gustave have sure helped ol' Zada. I'm planning on buying my first car." Her warm laughter shook their bodies, and Regan pulled back to assess her friend. Zada was a part of her chosen family now, and she knew in her heart they would always share a bond. There was comfort in knowing they would continue to see each other after this closure with her past. They had journeyed too far together to part ways. She was free to be herself now, and that meant assuming her identity as Rain.

She turned to Jorge, smiling. "Everything's okay. I'll explain later."

Zada's warm voice broke in behind them. "You kids go have fun. I think these old bones need to rest."

Regan could see how heavy the session had been. Zada's gift took a toll on her. Each session was draining, and this one was no exception. Regan wondered if the gift to channel energy was shortening the older woman's life, but the smile on the seer's face said it was all worth it. Regan wished she could have seen everything through Zada's eyes.

"Okay, is there anything we can help you with before we go?"

"No chile. I'll be okay. I just need to lie down a bit."

"Zada," Regan's voice called back in question.

The older woman wrapped a crocheted afghan around her shoulders with a shiver. Regan was perplexed. The room must have been seventy-five degrees. "Yes, Rain?"

"What about Gustave? Will he find the light? He has helped us, too. Shouldn't that count for something?"

Zada shook her head. "I don't know, chile. God has a plan for everyone. I didn't see our ol' friend, Gustave, today. I'll ask him how he's doing next time he calls." The seer smiled gently. Regan knew she understood her concern. If it was possible to be friends with someone of the spirit world, Gustave had become their best.

She smiled back at Zada as Jorge clasped her hand in his. She knew he was ready to leave. "Tell him I said hello and tell him about—" She'd almost said Rain. That would have been hard to explain to Jorge who only knew her as *Rain*. "—about my sister."

Zada nodded. "I will. Now go on and be young. It doesn't last forever. When you're my age, you'll understand. Nothing lasts long, so don't look over your shoulder. Soon, it'll all be gone."

CHAPTER 33

I t had been three grueling months of practicing with the band, and school had started again. At least she was now a sophomore. Regan was meeting with a tutor twice a week to prepare for when they started touring. Having a tutor was way more difficult than attending Louisiana public school. If they didn't go on tour before May, she would attend the rest of the year at Bonne Fete High. The album would be released next month, and radio stations across the nation were being petitioned to push "Walk on Water" across the airwaves.

She'd agreed to finish out her year of dance and could now drive herself to the additional practices that Mrs. Danskin said she needed to catch up. She was admittedly better, and she actually enjoyed the exercise, but it was more of a hobby for her. The producers had given her mother an advance, and it seemed to take care of any financial concerns Rona had. The band's accountant told them they could write the dance lessons off on their taxes as performance training. Apparently, Regan was supposed to dance and sing at the same time.

She was meeting with a clothing designer today after the walk-through with a choreographer for the video they planned to shoot next week. *Great, more dancing.* Regan hadn't seen Chase very often since the day he'd been with Emily at his apartment. He showed up for band practice twice a week but left with Emily right after. Regan tried to focus on her relationship with Jorge and ignore the shattering of her heart. She didn't see what was so great about Emily besides her blonde hair and large breasts, but then again, Regan was biased. She tried to suck it up and hide her feelings since Chase and Emily had become an item. There weren't many opportunities to pretend she had a chance with him, and as the band's popularity grew, she could only hope that Chase's connection to Emily would be severed by the weight of other, more glamorous, interests. Regan had a few years to grow up before she was legally old enough for him to express his affection. She understood the hurdles they faced, but she would like to know he at least thought about her.

Rona rode in the Mustang with her to the Crescent City. Regan didn't need a chaperone, but it was her mother's day off, and she needed to see the environment Regan was submerged in. It wasn't that her mother was smothering her. Rona worked too many hours, and Regan had a lot of free time without parental guidance. She felt the underlying fear her mother carried since losing a daughter. It was for this reason that Regan hadn't complained about her mother tagging along. She had grown a lot closer to Rona since the body switch. She still remembered that she was Regan inside, but she didn't remember the things from the past that separated her old existence from her new one. Her long, strawberry-blonde hair was familiar to her now, a stark contrast to her former chocolate tresses. Her mother noticed a slight difference in the color of her eyes but had written it off to teen hormones and growth. Regan's body was two inches shorter now, which probably made her a better ballerina, but the film director wasn't pleased with her petite stature.

"She's going to look like a Smurf. She's too short! And this blue dress.... Who's the costume designer?"

"Hanna," the choreographer called out.

"Tell Hanna to switch colors, show a lot of midriff and hike up the slits on the side to make her legs look longer."

Regan watched her mother jump to her feet with the scowl of a Pitbull on her face. "No, sir! She is just fifteen. I think those costumes are skimpy enough."

The director looked at her with distaste. "I guess you're the mother?"

"Damn straight, I'm the mother, and I have the final say in what she can or can't wear. It's in our contract." Rona held her shoulders back in a demanding stance. Her chin jutted out, challenging the director to defy her words.

"Look, Mrs. Landry. I'm not trying to sell your daughter into the sex trade, but she's a mere five-two. That may be great for a ballerina, but on camera, she's going to look like a kid. Hell, she is a kid, but for the purpose of promoting this song, we need her to look a bit older and taller." He emphasized the last word. "I promise you we will keep it clean. MTV wouldn't allow anything that belongs on Cinemax. So, can you trust me on this? If you can't live with the final product, we won't air it." He waited for

Rona to agree, but she stood there, staring at the producer's face as if she was sizing up whether to believe him or not. "I promise."

"It's Ms. Landry. I'm divorced." Without another word, she went back to her seat and watched Regan go through the steps again. The routine was pretty simple. Regan had mastered more complex choreography over the past few months and was grateful that her memories as Rain had helped her to learn the steps. Mrs. Danskin complained that she wasn't as good as before and was convinced it was some psychosomatic block that Rain was having due to the loss of her sister. *Maybe it was.*

Regan would never get over losing Rain, but she'd finally accepted being her. To do otherwise was a sign of disrespect for the second chance she was given. Rain's gift was immeasurable. Regan would get to live out the life she'd been meant to live and now had three extra years to prepare. The film director might have been put off by her age, but she knew that her youth was part of the reason the producer had picked her. There were a handful of teen musicians on the rise. Society wanted to be young and celebrate youth. With "Like a Virgin" topping the charts and shows like Star Search turning unknowns into celebrities, there was a new road ahead, and her age was just right. It would give her time to train and grow into the megastar she wanted to be. She'd already altered Chase's songs and written three more of her own. "Walk on Water" was the title of the album and the anchor of their first debut, but the producer was clamoring over the new songs and touting their future success. It made her almost completely happy, except for the loss of her sister and Chase's friendship. She missed them both terribly.

When Emily appeared in a skimpy red leotard and high-heeled dance shoes, Regan missed a step and was chastised by the instructor.

"What's wrong? You had it perfect before. Take a break. We resume in five." Tossing his hands in the air, the choreographer, who introduced himself as Antoine, left bristling.

Emily smirked and waved. Regan ignored her. They hadn't spoken to each other since the argument Emily had with Rain at the initial audition. Regan didn't remember being there, but through Rain's irritated recollection, she knew Emily had used her. She wasn't sure if it was that day that irked her or the nettling anxiety she felt because she never liked Emily anyway. The popular blonde had always been a suck-up.

Regan looked at Emily, now stretching as she smiled at Chase suggestively. "And she still is," Regan said under her breath. Emily had always wanted whoever Regan was into. She supposed it went back to Regan sleeping with Emily's boyfriend. She hadn't known he was Emily's until afterward, but she'd paid for that mistake the hard way, and she supposed Emily never forgave her. Turnabout was fair play, and Chase was the payback, but the story wasn't over yet. Besides, Emily was putting on weight. She wasn't fat by any means, but she was losing that tits-on-a-stick look that she'd had back in high school. She was in college now, so Regan supposed it was the freshman fifteen that people always talked about. Apparently, Chase didn't mind. Regan watched as he slid up behind Emily, embracing her and nuzzling her neck. As if sensing Regan's stare, he looked up, meeting her gaze. *Damn.* She hadn't wanted him to see her gawking at them like a lovesick puppy. It wasn't her style.

Antoine stepped into her line of sight, blocking out Chase's expression before she could discern it. "Girl, where is your head? I've been talking to you for two minutes. Are you deaf, or are you ignoring me?"

Regan shook out her arms and rolled her neck. "Sorry, I didn't hear you. There's so much noise in here. Too much going on," she said, feeling lame.

They started going over the routine again, but they were quickly interrupted by Emily.

"Hel-lo!" she called to Antoine, waving. "The producer said I should get with you for training."

Antoine's smile didn't meet his eyes. "You must be Emily." He looked back at Regan and shrugged his shoulders. "Okay, get behind Rain. You can follow her lead."

Regan wanted to ask questions but knew it would make her look as petty as she felt. She couldn't have Chase, so she needed to set aside her animosity and keep things on a professional level with him. She couldn't ask him, "What the hell do you see in her?" She didn't hide her smile as she stretched out her arms, blocking Emily's view. She performed the movement quickly and perfectly, leaving no time for Emily to catch up.

Antoine nodded his approval to Rain. "Again."

She could see their reflection in the studio mirror. Emily stumbled around and fell, whining about the pace being too fast. "If you could just walk me through it first, then it would be easier to learn. I used to be captain of the dance team."

"Really?" Antoine looked surprised. "Well, this isn't high school, sweetheart. This will be on MTV, and if you can't cut it, there is a line of fresh ladies out the door waiting to take your place." He snapped his fingers as his head moved from side to side. His short-cropped hair against his perfectly shaped head showed off aquiline features. His black complexion was cocoa butter smooth, and Regan guessed him to be around Chase's age. He knew how to dance and had a wicked sense of humor. He didn't seem to care for Emily, and that was one more reason that Regan thought he was spectacular.

Emily huffed, and he started the count again. Regan added three extra moves at the end, and he clapped his hands together, yelling, "Stop!"

Oops. Maybe that was too much. Regan really liked the routine so far, but it was missing something. She should have asked before ad-libbing. Now she'd probably gotten on his bad side as well.

"Do that again." There wasn't a trace of humor in his voice, and she wasn't sure if it was a request or a dare.

She decided to entertain them, repeating the entire choreography, plus her added steps, then she tagged on an extra three movements that she felt were a perfect ending.

"I like it." Antoine smiled broadly. "I thought you were kind of an odd choice for this video at first, but now I can see why they chose you." He paused, doing a little spin with a pose, creating a frame around his face with his hands. "Girl's got talent."

Emily rolled her eyes, looking weary.

Antoine snorted. "You," he pointed to Emily." "Take fifteen. You," he pointed to Regan. "Show me that again. I want it in the video."

CHAPTER 34

She loved the outfit, but after the seamstress pinned her dress for the costume designer, and Regan twirled around in excitement, she couldn't help but notice the frown on her mother's face.

"It's okay, mom. I promise it'll all be great."

Her mother smiled from a nearby seat. "Let's hope so. I'd hate for the producer to have to throw the entire video out because your skirt was too short."

The seamstress approached Regan, adjusting the dress and pinning the hem longer. The fair woman looked back at Rona for approval. She nodded and Regan smiled. Her mother was like a bear hovering over a new cub.

The final fitting was for a long white evening gown. Regan couldn't fathom what part of the video it was in since there was no way she could dance in it. When they zipped her up, she could barely walk.

Emily complained from the small stand next to her. "Where's my gown? Why does she get a gown and I don't?"

The designer poked a pin in the cushion she wore on her wrist. "Because Rain is the star, because you are just a back-up singer, and this isn't for the video. It's for the party in L.A." The self-satisfied smile that tilted the designer's lips upward was anything but kind.

Regan couldn't help it. "L.A.?" she blurted out in unison with her mother and Emily.

"Yes, it's part of the producer's marketing plan. You'll be in L.A. the week after the video is shot. The party is at The Playboy Mansion. Important people will be there, and you are expected to perform. Just the one song, so don't worry. Consider it a test run."

Regan gaped. L.A.? The only L.A. she'd ever seen was Louisiana. What would she do in California at The Playboy Mansion of all places? She didn't have to look at her mother to see Rona was blowing a gasket.

Without a word, her mother shot out of her chair and headed for the front of the studio where the offices were located. Emily was fast on her heels. Regan was being stitched into her gown and couldn't move. The powers that be would have to decide this one all on their own. She doubted her opinion would weigh much in the debate anyway. It was just cool to see Emily launch herself at the door. What she would give to be a fly on the wall and see that temper tantrum. All Regan could think about was that she was going to a party at a mansion with Chase, and Emily couldn't go. Maybe there would finally be time to talk to him. It occurred to her that Jorge probably wouldn't like the idea of her traveling, but he knew her plans to go on tour, so hopefully, he was prepared. She wouldn't change her future for anyone. She had literally died to be where she was right now, and no one could take this away.

Standing in the Playboy Mansion with its white marble and parquet floors against warm maple syrup colored paneling and rich wood trim was a dream come true. The beautiful women in their satin bunny costumes were the most beautiful people she'd seen in all her life. Her white satin gown made her look older than her fifteen years, but the white was also a beacon of chastity. Regan supposed she was a virgin again. Rain had never had a boyfriend, and the relationship Regan shared with Jorge was limited to hand-holding and kissing. She wasn't making the same mistakes in this life as she had in her last. Though it was silly, she was saving herself for Chase. Her mother had noticed her watching him the day of the rehearsal and asked Regan about her feelings for Jorge. Shrugging her shoulders, she said Jorge was just a friend.

Her mother's concerned look was followed by, "Does Jorge know how you feel?"

Regan had answered her with another shrug.

"Well, just remember, he has feelings. He's a nice young man, Rain. Don't break his heart over something you can't have." Rona had looked at Emily when she said it. Emily, who was complaining to Chase about not being invited to L.A.

Regan didn't want to think about Jorge right now. This was the moment she'd been waiting for. Though the only way she'd gotten to L.A. was by the producer promising Rona that Regan's tutor, Jane, would chaperone the whole trip and that he wouldn't leave their side at the party. He also promised that he would have Regan back at the hotel and in her room by eleven. She knew it had been a hard decision for her mother to make. Rona hugged her tight as she dropped her off at the airport, telling her to be good and to break a leg.

Regan was nervous. The crowd was older, and she felt self-conscious as other guests gazed at her formal attire. It set her aside from the bunnies and other female guests in their little black cocktail dresses. Regan thought she saw Rob Lowe at the other end of the room surrounded by beautiful women—she even spotted Hef himself. She really didn't see the attraction to Hugh Hefner. Women hung on his every word, and it looked like he had a long glittery tail as he moved across the room with his bunny entourage. The flashes of gold, peacock-blue, magenta and pristine ivory silk bunny costumes followed him wherever he went. It must be a special occasion. Regan thought all the bunny costumes were black with a white cottontail and collar. Tonight, she didn't think any two bunnies wore the same shade. Turquoise, fuchsia, and periwinkle swirled through the room, overwhelming her senses with all the extravagant decorations and well-dressed people that she would perform in front of. Grand tropical plumes and flowers graced every table and flat surface in the mansion. Regan wasn't sure if the heady scent that blew through the corridors on a breeze was from the beautiful flowers or the array of fresh fragrances the guests wore.

Cascading water drew her attention outside, and Regan wondered who might be swimming in the grotto. She was young, but she'd heard about the Playboy Mansion and all its sensational parties. It would have been nice to be an eighteen-year-old Regan right now, but admittedly, Rain was actually prettier. She didn't feel vain thinking it as she looked at her reflection in the mirror that covered one entire wall. Lost in its gold frame and the sea of people surrounding her, she felt surreal. Her strawberry-blonde hair was swept up high, cascading down her back in a waterfall of beautifully set curls. She'd been instructed not to cut her hair, and it was now almost to her waist. She didn't miss the glances she received from several admiring men, but most were old enough to be her father.

A white stretch limousine had brought her to the party. The producer stayed on the car phone most of the short ride, sounding terribly important as he governed the record label from such a great distance. Rodney had a New York accent, but she'd never spoken to him long enough to ask where he was from. It was only now that she felt slightly out of place with the stranger that he was to her. She'd always dealt with Chase, Antoine, Hanna, Jane, or Guidry. Lately, Jane had become her go-between for most questions about their travels or tonight's party. For whatever reason, Jane didn't get an invitation to attend, and the band must have come in a different car. She searched for them now while Rodney interacted with a few of the guests who chatted him up. The lively producer had forgotten her existence entirely.

Regan felt a hand on her shoulder and turned in surprise. Hugh Hefner was smiling down at her.

"You must be tonight's entertainment." His eyes sparkled, and the creases around his mouth showed that he liked to smile often.

Regan could have taken his comment as suggestive, but his warm energy conveyed sincere interest in her talent. She smiled back at him with excitement. "I'm Rain Landry."

He winked at her, taking her hand and squeezing it with reassurance. "I thought so. You are as lovely as your photo and then some. Are you excited about performing tonight?" His positive aura was just the balm she needed. His entourage was pleasantly supportive. She'd expected catty pettiness or remarks of jealousy on the heels of Hef's praise.

Regan tried to rein in her enthusiasm. "Are you kidding? This is my dream."

"Like I always say, life is too short to be living somebody else's dream. Shoot for the stars, kid. I hear you're going to be big." His eyes were wide, intensifying his words. He nodded and squeezed Regan's hand again before greeting Rodney, who quickly introduced Rain again before leaving her to follow Hef to another set of guests nearby. Regan wanted to laugh. Apparently, the promise to guard over her like his own child didn't mean much to Rodney. She approached one of the many bars and ordered a soda without ice. Her grandmother told her long ago that warm soda soothed the vocal cords, and it now was a ritual to drink warm soda before all of her singing engagements.

"How's it going?" Chase's beautiful voice was a balm to her soul. She felt her nervousness was manageable as long as he was by her side.

"It's going," she said, trying to think of how to say what she really thought, that it was amazing, like waking up in a dream, being a part of an exclusive Hollywood party where most celebrities would give their eyeteeth to be seen.

"That's all you can say?" He chuckled.

Regan supposed she was showing her age, lack of experience, and uncultivated social skills. She was a backwater, Louisiana, bayou girl, and this was her big ticket. She needed to drum up some adjectives.

She arched a brow. "I've always been better at singing my emotions, not wearing them on my sleeve."

Chase's chin dropped as he grasped his chest. "Damn, was that a shot at me?"

Regan quickly apologized. "No, sorry. Not you. I was thinking of someone else."

He nodded. His face said that he knew exactly who the barb was meant for. "If you just give Emily a chance. She's not that bad, you know. She was best friends with your sister, Regan. Is that what you hold against her?"

Regan was aghast. "Is that what she told you? Huh," she scoffed. "I'm sorry if I offend you by saying this, but Emily wasn't anywhere near the same league as Regan. She was a social butterfly, Miss Popularity, captain of the dance team slut that tried to take away Mark because Regan slept with Emily's boyfriend, and she never got over being dumped."

Chase's eyebrows went up and a few people nearby stopped their conversations to listen. Chase took his drink and grasped her arm, leading them out to the patio, by the pool. "You don't hold anything back, do you?" He shook his head in annoyance.

"Sorry, I didn't mean to spill all that, but that's what I don't like about Emily. She lies. My sister tolerated her because she didn't give a crap." Regan paused for a moment, asking herself why she cared now. *Because now it hurt.*

As if the question was obvious to them both, he asked, "Then why do you hate her so much?"

Regan paused, sipping the remainder of her soda. Should she lay it all out—say how she felt. Zada had warned her against throwing herself at a man that wasn't hers. The constant debate had felt like a conversation between two Ping-Pong paddles.

The banter with the seer echoed in her mind. "Don't go throwin' yourself at a man that's just not into you, chile. You'll only get hurt, and if he is into you, then he's a pervert, and you shouldn't want nothing to do with him any-hoo."

Regan looked up into the depth of his hazel eyes. "I suppose I'm jealous."

The muscle in his jaw jumped, showing his discomfort. "We've been over this Rain. What about Jorge?" He smiled.

Regan supposed he was trying to soften the blow. "He's great," she nodded, trying to sound indifferent to Chase's rejection.

"Rain, you are a beautiful, talented young girl, and I should be the one who's jealous. Jorge or some other great guy is going to come along and have you all to himself. They will get to grow old with you, and I'll be just some old guy you used to sing with, drowning in whiskey and the wake of your success. People never remember the band when you get to this level, Rain. They will remember your songs, your voice, and your beauty. You're going to have it all. Don't waste your time wanting someone like me."

Chase squeezed her hand between his. His words were sincere, and Regan thought she saw a hint of interest sparking in the depths of his gaze. She was sure that he would be hers if their age difference wasn't taboo.

"What about in three years, when I'm old enough?" She challenged. Regan knew she sounded young, inexperienced, and desperate, but she couldn't help herself. There might not be another moment like this one.

His eyes glazed over with introspective thought, and he let out a long breath. "I tried to break up with Emily last week." He pressed his lips together, studying the night sky above. The muscle worked in his jaw again as he swallowed hard. He looked at the stars twinkling above them.

Regan grasped at his bicep. "She can't make you love her. You don't love her."

Chase shook his head. "It's not that simple, Rain. She's pregnant." He tilted his head further back like he was trying to fly above the atmosphere and escape the words he'd just uttered.

Regan was silent. Emily was pregnant. Chase was Catholic. They would have a baby together. He would have a life with Emily, and three years from now, he would probably be knee-deep in babies, family functions, and a life with a wife he didn't love.

Rain held back the tears that threatened to fall. "You don't have to marry her."

Chase was about to say something, but Rodney approached them, spouting rapid orders about where the instruments were set up and when to start. Hanna approached her, picking at her gown and hair, pulling a tube of gloss out of her handbag and dragging Regan to the lady's room.

The conversation was finished. Regan would be whisked away in the limo after their performance, and she wouldn't see Chase until the next time they met at the studio. It was all over. She'd lost him. He might even be married before she saw him next. She could almost hear her heart breaking as she took the stage. The music started with a slow beat, and she quickly took the crowd, careening over the edge as she beat out the chorus with her lungs. No one was dancing. Everyone was watching her as she writhed in song. She would later see a video of this moment and think how the dress had made her look like she was floating. The large white wings of an angel hung behind the stage made her look like a celestial being. Regan had almost forgotten that she had once had a guardian angel. A presence whose mistake cost Regan her life. The heavenly being took her from her soulmate, then cast her in a form that ensured they'd live a life apart or at least not together the way she wanted. It was cruel. Why? What sin was Regan paying for in this life? Maybe it was for taking a body that was not hers.

She had dreamed about the angel after the séance with Zada, when Rain had found the light. The angel flew to her with white feathered wings and a golden sword. She placed it in Regan's hands and told her that life wouldn't be easy. She warned her there would always be darkness beside the light.

Regan's slumber had made her own speech slurred as if she were back between worlds, in the cave where water had garbled her words and their meaning. "What war am I to fight?" she had asked in the haze of sleep.

The Angel's words were soft but she remembered them still. "War comes in every lifetime. It's a matter of whether you choose to pick up the sword and wield it."

Now, steeped in the present, her dream had become reality. At the end of the song, Regan's voice reached a pinnacle of clarity. The crowd was as mesmerized by her voice as she was by the golden sword in her dream. She imagined herself drawing the blade from its sheath and holding it high above her head. She would win this battle of the soul. She would fight for her eternity. The gift of life held meaning in every event that passed. Regan had to believe there was a purpose for her presence in this moment, this body, and this time. She would follow the light in this world and overcome her fear of darkness. Time would pass, and the pain in her heart would heal. There was a future for her within herself, and for that she would be strong. She would battle and win the war within her soul.

CHAPTER 35

Her mother's voice on the other end of the line was a soothing balm to her night.

"So, how was everything? Tell me all about it."

Regan smiled, tugging at the bedsheets in her hotel and flopping onto the mattress. She coiled the phone cord around her hand and wondered why the chic hotel didn't have cordless models.

"It was fabulous, great, stupendous. I can't believe it all happened. It's like a dream. The best dream ever." Besides Chase crushing her heart, she'd had one of the best nights of her life.

"Did you meet any celebrities, eat any swanky food? How did you sing? Did it all turn out okay without the sound equipment?"

"We had all the equipment we needed, but I think I've gotten better. Everyone seemed to love the song. We played it twice. It was so cool. I met Hugh Hefner, a score of bunnies, and I think I even saw Rob Lowe!"

Rona chuckled then made a woo-hoo sound. "Well, that sounds truly amazing. What time is your flight landing?"

Regan looked at her ticket on the nightstand. "Three o'clock."

"Why so late?" Her mother complained.

"It's two hours earlier here than there, so we leave at ten AM Louisiana time. It's a five-hour flight, mom."

"I still can't believe that modern man has a way to travel from one side of the continent to the other in a few short hours. My daughter, the celebrity." Regan loved how her mother's voice bubbled through the phone. It felt good to have her support.

"Not yet. The song comes out Monday."

Rona made a grunting sound. "That seems like such an odd day to release. Why not over the weekend?"

"I don't know, Mom. That's just what Rodney told me."

Rona grunted again. "Speaking of which, was Rodney a good chaperone?"

Regan thought about the truth, then said, "He was the best. No worries, I was barely there before the first performance and then in the makeshift dressing room most of the time."

"Good. Very good."

"Mom, why are you breathing funny. Are you okay?"

Her mother laughed. "Ha, it's a surprise. You better go to sleep. You have an early morning, and I won't accept any excuses for missing your plane. So off to bed."

Regan laughed. "Even from this far away, you try to mother me."

"I'm your mother. What else am I supposed to do?" She laughed and then paused. "I love you, Rain. You're all I got, so be safe. See you tomorrow."

Regan wasn't afraid to fly because she had never flown before. It was amazing how the plane sped up and the air lifted the wings, pointing the metal nose into the sky. She sat in first class this leg of the flight. Rodney had been able to get her an upgrade from her original coach class seat. He'd told her if she performed every time like she did at the party, she'd never fly coach again. That sounded great, but she hadn't minded the coach seat on the way there. The flight attendant was kind and kept her glass full of soda, even when they flew through turbulent weather. The pilot took the plane farther up to avoid the bumps, but the seat belt light was on most of the flight, making it hard to go to the tiny lavatory. She decided to slow down on the soda for fear of wetting her pants.

She wished Zada could be there with her. The billowing white clouds they flew above were what Regan imagined heaven to be like. Blue stretched as far as the eye could see above them, turning a deep purple at the edges of the atmosphere. Huge thunderheads looked like atomic eruptions floating all around them as they flew over Houston. Regan wondered in amazement how the weight of so many people, luggage, and metal could stay afloat as the plane picked its way between the large, mushroom-shaped clouds. The seat next to her was unoccupied. Jane was somewhere back in coach, and Rodney got delayed by another booking. He was catching a later flight home. Chase and the band were dispersed some rows back and every now and then, she could hear Guidry's great bellows. He kept the attendants shaking their heads and laughing at every turn.

The plane dipped and shuddered, and Regan peered out the small port-hole, wishing the weather would smooth out so she could see the landscape beneath them.

"Hey, how'd you get the luxury accommodations while us guys have to sit in the cheap seats?"

Regan smiled at Chase. She wasn't angry at him. She felt sorry for them both. She was losing what should be the perfect love, and he was trapped in a life he didn't want to commit to.

"Sorry, Rodney could only get one upgrade. I guess he felt like it should go to a lady. He's such a gentleman, you know." She batted her eyes as she tilted her head toward him, smiling at her own sarcasm. "But there's no one sitting here, so I don't see why you can't join me."

He'd already sat down. "Great, I think I will. Those seats are made for midgets."

Regan laughed and he smiled as his head lolled back in the headrest. He stretched his legs, and she heard his knee pop.

"Wow, I guess you really were cramped."

Chase laughed. "Yeah, there isn't much leg room for anyone over five foot."

She was amused at his light conversation, contemplating how differ-ent it was from their much heavier one last night. She took in his long legs, stretched to the row in front of them. He was just over six feet tall. If the flight attendant asked him to move, Regan would take Chase's seat. It must be horribly uncomfortable for him in the back.

Braving the waters, she asked, "How are you?"

He raised an eyebrow at her. "Back there?"

She shook her head.

He pressed his lips together as if contemplating what he wanted to say. "That's why I came up here. I wanted to apologize for last night. I shouldn't have dumped all that on you. I don't know what I was thinking. Nobody knows." His words trailed off as he stared ahead.

The attendant came by, gave him a surprised look, then asked him if he cared for a drink. The lady winked at Regan over Chase's head. Regan liked her even more now. There was an extra demo CD in her bag that she was supposed to use for promotions. She would give it to the attendant before leaving the plane.

When the attendant went back to the galley, Regan placed her hand on Chase's. Her fingers interlaced with his. "I won't tell anyone."

He looked at her with a sad smile. Flipping his hand over in hers, he squeezed her fingers. "Thanks." He was silent for a moment. He seemed to take in all the planes and angles of her features. At last, he stared into her eyes. He leaned forward, and Regan thought he might kiss her. When he was close, she felt his breath on her ear. "If I were only seventeen, life would be different." He kissed her on the cheek. The warmth of his lips seared her skin, and she tingled from her hands to her heart. He sat back, smiling at her. His eyes danced with sincerity, and Regan realized that it was all he could give. Chase was a good guy. He would do the right thing by society's standards, and he would do the right thing by Emily.

Regan swallowed hard. "What if I were eighteen?"

Chase smiled at her. Regret shining in the depths of his green-flecked eyes. "You're perfect just the way you are. Don't change anything about yourself for me or anyone else."

Something sparked between them. She felt his energy tinged with regret for what could have been, but then there was an actual flash.

The guy in the row beside them apologized. "Sorry, it looked like a moment you might want to save. Give me your address and I'll mail you a copy." The man in the suit looked familiar to her and she wondered if he'd been at the party last night.

He apologized again when Chase stared daggers at him. After a long pause, Chase finally found his voice, "No man, that's all right. Thanks, but no pictures, please."

The guy nodded and put his camera back in its case. He was obviously serious about his hobby. The Canon looked expensive. Chase turned back to her, rolling his eyes. "Better get used to it. Eventually, the tabloids will be all over you." They both laughed, breaking any chance of resuming the moment they'd shared. The attendant set Chase's beverage down on his foldout tray and they clinked glasses.

"Cheers! To our futures and our success."

CHAPTER 36

Regan arrived home to a house full of boxes.

As Rona put her key in the front door and opened it, she squeaked, "Surprise! We're moving."

Regan blanched, fear gripping her heart. "Moving where? When?"

"Rodney found this great place in Redondo Beach. He says that we should all move to California since that's where the record label is based. Can you believe it?" Her mother bobbed up and down with a youthful excitement that Regan hadn't seen in years. The advance they'd deposited upon signing the contract had a lot of zeros, and it had made Rona a lot happier and more relaxed. Regan guessed the anxiety of making enough money to support them since her father left had taken a toll on her mother. She loved seeing her so invigorated, but what would this mean for the future?

"What about Chase? I mean the band. Is everyone moving?"

Her mother came to her, grasping her shoulders with a soft smile. "Oh honey, I don't know about everyone else. Maybe they'll choose to fly back and forth, but I have you to think about, and I'm not going to sit here worrying about you flying across the country every time there is some event in L.A. they want you to attend."

"Will there be lots of events in California?" This was news to her. Rodney had babbled a bit after the party and before she left the hotel to catch the plane, but Regan had only been half-listening. She'd been reeling from the high of the evening at the Playboy Mansion.

"Rodney says that everything is in L.A. and we're going to love it!" Rona's excitement was evident by her permanent smile and the way she swished past all the boxes to the kitchen, where she pulled two Cokes from the fridge. They were the individual glass bottle kind that was more expensive. A mere month ago, they'd bought two liters when they were on sale. Her mother opened the fridge wide, showing Regan a whole shelf of bottled sodas. "Ta-da!"

Regan chuckled. "Oh, my God! I guess we're rich."

They both laughed and her mother came to hug her. The mood changed from laughter to sensitive emotion. She couldn't see her mother's face, but she felt the strength in her arms as she said, "We are going to be happy, Rain. I didn't think it was possible, but you are all I have left. For that, I have to be thankful, and we have to live. I promise you, California will be a new start for us, and we are both going to love it."

Regan knew in that moment that Rona had been struggling as much as she'd been, trying to find her place in this post-Regan existence. She also knew that her mother was right. If Chase was going to marry Emily and start a new life, she had to move on. She loved the warm weather in L.A. and the bright future that lay ahead of them. Living near the ocean would be amazing. Maybe a new start was just what they both needed.

Monday at school was anticlimactic. The song was released, but Regan hadn't heard it on the radio yet, and she hadn't shared the news with any of her classmates. Only Jorge and her mother knew about the weekend in L.A., the Playboy Mansion and the new album. Rona was at work, Jorge was teaching swimming lessons to toddlers, and she was back in the tenth grade. How exciting, she thought to herself with sarcasm. She hadn't told Jorge about the move yet, but she needed to soon. They had committed to not seeing anyone else. He'd asked her to "go together," but she'd never really understood the expression that defined two people dating. They weren't *going* anywhere. Regan hoped they could remain friends when the miles separated them. She would miss his companionship along with his warm reassuring hugs. Jorge was a great listener and he was so handsome. Most girls would think she was an idiot for letting him go, but the truth was, he deserved better. He deserved someone who loved him, and Regan knew she didn't care for him in the way that he wanted.

The school had a pep rally for final period to engage the students in the upcoming game. Homecoming was just around the corner and she wondered if she should bother to go. The cheerleaders went through several cheers and the football players were introduced. The coach talked about the year ahead and how they would annihilate the opposing teams. Regan was never into sports and grew bored with all the chants. She doodled on her notebook as the school principal took the stage. It wasn't until her name was announced across the loudspeaker that her head flew up. She scanned the gymnasium, confused.

The curtains of the stage were drawn back and a slew of instruments were exposed. Something was said about a band coming to play and that everyone should give a hand to their fellow student, "Rain Landry and the band, Quarter Rain."

Regan felt her classmates' hands upon her, nudging her from the bleachers. She stood on wobbly legs, shocked at this request for an impromptu performance. She wondered just whose idea it was to surprise her. Chase, Guidry, and the guys took the stage and the applause shook the bleachers. She didn't have to be a genius to realize whoever's idea it was had just sent her to the top of the school popularity chart. Regan wasn't sure if that's where she wanted to be. Being famous would be okay since people would like her from afar, but her peers saw her get dressed in the girls' locker room for PE. They would see her miss a question in class or stumble with her books at her locker. This was a little too personal, but she was in the spotlight now, and there was no turning back.

Without giving her any time to think about it, the band started the moment she hit the stage. Chase nodded to her, and she nodded back. Even though her hands shook, and her legs felt like water, she couldn't help but smile. It was the first time she'd seen him since the plane. It was the release day of their album. He'd single-handedly given Regan her dream. He might not be able to give her his heart, but she hoped they'd still be friends. Flowing into the music, she brought the house down with "Walk on Water." If her classmates' enthusiasm was any indication of their success, the song was destined to hit the top forty.

The students cheered for more and she looked to the principal, who nodded with a broad smile.

"Wow," Regan paused, looking into the crowd of the faces she saw every day. Today they looked different. They looked at her differently. She saw the excitement, admiration, and envy. "What a surprise it is for me to stand here today. I wasn't supposed to be the singer in the family, but sometimes dreams still evolve from tragic situations. If you ever think that luck has deserted you and that truly there is no way out, I want you to turn it around and know that there is a greater plan for us all. A few months ago, I thought my life was over, but time changes everything. So, if you ever feel desperate for change, know that it will happen. Nothing lasts forever, and even the bad has to end." She looked at Chase. She hoped he, too, would hear her words as a concerned friend. His eyes shone in the natural sunlight filtering in from the high skylights of the gymnasium. He nodded to her as he began to play. She nodded back to him, turning toward the bleachers. "This is another song from our album, but it won't be released until next month. We hope you enjoy it."

Delila breezed through the house filled with boxes. She'd loved watching Regan perform, but she felt the brewing of a great storm. It wasn't the barometer pressure changing that alerted her to what was coming, but the intuition of a guardian angel before a bullet was aimed at her ward. The song had played over and over on all the popular stations, and even the local TV stations played a clip of Regan singing at her school. Delila was proud of what Regan had accomplished. The journey to success hadn't been easy for her ward, but Regan was willing to fight for it. The angel watched as her ward put clothes into a box, lingering over a t-shirt that Rain had worn often when she was alive.

Rona called from the living room for Rain to come see the news. One minute they were showing the school gymnasium and the next they were showing a picture of Chase and her, sitting on the plane together. They looked like a couple as they held hands. Regan remembered the short moment of reassurance she'd given him when making her promise to keep his secret. Chase was close and the look in Rain's eyes said it all. Her mother gave her an accusing glare. The media was saying something about their illicit relationship and the ongoing inappropriate acts that reportedly happened after the Playboy Mansion party at their hotel.

"Rain, is there something you want to tell me?" Her mother had tears in her eyes, but her voice was calm. Regan knew her mom understood how much she cared for Chase.

"Mom, I swear, nothing happened. Chase is with Emily. He was telling me about—" She'd promised Chase she wouldn't tell anyone about the pregnancy. "—how he plans to marry Emily. The stupid guy on the plane thought we were a couple. I think he was at the party the night before. Nothing happened between Chase and me. I promise."

Rona sighed with relief. "You better call Jorge and warn him. This won't be a nice image to be blind-sided by."

"I need to call Chase first. This looks worse for him."

"I guess you're right. People only see what they want."

Regan picked up the phone in the kitchen as it rang. "Hello."

It was a reporter from the *Times-Picayune*. "Rain Landry? How long have you been having relations with the lead singer of Quarter Rain?"

"That photo is bogus. You people need to get a life." She held down the receiver, but the phone rang again. "Stop calling. No comment."

"Rain?" It was Chase.

"Oh God, Chase. Did you see the news?"

"Yeah. I have to get ready for a press conference now. Rodney insisted." He took a deep breath, and there was a long pause. "Look, you're going to hear some things about me, and you're not going to like it. I just wanted to tell you before the conference that I'm quitting the band."

The glass castle she'd built around all her dreams shattered. What would the band do without Chase?

Her hand flew to her head as if she could ward off the news. Tears brimmed in her eyes. "No!"

"Look, Rain, I was going to have to quit anyway once Emily and I got married. When the baby is born, Rodney would have had to find a sub. I don't like any of this bullshit, but Quarter Rain can't take a chance with all the negative publicity. If Rodney does this and plays the media right, this will get the band seen and heard. It won't matter who plays the guitar, the fans will only care about you." There was a pause and Regan tried to jump in to stop him. "No, Rain. This is for the best, trust me. The guys have worked so hard for this. Regan's song needs to be celebrated and we can't let this reporter rip it to shreds."

She was quiet. He was right and she knew it, but it was so unfair. Nothing meant anything to her without him in her life. She'd lost his love to a life with Emily. Regan didn't want to lose him and her music, too.

"Look, I know it's hard, but I was never going to be able to move to California with a wife and kid. Emily's dad offered me a great position at his company. This music thing, who knows, but a steady job, with a company that offers great benefits and..." a catch in his words stopped his tirade.

"Chase, please don't do this."

"It's already done, kid. Guidry's little brother has already signed the contract. He'll be great. You'll see. I just wanted to tell you before you saw it all in the news."

"Chase."

"Yeah?"

"I'm sorry. This is all my fault."

He chuckled softly. "Naw, kid. This is the way it's supposed to be, but don't worry. There's a greater plan."

She supposed he was referring to her speech in the gymnasium. He said good-bye and the dial tone blared as the line went dead. She wanted to throw the phone at the wall but knew her mom was trying to fix up the house to sell. She felt defeated. What was she supposed to do now?

She called Jorge. "Don't worry. I didn't believe it anyway. The dude's twice your age."

"Chase is twenty-six, but that's not the point." Regan found herself losing her temper. What was it with everyone? She might be underage, but she wasn't an idiot. Chase had been a perfect gentleman. He'd turned her down more than once, to her ego's dismay. "He never laid a hand on me. The picture was him whispering something he didn't want anyone else to hear."

"Yeah, what was that?" Jorge challenged.

"None of anyone's business." Regan parried.

"I'm your boyfriend, Rain. I have a right to know."

Regan tried to calm herself. Mark's memory danced in her mind. She'd driven him mad with jealousy. "About that. We need to talk."

There was a long pause between them. "What, you're breaking up with me? Is it because of this? Because of him?"

"No, it's nothing to do with Chase. He has Emily, so chill." She took a pause, then said, "We're moving to California as soon as Mom sells the house. The whole place is in boxes already." There was dead silence on the other end of the line. "Jorge?"

"How long have you known?"

"Since yesterday when I got back. It's not my decision, but I think it might be good for us."

Jorge's voice was hoarse. "For you and me?"

Regan shook her head. Knowing he couldn't see her, she cleared her throat. "No, for Mom and me. She needs to start over, and…maybe I do too."

"What about us?"

Regan chose her words carefully. "I hope there will always be an us, but maybe not right now."

"Are you asking me to wait?" His voice sounded hopeful.

"No. I wouldn't do that. I don't know what all this music business stuff will bring." She leaned into the kitchen counter, wishing she'd called him from her room. Her mother kissed her on the forehead as she went off to her own bedroom, waving good night as she shuffled down the hall in her furry slippers. Regan smiled.

"The band…." He blew out a deep sigh. "They come first?"

"Yeah. This is what I want right now, and I'll need a friend along the way." She tried to sound positive. She cared a lot about Jorge, just not in the way he hoped for. "I don't know anyone in Cali. Will you still take my calls?"

"Yeah," he said readily. "I'm not giving up on you just because you're thousands of miles away."

Regan smiled. "Thanks."

"I love you, Rain." There it was — the moment of truth.

"I—"

Jorge breathed deeply into the phone. "It's okay. You don't have to say it back if you're not ready. I'll wait."

CHAPTER 37

Regan couldn't go to school the next day. Reporters waited at the end of the drive, and it would draw too much attention if she tried to go to class. Her mother and Rodney might have thought it was cool to have Rain perform at her own school on the day of the release, but they had caught her tail in a trap. Everyone knew she was the lead singer of Quarter Rain. There was no way Rona would allow her to attend with the media circus dogging her, plus now everyone thought she was having an affair with an older guy. Her reputation would be ruined, but it was nothing compared to what Chase would have to go through. Regan wondered how Emily and her family were taking the news. Chase was branded a pedophile even after he and his lawyers made a public statement denying the media's claims. Rodney pointed out to the reporters that there weren't any legal charges against the band or any of its members, and that all the allegations were false.

She was going to meet with the New Orleans Police Department. They'd summoned her and her mother to give sworn statements. After today's fiasco, Regan would finish out the school year with her private tutor. She really wanted to see Chase but knew it was impossible at the moment. She had been coached what to say by Rodney's leading HR associate. The entire day was nothing but a blur of appointments and meetings. As she was ushered outside of the studio to a podium with microphones, she blinked at the multitude of flashes.

A blonde reporter in a red suit didn't wait for any introductions. "Rain, is it true that you met with Chase in your hotel after the Playboy Mansion party?"

Another reporter chimed in. "Is it true that you believe he's your soulmate?"

A man in a navy suit added, "Did your mother sell you to the record label and allow this older man to have sexual relations with you in exchange for money and fame?"

Rodney stood in front of the podium, blocking the microphone. "I'll remind the press that Rain is a young adult, and questions should be posed with respect."

People in the crowd nodded and made affirmative murmurs.

Regan stepped to the microphone once again and waited until the media settled. "People say that a picture is worth a thousand words, but they don't tell you if those words are true." Bystanders started to buzz with chatter. She waited for everyone to quiet and soak in the meaning. "It saddens me that in an instant, one person's misinterpretation could so easily ruin another person's dream. Chase took a song that my sister wrote before she died and made our family's dream a reality, and anyone who questions the parental guardianship of my mother, Rona Landry, obviously doesn't know her. Chase has stepped down from his dream because he didn't want the rest of the band to lose theirs. I think his actions are chivalrous and kind. He has a relationship with someone and that someone is not me. He has always treated me with the kindness of friendship and has respected me as a co-writer for the band, and anyone who alludes to anything more is just wanting to stir up trouble.

"The police have investigated and cleared Chase of any suspicion of wrongdoing. If you have honor in the news you tell, you will relay the truth. The truth is that Chase never treated me in any way that was inappropriate." She held her shoulders back and her spine straight. She wanted to scream out that she loved Chase. That he *was* her soulmate and who were they to judge right from wrong, but that wouldn't help anyone. Instead, she concluded with, "Thank you for your time."

A flurry of flashes blinded Regan, and she held onto Rodney's arm as she made her way to the car. Her mother was already inside, waiting for her. Rodney climbed in beside them both and grasped Rona's hand as the driver maneuvered the car onto the highway.

Regan suspected that something else was adding to the bloom in her mother's cheeks. She saw Rodney's hand squeeze her mother's again before letting it go. Her mother smiled awkwardly and then she looked away. Regan stared at them both. Yes, they were the ones with the secret relationship, but no one gave a hoot besides her. She supposed no one was talking about it since her mother had said she was divorced. She wondered if Rodney knew that her father had never signed the papers. It's not like Regan would judge her mother for falling in love with someone else. The heart wants what it wants. Rona knew how Regan felt about her dad, but what had Rain felt? Maybe that's why it was still kept quiet. Regan didn't feel like confronting her mother about it. She had her own secrets and sorrows. She now wished for the move to come sooner. It looked like her life was officially over in Bonne Fete, Louisiana.

CHAPTER 38

In the weeks that followed, she studied hard, went to dance practice to say good-bye to Mrs. Danskin, and tied up the loose ends of her young life. There weren't many, but she did have Jorge and Zada. She was forbidden to see Chase under any circumstance, and she respected that the effect would be detrimental to him if she tried. He no longer came to band practice, and most of her extra work time was spent with Antoine and Hanna, who apparently were following the mass exodus to L.A. Those going to California were bubbling with energy, and it seemed to be the topic on everyone's tongue, along with the album's success and the upcoming tour. They had landed a gig opening for the Eurythmics, and even she knew that it said something huge about their futures. The tour started in late spring, so they had plenty of time to move and get their lives started before taking off. She would see Canada, England, France, Italy, and Greece, plus a dozen other countries before the tour was over.

It helped to have something exciting to focus on while she mourned the loss of Chase. Regan heard through the grapevine that he was getting married soon and a baby was on the way. She was glad he'd told her the news himself. It prepared her so that she wouldn't fall apart the first time it was mentioned. The news was hard enough to stomach with so many people talking about going to the wedding. She didn't receive an invitation, and though she didn't want to see Chase marry Emily, it hurt that he hadn't invited her.

Jorge clung to her as often as he could, and she felt as if she were suffocating. Her emotions toward him had changed, and she was already severing the ties that bound her to Bonne Fete.

She told Jorge she needed a day off, and she drove to New Orleans alone. She didn't want to be rushed into saying goodbye to Zada and Gustave as well. The seer was waiting for her on the front porch of her newly painted home. The place had taken on new life, and though the first cool snap was upon them, the sun shone brightly overhead, making Zada's newly cropped hair sparkle.

"Hey, hey, little lady. You lookin' good! I thought you'd never come back for your ol' friend Zada."

Regan ran to her friend and threw her arms around the older woman's neck. "I'm sorry, Zada. I've been busy. The practice, school, the upcoming tour." She hadn't mentioned the move yet. It was the reason she came to visit.

"It's okay. Young people gotsta be young. I told you and your boyfriend that. How you two doing?" She lifted her brows in question.

Regan shrugged her shoulders, not sure if Zada was talking about Jorge or Chase.

"That's okay. We don't have to talk about men. We is strong women." Zada put her arm around Regan's shoulders, guiding her into the house. "I got us some cold Cokes in the fridge."

They went into the kitchen, and it felt like yesterday they had seen Rain ascend. It was the last time she'd seen Zada. They talked on the phone from time to time, but her life had shifted to full speed ahead since the party in L.A.

Regan told Zada again about the party, the day at school, and then the media explosion with Chase.

"Um-hm, I seen that on the news. I didn't think he was guilty of anything, but then I know you." She smiled teasingly.

Regan tipped the cool bottle to her lips, taking her time to enjoy the fizz that danced on her tongue and in the back of her throat. "He's marrying Emily. They're having a baby." She heard the pitifulness of her own voice and shut her eyes against the sting. She would not cry again.

Zada placed her hand over Regan's. "Oh honey, I'm sorry, but you know he's too old for you in this life, or for now anyway. I know it doesn't help your broken heart to hear it, but it's probably for the best."

Regan took a deep breath and sighed. "I know, Zada. I'll be okay. This is just the beginning of what it's like to be an adult. I was eighteen before…. The truth is that I am old enough for Chase, but the world can't see it. I think he cares about me, but he's too damn much of a rule follower to admit it." Regan remembered what he said on the plane. If he was only seventeen. That was all the admission she would ever get.

Zada's mouth twitched. "I believe he's meant for you chile, and I believe you will find each other again, but these things take time to work themselves out. Until then, maybe you can find another friend for a while. How's your Mexican friend?"

Regan smiled at Zada. "What makes you think he's from Mexico?"

Zada made a pfft sound, waving her hand. "Whatever."

Regan wouldn't lecture her on the politically correct labels she should use. Zada was a grown woman. She wasn't about to change old habits now.

"I'm moving to California, Zada. I have to say goodbye to Jorge when I leave, and I've come to say goodbye to you today." She could feel the tightness in her throat and knew she felt more pained than Zada looked.

"Well, now I just won't accept that." The old woman shook her head. Standing abruptly, she went to the sink and fiddled with a dishcloth.

Regan stood, too. "I don't have a choice in the matter. My mom's sold the house already and the closing is next week. We're driving the Mustang to California, and a moving company is taking the boxes. Mom sold her car."

"I know you have to go, but I don't accept it's goodbye. You will come back and see your old friend Zada. I know it."

Regan smiled. "Of course, I will." She walked to the sink and put her arms around her friend.

Zada patted Regan's hands that were settled around her middle. "Okay, then. That's settled. This is not goodbye. This is just the beginning of a long-distance friendship that you won't forget." Zada turned on the water and washed her hands. "Now, there's someone else that we need to visit."

They moved to the lavender room and Zada grabbed her sage, waving it around. Gustave entered Zada's form almost as quickly as she sat down. He had been lurking in the shadows, listening to their conversation, so Regan didn't have to fill him in on the particulars.

"Oh, what I would give to have your life, Regan. The things you will see, the places you will go."

Regan laughed, shrugging her shoulders. "It's everything I ever wanted, almost."

"Hm, I heard about your loverboy marrying some tart. Sorry about that, but don't fret. There are certainly more fish in the sea." They laughed together. Gustave laughed at his own humor, but Regan was laughing at Zada as she took on Gustave's mannerism, waving her hands wildly like she held a kerchief.

"So I've heard. Anyway, I don't know when I'll get back to the city to see you or Zada. I wanted to say goodbye, in case…"

He laughed heartily. "In case I should find the light or my own demise?"

Regan didn't smile. "Well, yeah."

"Darling—don't you worry about dusty old Gustave. I've been helping poor souls find Zada, and they are all discovering their destiny. It's only a matter of time before the heavens open up and beckon me home. Call me the in-between world social worker. I'm linking souls with the closure they desire, and I feel useful for once in my existence. Maybe I haven't found my destiny yet, but trust me, young one, it finds us all eventually." Zada slapped her hands down on the table with a clap. "Now, go out there and find yours!"

The seer's eyes were closed, but the smile on her face looked like she'd just been served a huge serving of white cake with thick frosting—her favorite.

"Um-um-um. If I can ever find a way to bottle up that man's spirit and stick it under my pillow, I will. Today he smelled like sugar-coated beignets with honey drizzled all over the top."

Zada cackled and Regan laughed. "You have a very interesting relation-ship with food, Zada. I think we better go eat. Pick any place you want. I'm buying." Regan pulled a hundred-dollar bill out of her pocket and slapped it on the lavender silk cloth.

Zada's eyes widened. "Give me five minutes to change. I know just the place."

CHAPTER 39

Regan stood on the beach with her toes in the sand. It wasn't warm enough to swim, but the weather was a perfect seventy degrees and sunny. She understood why people flocked to the Golden State with all its beauty. She'd been living there for a month with her mother, and there were still boxes in the garage she should be unpacking. It seemed unfair to do work on such a beautiful Saturday. Dance practice with Antoine wasn't for another three hours, and her geometry lesson with Jane was tomorrow.

Her mother and Rodney were on an official date. Since Rona claimed desertion, the divorce papers had finally been filed. Her father never showed up again, and they didn't know how to reach him. It might take time for the divorce to go through, but Regan had given her mother her blessing. It was good to see Rona in this new life. California was a literal breath of fresh air for them both. Regan wasn't sure if it was the sunlight, the beach or maybe Rodney who influenced her mother to give up cigarettes, to take morning jogs on the beach, and to let her hair flow freely around her face, but her mother looked younger, healthier and happier than she'd ever been back in Bonne Fete. Here, it was easier for both of them to forget the past. She hadn't seen Rain again since her soul ascended into the light, and it was actually a relief since it meant that Rain had met her destiny and was no longer in danger. Regan's guilt would never be entirely washed away, and she was sad that there was no one to share her grief with, but life went on, she was still here for now.

She talked to Zada on the phone at least once a week to hear the local gossip. The fortune teller's business was booming. Some other seer had first dibs on being Psychic to the Stars, but when anyone ever asked Regan when was the first time that she knew she would be famous, she always mentioned that first meeting with Zada. She didn't tell them she'd been Regan back then. The first interview on Johnny Carson had started a hotline business, Zada's Tell-All Call, and Regan was sure the money was now flowing in. Hotlines were all the rage of the eighties, and Regan could see a booming enterprise for the seer's future.

Waves lapped at the shore, and she watched the green-glass colored water churn in the white surf. A big yellow lab raced toward her and she waited to be tackled. As a frisbee whizzed by, Regan laughed at the dog's near miss of her and its airborne catch. A sun-bronzed guy in swimming trunks approached her as the lab turned and barreled back their way.

"Sorry, I didn't mean to throw it so close. The wind picked up, and you were in the way."

Regan's mouth opened in shock and she laughed. "I was in your way?"

He smiled. "Sorry, that's not how I meant it. I'm Cole. This is Gardener."

Regan bent down to pet the drooling lab holding the red frisbee. "Gardener. That's an interesting name for a dog."

"You should ask my neighbors. The dog's dug up every one of their calla lilies."

They both laughed. Regan put her hand over her mouth in mock surprise. "Oh, I bet they just love you, Gardener."

"What's your name?" His golden skin glistened in the sun and she admired his perfect white toothpaste smile. He looked like an ad for California tourism. She wondered where he'd stashed his surfboard.

"I'm Regan."

He stuck out his hand before she could correct herself. "Hi, Regan, Nice to meet you."

"Um, sorry. I'm Rain. I don't know why I said Regan." She didn't want to talk about her dead sister right now. It was awkward, and she hoped the conversation wasn't repeated at some later date to her mother. She'd end up in therapy.

He looked at her with an odd expression. "Okay. Either way. Both names are cool. Wait, you're not making up a name to blow me off, are you?"

She laughed. At least he had a sense of humor. "No, really. I just moved here. I guess I'm a little tired."

Gardener dropped the frisbee at her feet and barked, breaking the awkward moment. She bent down, picked it up, and threw it. The red disc went up on its side and fell quickly to the ground, rolling just a short distance away.

She put a hand to her forehead, half-covering her eyes. "I guess I suck at this. I've never thrown one before." She felt heat creep into her cheeks.

"Are you kidding? Where are you from, Mars?" He laughed, teasing her with his perfect smile. She liked the warmth his personality emitted. He seemed so carefree.

"Louisiana, outside of New Orleans. I just moved here a month ago."

He smiled broadly, "Really? That's awesome! I love soul, jazz. You know the great Sam Cooke died just a short drive from here. Have you been to Long Beach yet?"

"No," she shook her head.

"Come on, Gardener and I'll show you." He started to turn toward the parking lot. Regan was shocked by his willingness to show a stranger around.

"Hey, sorry, I can't." She called out. "I have dance lessons in a few hours and I probably should get home to change."

He looked crestfallen. "Oh, yeah, okay." He paused.

Not knowing what to say next, she offered. "I can give you my number. Maybe later in the week?" She wouldn't tell him about the band or the tour coming up. It was too soon, but she had hopes they might become friends. Gardener nosed her hand and she petted him again.

Cole's energy renewed as he tapped his head. "I don't have a pen, but I never forget a pretty girl's phone number."

"Got a lot of those stored away?" Regan tapped her head with sarcasm. He gave her a sheepish grin.

After she gave him her new number, they parted ways. She walked up the beach in the opposite direction from Cole and Gardener and found the path that wound back up the hill to the neighborhood where she lived. Their rental overlooked the ocean. As she rounded the front of the house, she noticed a strange car in the drive.

"Hey, kid."

Regan spun around, looking at the porch. Chase stood there in faded blue denim jeans and a well-worn t-shirt, looking every bit as handsome as he always had. He held two glass-bottled sodas in one hand as she remembered him doing so many months ago. His hair was cut much shorter now, and there were more creases around his eyes than she remembered.

"You're here." She didn't know what else to say.

"Yeah, well, you didn't say goodbye."

"You were getting married, and I didn't get an invitation to the wedding." She shrugged.

He pressed his lips together as if caught up in a deep thought. "Yeah, I know. Sorry about that. Rodney thought it was for the best."

Regan tried to control the beating of her heart. He was here. He was really here, and they were alone. She looked over her shoulder, scanning the trees and leafy bushes to see if anyone was watching them. She half-feared a reporter would spring from the foliage.

"It's okay. Rodney knows I'm here, and I promised I'd stay outside." He walked toward her, and they both sat in the Adirondack chairs looking out at the calla lilies and bamboo along the drive.

Regan wanted to throw her arms around him and tell him how much she'd missed him. It was all she could do to play it cool, after everything they'd been through. "How long are you here for?"

"That's a good question." He paused, taking a long drink of his Coke.

"Emily lost the baby. I couldn't cut it working for her dad, and in the end, he wrote me a fat check to leave her and get a divorce."

Regan's mouth opened in surprise and horror. "What? Are you being serious?"

"I didn't take the check. But after Em lost the baby, we didn't seem to have much to talk about. I didn't want to quit the band, but I wanted to do the right thing. Now I don't know what's right anymore." He shook his head, watching Rodney and Mom pulling into the driveway. "Yeah, I knew we didn't have much time." He winced.

Regan's heart sank as her mother and Rodney rushed out of the car toward the porch.

"Chase." Her mother's voice didn't sound too happy. Regan knew that Rona didn't believe in the tabloids, but her protection level had spiked since then. Her nerves hadn't settled down entirely since leaving the scandal behind in Bonne Fete. Regan's schedule and who she spent time with were inspected daily. Thank God for her mother's interest in Rodney.

Rodney approached Chase with sincere pleasure, clapping him on the back and clasping him in a one-armed hug. Regan had dubbed it the California hug.

After a few pleasantries were exchanged, Rodney looked at him sincerely. "I was sorry to hear about the baby."

Chase nodded. He looked hurt by the loss. He might not have been in love with Emily, but she could see that he might have loved the idea of having a child. "These things happen, I'm told."

"What brings you to California?" Rona asked.

Chase's hands delved deep in his pockets. He rocked back on his battered Converse sneakers. "I'm hoping to get my old job back." He looked at Rodney hopefully.

Rodney beamed and then looked at Rona's concerned face. "Man, you are in luck. I was talking to Porter, the guy that owns that new label…" They started into the living room as Rodney chatted nonstop industry news. He had a job for Chase, but it wasn't with Quarter Rain.

Regan should be disappointed, but she knew there was a lot of ground to cover before she turned eighteen and a lot of life between now and her future. She was like a butterfly, breaking free from her cocoon and soaring high on a dream. The future was ever-changing, and today she'd been given a glimpse of another destiny. Celebrating her small gift, she raised her soda to the air in a toast.

"To the next three years. Don't forget me, Angel."

Walk on Water

I look in your eyes
And when I do, I see paradise
You know I love the way you dance
Just give me another chance

You walk on water, baby
You're just too good for me, lady

You stole my hand
You stole my heart
You said that we'd never part

You walk on water, baby
You know you're driving me crazy

You're my angel, and I love you
Always be by my side
You're my heart, and I need you
Just to make me smile
Spread your wings and fly, I don't want to die
Protect me with your touch
You can never be too much

It's the little things that you do
The big things that tear my heart in two
Guide and guard me, baby
Don't be too hard on me, lady

You lift me up
Spin me around
Crash me to the ground
You walk on water, baby
Ain't no crying this time, lady

You stole my heart
You stole my mind
Think about you all the time
You walk on water, baby
Don't leave me lonely here, lady

With you I see paradise
Our lives stretched over fire and ice
And I'll see you again,
We're so much more than just friends

You walk on water, baby
You drive me crazy, lady

I hope you liked *Chase the Moon*. You can also check out my companion series *Race for the Sun* (The Soul Watcher Series Book 1) on Amazon. Or visit minettelauren.com to find out more.

ABOUT THE AUTHOR

As soon as Minette Lauren was old enough to write, she composed a play in one act about the love of Seth and Beth, inspired by the movie, *Gone with the Wind*. Not deterred by the play's questionable success, she has been in love with writing ever since. Growing up in a small town outside of New Orleans, Louisiana, has fueled a lot of her creative endeavors. She travels often and takes advantage of anyplace with a view that inspires her to write. Lauren now resides in Texas, where she loves to write outdoors by her pool, with her six furry writing muses. Besides her menagerie of tail-wagging pooches, she also has a loving husband, three turtles, and four sassy parrots to keep her company. Together, they make all of her dreams come true.

www.ingramcontent.com/pod-product-compliance
Lightning Source LLC
Chambersburg PA
CBHW070906180626
46817CB00003B/938